"Tell me

Samuel said, breaking the strained silence. He met her surprised gaze without wavering. "You want me to help you uncover your past. I know who you were when you used to live on this island. I'd like to know who you are *now*, the person you've become."

Jessie bit her lip, considering her answer. How much did she want to tell him? That she was haunted by dreams she couldn't explain? That she'd never been able to make a relationship last because she wouldn't allow herself to trust anyone? That she'd come to the island in search of a past, because she was desperate to save herself from a dismal future?

No, she couldn't tell him the truth. No matter how much she might want to confide in him, she wasn't ready to reveal that much about herself to anyone.

Dear Reader,

This is a very special month here at Intimate Moments. We're celebrating the publication of our 1000th novel, and what a book it is! *Angel Meets the Badman* is the latest from award-winning and bestselling Maggie Shayne, and it's part of her ongoing miniseries, THE TEXAS BRAND. It's a page-turner par excellence, so take it home, sit back and prepare to be enthralled.

Ruth Langan's back, and Intimate Moments has got her. This month this historical romance star continues to win contemporary readers' hearts with *The Wildes of Wyoming— Hazard,* the latest in her wonderful contemporary miniseries about the three Wilde brothers. Paula Detmer Riggs returns to MATERNITY ROW, the site of so many births—and so many happy endings—with *Daddy by Choice.* And look for the connected MATERNITY ROW short story, "Family by Fate," in our new Mother's Day collection, *A Bouquet of Babies.* Merline Lovelace brings readers another of the MEN OF THE BAR H in *The Harder They Fall*—and you're definitely going to fall for hero Evan Henderson. *Cinderella and the Spy* is the latest from Sally Tyler Hayes, an author with a real knack for mixing romance and suspense in just the right proportions. And finally, there's *Safe in His Arms,* a wonderful amnesia story from Christine Scott.

Enjoy them all, and we'll see you again next month, when you can once again find some of the best and most exciting romance reading around, right here in Silhouette Intimate Moments.

Yours,

Leslie J. Wainger

Leslie J. Wainger
Executive Senior Editor

Please address questions and book requests to:
Silhouette Reader Service
U.S.: 3010 Walden Ave., P.O. Box 1325, Buffalo, NY 14269
Canadian: P.O. Box 609, Fort Erie, Ont. L2A 5X3

SAFE IN
HIS ARMS
CHRISTINE SCOTT

Published by Silhouette Books

America's Publisher of Contemporary Romance

To my mother-in-law, Dutch.
Thank you for your wonderful son, and for being
such a loyal supporter of my work.

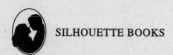 SILHOUETTE BOOKS

ISBN 0-373-27072-0

SAFE IN HIS ARMS

This edition published by arrangement with Harlequin Books S.A.

® and TM are trademarks of Harlequin Books S.A., used under license.
Trademarks indicated with ® are registered in the United States Patent
and Trademark Office, the Canadian Trade Marks Office and in other
countries.

Visit Silhouette at www.eHarlequin.com

Printed in U.S.A.

Books by Christine Scott

Silhouette Intimate Moments

Her Second Chance Family #929
Safe in His Arms #1002

Silhouette Romance

Hazardous Husband #1077
Imitation Bride #1099
Cinderella Bride #1134
I Do? I Don't? #1176
Groom on the Loose #1203
Her Best Man #1321
A Cowboy Comes a Courting #1364

CHRISTINE SCOTT

grew up in Illinois but currently lives in St. Louis, Missouri. A former teacher, she now writes full-time. When she isn't writing romances, she spends her time caring for her husband and three children. In between car pools, baseball games and dance lessons, Christine always finds time to pick up a good book and read about…love. She loves to hear from readers. Write to her at Box 283, Grover, MO 63040-0283.

IT'S OUR 20th ANNIVERSARY!
We'll be celebrating all year,
Continuing with these fabulous titles,
On sale in April 2000.

Romance

#1438 Carried Away
Kasey Michaels/Joan Hohl

#1439 An Eligible Stranger
Tracy Sinclair

#1440 A Royal Marriage
Cara Colter

#1441 His Wild Young
Bride
Donna Clayton

#1442 At the Billionaire's
Bidding
Myrna Mackenzie

#1443 The Marriage Badge
Sharon De Vita

Desire

#1285 Last Dance
Cait London

#1286 Night Music
BJ James

#1287 Seduction, Cowboy
Style
Anne Marie Winston

#1288 The Barons of
Texas: Jill
Fayrene Preston

#1289 Her Baby's
Father
Katherine Garbera

#1290 Callan's Proposition
Barbara McCauley

Intimate Moments

#997 The Wildes of
Wyoming—Hazard
Ruth Langan

#998 Daddy by Choice
Paula Detmer Riggs

#999 The Harder They Fall
Merline Lovelace

#1000 Angel Meets the
Badman
Maggie Shayne

#1001 Cinderella and the Spy
Sally Tyler Hayes

#1002 Safe in His Arms
Christine Scott

Special Edition

#1315 Beginning with Baby
Christie Ridgway

#1316 The Sheik's
Kidnapped Bride
Susan Mallery

#1317 Make Way for
Babies!
Laurie Paige

#1318 Surprise Partners
Gina Wilkins

#1319 Her Wildest
Wedding Dreams
Celeste Hamilton

#1320 Soul Mates
Carol Finch

Prologue

Voices.

Loud, angry voices woke her.

Confused and uncertain, Jessie Pierce climbed out of bed. Stumbling, following a night-darkened, long and unfamiliar hallway, she hurried toward the sound of shouting. Her movements were clumsy, her feet leaden, as though she was walking in slow motion. She was disoriented, uncertain where she was headed. Her heart raced, fluttering in her chest like a butterfly's wings.

The angry voices grew louder. Emotion distorted their timbre, making it hard for her to identify them.

A beam of light sliced through the inky night, blinding her, paralyzing her with fear....

A shape emerged from the shadows.

A shape large and frightening, coming closer, closer...

*Her heart leaping in her chest, she stumbled back,
one step, two, until she couldn't go any farther....*

And then there was nothing but darkness. All-encompassing darkness.

With a start Jessie's eyes flew open. She was trembling. Her teeth were chattering—the only sound in the stillness of the night. Her lungs burned in her chest, and she realized she was holding her breath. Releasing the pent-up breath with a whoosh, she gulped in cooling drafts of air and desperately tried to still her shaking limbs.

Perspiration drenched her body. Her silky nightgown clung to her slender body like a second skin. The light from the bathroom cut through the darkness, reassuring her. She glanced from one shadowy corner to the next—nothing appeared out of place. Straining her ears, she heard no angry voices. No sound at all.

All was well.

Or was it?

Feeling foolish, she realized she'd been dreaming once again. A dream as familiar as life itself, as unwanted as uninvited guests who had overstayed their welcome.

A lump of emotion caught painfully in her throat. She swallowed hard, trying to ease an overwhelming sense of dread, of loss. Jessie closed her eyes, fighting the fear that gripped her. When would she ever be free of the dream's tenacious hold upon her?

At one time she'd sought professional help for the recurring nightmare. But the doctors had no answer, no cure for what ailed her. The thought chilled her, sending a long shiver down her spine. Opening her eyes, she noted the early hour on her bedside clock. It was only four in the morning, but she knew she wouldn't be able to fall asleep again. Tossing the blankets aside, she scrambled out of bed and reached for her robe. She tied its satiny belt securely around her waist, stepped into a pair of house slippers and hurried from her bedroom.

Muted light coming from a small table lamp lit the hallway leading to the living room. In her world there was never complete darkness. Since she was a child, Jessie had feared the night and what it might bring. As an adult she was embarrassed to admit to anyone that she'd been unable to overcome the weakness.

Snapping on the light over her desk, Jessie stared at the drawing she'd been working on before she'd gone to bed. It was a dark and mysterious illustration, one of many she'd been commissioned to draw for a children's book. The book was a quixotic tale of one young boy's quest to slay dragons. A tale of good overcoming evil, a tale of strength and courage. One that she found herself envying.

Goodness only knew, she had her own dragons to slay.

Jessie shivered, the memory of her nightmare still too fresh. It pained her to admit that she hadn't the courage to face the monster of her own dreams.

Pushing the disturbing thought from her mind, she picked up one of the illustrations. Known for her eye for detail and her talent for bringing a story to life, she'd become quite successful as an illustrator at a relatively young age. It was a job that allowed her to work out of her apartment in Atlanta, letting her set her own hours. It also kept her isolated from others.

Which she desired most.

The truth was, she found more comfort in her art

than she did with people. Jessie sighed. Her mother, bless her heart, worried about her solitary life. Since her father's death one year ago, her mother seemed even more determined to push Jessie out into the world. She needed to make more friends, her mother often chided her, to open her heart to new relationships, to fall in love so that she wouldn't ever have to be alone.

Jessie didn't try to argue. She knew her mother's intentions were good, though misguided. What her mother didn't understand was that Jessie wanted it all. A husband, a family...someone to love, someone who would love her.

She didn't want to live her life alone. But a solitary life was all she could handle. Opening up her heart, trusting others just wasn't as easy as it might seem.

For Jessie it was impossible.

Just a few days ago, on their last visit together, her mother had seemed inordinately preoccupied with Jessie's welfare, obsessing on her need for a secure future. Jessie had tried to laugh off the concern, telling her that, with a mother like her living nearby, she had all the love and security one person could handle. She remembered the worried expression that had flitted across her mother's face at her flippant response.

Jessie pushed the disturbing image from her mind, picking up a charcoal pencil. Trying not to notice the trembling of her hand, she forced herself to work on the illustration. Purposefully she cleared her mind and focused her attention on the drawing, not stopping until she was finished.

Later, her fingers stiff with overuse, she laid her pencil down on the desktop and sighed with relief, satisfied with what she'd accomplished. Flexing her fingers, stretching the kinks from her muscles, she glanced outside the apartment's large picture window and was surprised to see the early rays of dawn filtering through the cloud-laden sky. She must have been working for over an hour, though it had only seemed like minutes.

The phone rang, jarring her out of her reverie.

Startled by the early-morning call, she snatched the receiver from its cradle, anxious to still its insistent peal. "Hello?"

"Jessie?" It was Eugenia, her mother's housekeeper. More than a housekeeper, she was her mother's loyal friend, a valued member of the family. The pain shadowing Eugenia's voice sent an arrow of dread darting through Jessie's heart.

"Eugenia, what is it?" Jessie demanded. "What's wrong?"

"It's your mother," Eugenia said carefully, regret lacing her tone. "She's gone, Jessie."

"Gone? I don't understand. Gone where?"

A strained silence followed.

"No, you can't mean—" Jessie's voice broke beneath the heavy weight of disbelief. "She can't be—"

"I'm so sorry, darling. The best we can figure, it happened early this morning. She went to sleep last night and never woke up. The doctor thinks it was her heart. It…it just gave out on her."

Early this morning Jessie's dream…she'd been awakened by an unbearable sense of dread, of loss. Her first thoughts had been of her mother. Surely it had been merely a coincidence.

Or had it?

Jessie closed her eyes against the hot sting of tears. Coincidence or not, her mother's worst fear had just been realized. For the first time in her life, she was truly, completely alone.

Chapter 1

"I don't understand." Jessie pointed to the documents spilling out onto the shiny surface of the lawyer's mahogany desktop. "What are you trying to tell me?"

The lawyer for her parents' estate shifted uncomfortably in his seat. His round glasses reflected the light of the desk lamp as he looked to Eugenia for guidance.

Eugenia refused to meet his gaze. Instead, she sat stiffly in her chair, her faded-blue eyes, moist with tears, trained on the handkerchief clenched in her trembling hand.

Sighing, the lawyer began, "Miss Pierce, I'm sorry to be the one to have to tell you—"

"I...I told Louise that you needed to know the truth," Eugenia interrupted, her voice sounding strange, thick with emotion. "But she wouldn't...she couldn't bring herself to tell you."

Jessie stared at the older woman in disbelief. "Then it's true?"

"I—I'm afraid so, darling. Louise and Malcom Pierce weren't your real parents. They adopted you when you were five years old."

The admission struck with a stunning blow. Jessie couldn't breathe. She couldn't think. Her life, everything she'd believed to be true had been built on a lie.

"Why—" Her voice broke beneath the weight of tension. She forced herself to continue. "Why didn't they tell me?"

Eugenia hesitated, glancing at the lawyer. He shrugged, looking lost, discomfited by the personal turn of the meeting. Finally she said, "I don't know all the details. But I suppose they were trying to protect you."

"From what? Being adopted isn't a crime." Jessie noted that the pitch of her voice rose as she spoke. But she couldn't seem to help herself. In the three days since her mother's death, she'd been under an enormous strain. Grief had all but overwhelmed her. Now she had to deal with the fact that the parents she had believed to be hers weren't really hers, after all. "Adoption isn't the social stigma it might have once been. What's the point of hiding something like this?"

Eugenia shook her head. "It wasn't like that. Malcom and Louise didn't care what others thought. Their only concern was for you."

From the stack of papers Jessie picked up a birth certificate naming her as Jessica Pierce, daughter of Evelyn and Jonathan Pierce. Her hand shook as she read the document stating that she was born in Charleston, South Carolina. Not in Atlanta, where she'd lived all of her life. An unwanted anger built inside her. She felt betrayed by those who were supposed to have loved her most. "I don't understand any of this. My name on my birth certificate…it's the same as the one I have now."

"It would be, wouldn't it?" Eugenia said quietly. "Since Malcom and Louise were already your aunt and uncle."

"My aunt and uncle?" She stared at the other woman, her incredulity growing.

Eugenia released an unsteady breath, suddenly looking older than her sixty years. "Darling, Malcom's younger brother was your birth father."

If she thought she'd been surprised before, nothing compared to the shock of that single statement. Tears welled in Jessie's eyes. She blinked hard, fighting the flow. Now, more than ever, she needed a clear head, not one clouded with emotion. "I still don't understand. Why didn't they just tell me the truth?"

"Jessie, I'm sorry." Eugenia started to reach out to her, then stopped. Looking uncertain, she let her hand fall helplessly onto her lap. "I know how upsetting this is…. I'm handling it so badly."

Numbly Jessie shook her head. "It's not your fault."

"I…I just wish I knew more what to tell you," she said. "All I can remember is that your birth father died before you were born. And your mother died when you were only five. When Malcom brought you home, you were terribly traumatized. Both he and Louise were beside themselves, at a loss how to help you—"

"The nightmares," Jessie said, her voice trembling.

"Yes, they were horrible. Every night for months you woke up screaming, so frightened. And then the dreams came less often. It was as though you'd put whatever had caused them out of your mind. You even forgot about your mother. I truly believe Malcom and

Louise were too afraid to do anything to upset the peace that you'd found."

Not so peaceful, Jessie admitted silently. The nightmares still haunted her, the latest occurring only days before. Aloud, she murmured, "My parents were always too protective."

"They loved you, Jessie. They tried to be the best parents they could."

"I know they did," Jessie said. The tears she'd fought so hard escaped. They filled her eyes, blurring her vision. She blinked, and a single drop trickled down her cheek. "Now what am I supposed to do?"

"Get on with your life," Eugenia said, her voice firm yet gentle. Finally she allowed herself to reach for Jessie. She placed a hand on her arm, warming her with a reassuring touch. "Forget about the past."

"How can I?" Jessie almost laughed at the thought. "I don't even know who I really am. For God's sake, how could I have forgotten my own mother...or the first five years of my life?"

"Perhaps there's a reason for that, Jessie," Eugenia said, her voice quiet, the warning unmistakable.

Silence filled the lawyer's office.

The lawyer cleared his throat, cutting through the sudden tension. Adjusting the knot of his tie, he said, "There's still the matter of the house on Prudence Island, in South Carolina. A place called Gull's Cottage."

Jessie frowned in confusion. "Gull's Cottage?"

"It's yours," the lawyer said, holding up the property deed for her inspection.

Jessie stared at the document and wondered what other secrets awaited her.

Wearily Eugenia murmured, "Why Malcom

wouldn't sell the house, I never understood. Once he told me he couldn't. That it was your legacy.''

''My legacy?''

Eugenia looked at her, regret shining in her eyes. ''Gull's Cottage belonged to your birth mother. It's the house where you lived before she died.''

A fist of tension gripped Jessie's chest, making it difficult to breathe. She couldn't think, couldn't respond.

''Miss Pierce,'' the lawyer said, oblivious to her growing panic. ''The taxes have been paid, and the house has been well maintained over the years. All that is left for you to do is decide whether or not you'd like to keep it.''

Shaking her head, Jessie said, ''None of this is making any sense.''

''I know, dear. It's been a long and trying year,'' Eugenia said, her tone soothing. ''Perhaps now would be a good time to take a vacation. Why don't you go to Europe or the Caribbean? Somewhere that you can forget all about this and put it behind you.''

As tempting as the thought might be, Jessie knew in her heart she couldn't run away. No matter where she went, what she chose to do, she could not alter the past. Nor could she allow it to rule her future. ''It seems to me I've been hiding from my past for too long already. I need to find out the truth…I need to know who I really am.''

Alarm creased Eugenia's round face. ''Darling, I'm not sure if that's such a good idea.''

''I'm not sure, either,'' Jessie admitted. ''But it's something I must do. There are too many questions and not enough answers.''

''Then, why don't you let someone else handle this

problem?'' the lawyer suggested. ''We could hire a private investigator, a professional to check into your background.''

''No.'' Jessie shook her head. ''This is something I have to do on my own.''

Eugenia gave an exasperated sigh. ''Jessie, why must you be so stubborn? You don't always have to be independent.''

Jessie brushed a tear from her cheek, smiling despite herself. ''Now you're starting to sound like my mother. Next you'll be telling me that the only way I'll be happy is to find a man to settle down with and raise lots of babies.''

''Lord help me, that's one argument I won't be a part of. I've been a bystander once too often in the clashes you two had over your differences of opinion on men and marriage.''

Jessie's smile faltered at the memory. Her mother had wanted her to find roots—a husband to love, a home where she could settle down. She'd never understood why a woman of Jessie's age hadn't been able to make a relationship last. Why she hadn't been able to find that perfect man, her soul mate.

Neither did Jessie.

When it came to trusting anyone, especially a man, something always held her back. She'd been unable to make that final commitment.

Perhaps there was a reason for her wariness. A reason that was hidden in her past.

''I don't know how to explain it. But I've lost five years of my life, Eugenia. It feels as though there's a hole, as though something important is missing.'' She picked up the deed to Gull's Cottage. ''Maybe I'll find what I'm looking for on Prudence Island.''

"And what if you don't?" Eugenia asked, her silvery brows furrowed with concern.

"Surely I won't be any worse for trying," she said, feigning a confidence she did not feel.

The truth was, she had no idea what might await her on Prudence Island. All she knew was that something strong and impossible to resist drew her to the house that was her legacy.

Right or wrong, she was going to Gull's Cottage.

The thick stands of loblolly pine trees that stood sentinel over the length of the narrow, two-lane road gradually gave way to the graceful stretches of moss-covered live oaks. Sunlight broke through the trees, dappling her arms, warming her skin. With the top down on her BMW convertible, Jessie knew she was getting close to the coastline. A salty sea breeze peppered the sweet, magnolia-scented air.

An unexpected thrill of excitement buzzed in her chest. For the first time in the month since Louise's death, Jessie had no responsibilities. No lawyers to meet, no estate to settle. She'd even finished the illustrations on the book she'd been commissioned to draw. There was nothing to stand in the way of her quest for the truth. Before the summer's end, she fully intended to find the answers to her past.

Then, perhaps, she could get on with her future.

Her future...Jessie's heart thumped with an unwanted bout of trepidation. It wasn't her financial well-being that worried her. Her adoptive father had been a doctor. Through shrewd investments, he'd been a wealthy man. Now, with both of her parents gone, Jessie had inherited more money than she knew how to spend. Even after seeing to Eugenia's retirement, her future was financially secure. But she would trade it all, every penny of her estate, just to have her parents back.

Not to be alone.

Pain, sharp and unwanted, jigsawed through her heart, bringing tears to her eyes. She blinked hard, fighting the emotion. Oh, how she missed her mother, more than ever. She had been her best friend, her confidante. There was no one else to turn to, no one to lean on, no one who could explain her confusing past.

No one to make life worth living.

Impatiently Jessie ran a hand through her short, dark hair, trying to shake off the blue funk that threatened. If her mood sank any lower, she chided herself, she'd be stuck in the muck and mire of self-pity. She refused to allow herself to become maudlin. She'd shed enough tears this past month. It was time to stop feeling sorry for herself.

The narrow road curved unexpectedly. She tapped on the brakes, taking the bend fast but still maintaining perfect control. Glancing in her rearview mirror, breathing a quiet sigh of relief, she didn't notice the beat-up, red pickup truck looming in front of her until it was almost too late.

She slammed on the brakes, causing her seat belt to bite into her shoulder. But it wasn't enough. Her car still skidded toward a certain collision.

Somewhere in the deep recesses of her mind the will to survive resurfaced with a vengeance. She jerked the wheel sharply to the right, aiming for the side of the road, narrowly missing the slow-moving truck by inches. Her BMW bumped off the pavement, hitting the shoulder with a loud thump. The back end of her car spun out behind her. Crushed seashells crunched beneath the tires. Thick clouds of dust rose up around her, nearly choking her. Before the car finally settled to a wobbly stop, she heard the *pop-pop,* then the slow *hiss* of two tires going flat.

Coughing, covering her mouth to keep from swallowing any more dust, Jessie thanked the powers that be for saving her life. And then the tremors set in. Blaming the reaction on delayed shock, her hands shook so badly she barely managed to slip the car out of gear and turn off the engine. Even before the dust settled, she threw open the car door and scrambled outside, feeling the need for the anchoring strength of solid ground.

Her legs nearly buckled beneath her as she tried to stand. She leaned both arms against the door, giving herself a moment to calm her jittery nerves. A thick coat of dust covered her black sleeveless turtleneck and her white jeans. She didn't even have the strength to brush the grit away.

"Are you all right?"

Jessie whipped around, startled by the deep, male voice. She tore her sunglasses from the bridge of her nose and squinted at the man approaching her. The driver of the pickup truck, no doubt. Perhaps it was just a trick of the hazy sunlight, or perhaps it was just that—considering the circumstances—she was feeling a bit more vulnerable than usual, but he appeared larger than life, towering over her.

"I—I'm fine," she stammered.

"You took a bad skid," he said, narrowing his pale blue eyes as he scanned her body from head to toe. Jessie fought the urge to fidget beneath his assessing gaze.

"Really, I'm okay. There's no need to worry," she

said, struggling to collect her scattered aplomb, wondering what it was about him that had set her body tingling and her mind racing with awareness.

He stood an inch or two over six feet and was a hard-muscled, tawny-haired and powerful male. But she knew it wasn't only his size that drew her attention. There was something about the man, something that stirred recognition deep inside her.

She hesitated. Then, frowning, she asked, "Do I know you? You look so familiar."

For just a second, irritation flickered in his eyes. Then quickly he hid the emotion behind a polite smile. "No, I don't think so. I have that sort of face. So common, everyone thinks they've met me before."

Common wasn't the word she would use to describe the way he looked. Handsome, rugged, unforgettable, those were terms that came to mind as she studied him closely.

Realizing she was staring, she averted her eyes. What was wrong with her? No matter how good-looking he might be, it wasn't like her to ogle a man. Especially when the man was a complete stranger. "I'm sorry. It's just that I could have sworn—"

"It looks like your car's the one that suffered most of the damage," he said, abruptly changing the subject.

Not giving her a chance to answer, he strode past her, close enough that they brushed arms. She felt the heat of his body singe her bare skin. Sucking in a surprised breath, she inhaled the earthy, male scent of sweat and hard work. Jessie swallowed the lump in her throat, trying to ignore the sensations stirring in the pit of her stomach. What was happening to her? Never before had she experienced such a quick and intense awareness of a man.

The stranger glanced at her sharply, telling her he, too, had been affected by their brief contact. But he had the good grace not to comment. Instead, he focused his attention on her BMW's flat tires. He gave the first tire a kick for good measure, then hunkered down on bent knee for a closer look at the second. Chewing nervously on her lower lip, Jessie tried not to notice the way his faded jeans hugged the taut muscles of his thighs.

"The rim's bent on this tire. It'll have to be replaced. Where are you headed?"

He'd been quiet for so long, the sound of his deep voice startled her. She glanced over her shoulder, making sure no one else was there, that the question was directed at her. Then, feeling foolish, the heat of embarrassment rising on her cheeks, she said, "I'm on my way to Prudence Island."

His gaze slid from the BMW to her long legs encased in a pair of designer jeans, his lingering look one of pure male appreciation. "Are you staying at one of the resorts?"

"No, I'm not a tourist," she said, her flush deepening beneath the heat of his gaze. She wasn't sure why she felt the need to make the distinction. After all, this was her first trip to Prudence Island. Her stay hopefully would be brief, since she had no desire to keep the house on a permanent basis. To all intents and purposes, she was a tourist. "I own a house on the island."

Slowly he rose to his feet, a frown furrowing his brow. "I've lived on Prudence Island all of my life. I'm sure I would remember if I'd seen you before."

It was a statement of fact. One that did not offend her. Instinctively she knew it wasn't a matter of disbelief on his part. Rather, he merely seemed curious.

"That's because I've only recently inherited a cottage on the island. Though it's been in my family for quite some time."

"Which cottage is that?" he asked, his tone still polite, friendly, encouraging her to answer.

"Gull's Cottage."

His reaction was immediate. He flinched as though he'd been struck. She heard the sharp inhalation of his breath. His face paled beneath his tanned skin, his eyes widening in surprise. He looked stunned by the news. In a strained, almost harsh voice, he demanded, "What's your name?"

"M-my name?"

He stared at her, not saying another word, his lips pressed in a firm, unrelenting line.

"It's Jessie, Jessie Pierce. Why do you want—"

He didn't wait for her to finish. Turning on his heel, he strode toward his truck. Jessie stared at him in disbelief as he climbed into the cab and slammed the door behind him. When he gunned the motor to life, a hot flush of anger melted her frozen limbs.

Her Good Samaritan was abandoning her.

"W-wait," she called out, following after him. "Where are you going? My car...I've only got one spare tire. You can't just leave me here."

Glancing at her briefly, he forced his gaze to the road before him. His face stony with suppressed anger, he said, "I'll send out a tow truck, as soon as I get to town. That's all I can promise."

With that he threw the truck into gear and peeled away from the shoulder, sending up a spray of crushed shell and dust in his wake. Jessie waved a hand in front of her face, trying to clear the air as she stood at the side of the road, unable to believe what had just happened.

One minute the handsome stranger had seemed polite, friendly, ready to help; the next, he'd become cool, distant. He had abandoned her.

Growling her frustration, she stamped a foot in a useless show of self-righteous indignation. For his sake, as well her own, it had better be the last time she ever laid eyes on—

Dammit, she didn't even know the man's name.

Well, hell! Whoever he might be, he'd just better stay out of her way from now on.

Samuel Conners glanced out the side mirror of his truck at the woman standing alone on the shoulder of the road. An arrow of guilt pierced his heart when he saw how vulnerable she appeared. Tiny and petite, she couldn't have stood taller than five-three, or weighed much more than a hundred pounds. He almost smiled when she stamped her foot in a show of anger.

But he didn't.

Instead, despite the sultry heat of the day, he shivered. And he knew that the coldness that had enveloped him had nothing to do with the weather. It had to do with a chilling memory from the past.

Jessie Pierce, all grown up and beautiful...

What was she doing here? Why had she come back after all these years? Why couldn't she have just stayed wherever she'd gone?

If she had, he could have kept the past where it belonged...buried deep inside of him.

Her image disappeared as he rounded a corner. Taking the curve too fast, his tires squealed in protest. His load shifted in the bed, slamming against the side of the truck. Belatedly Samuel slowed to a more manageable speed.

Jessie had almost recognized him. After all these years, she'd seen his face and wondered if they'd met.

It would be only a matter of time before she figured out the rest.

Samuel's muscles tensed reflexively. His knuckles were white as his grip tightened on the steering wheel. Prudence Island wasn't very large, but it was big enough for two people to steer clear of each other if they really wanted.

For her sake, as well his own, he had no intention of ever crossing paths with Jessie Pierce again.

Chapter 2

"How long will it take to repair the tires?"

After waiting over an hour for the tow truck to arrive, plus enduring a long and bumpy ride over the bridge to Prudence Island, Jessie was impatient to get to Gull's Cottage before dark.

The mechanic lifted the brim of his baseball cap and scratched his head as he studied the BMW. "Well, it'll take me a while to get the tires off. Then I'll have to see if they can be fixed. If they can't, I'll have to find new ones to put on and—"

"Could you just give me a rough estimate?" she cut in, her patience wearing thin.

"Probably an hour, maybe a little longer," he said with a shrug, seeming in no rush to get started.

"Great," Jessie said, sighing, as she glanced at her wristwatch. The sun would be setting by the time she arrived at the cottage. Thanks to the handsome stranger who'd abandoned her along the side of the road without a word of explanation, she'd wasted precious time.

She should be miffed at the man and rightfully so. After all, it was his slow driving that had caused her near wreck in the first place. Then he'd had the nerve to leave her stranded. Most disconcerting of all, she didn't have a name on whom to pin the blame. While he'd insisted that she identify herself, he'd never bothered to return the favor.

Somehow that omission of common courtesy seemed an even worse offense than his unexplained abandonment, striking a blow to her feminine self-esteem. It was as though she were unimportant, as though she didn't matter to him.

No, Jessie told herself, with an uneasy frown, that wasn't true. The stranger cared. In fact, he'd cared a great deal who she was. She doubted if she would ever forget the look in his eyes when she'd told him her name—that stunned, almost devastated look—and she couldn't begin to understand its cause.

"There's a coffee shop around the corner. And the beach isn't too far, if you'd like to take a walk while you're waiting," the mechanic said, drawing her out of her thoughts.

Jessie considered the possibilities. "Is there a grocery store nearby?"

"Right down the street," he said, pointing to a weathered wood building a block away. "It's just a local store, nothing fancy. But it's got everything a person might need."

"Thanks, I'll be back when I'm finished."

As long as she was waiting, she might as well kill time by doing something constructive. It had been hours since she'd had a meal. She would be hungry by

the time she got to the cottage. Grabbing her purse
from the back seat of the BMW, she headed for the
store.

A rush of cool air met her at the door of the building,
evoking a sigh of delight from Jessie. After sitting outside in the hot sun, the air-conditioning was a welcome
relief. The building was older, nothing more than one
large room. The wood-planked floor was worn smooth
with age. But the store was clean, and the shelves appeared well stocked. Grabbing a basket, she made her
way down the narrow aisles.

There was a handful of shoppers in the store. Since
the store wasn't close to any of the resorts, Jessie assumed them to be locals. Their curious stares at her
appearance gave credence to her suspicions.

More than curiosity, Jessie corrected herself, their
reactions were out-and-out odd. A woman at the dairy
section nearly dropped a carton of eggs when she
looked up and saw Jessie standing beside her. An older
man rammed his cart into a display of stacked canned
goods as he watched her pass him by. For the first time
in her life, Jessie actually felt paranoid. First she'd been
slighted by one of the island's citizens on the highway.
Now, for apparently no other reason than her being
new to town, she was being ogled like a mermaid in a
fishbowl by her fellow shoppers.

What was wrong with the people in this town?

Unnerved by the unexpected attention, she concentrated on composing a mental shopping list. Deciding
it best to buy only enough supplies for a couple of
days, she picked up a small carton of milk, fresh fruit
and bread. For dinner she bought chicken, a potato for
baking and greens for a salad. Satisfied, she went to
the front counter to check out.

An older woman, with coarse, steel-gray hair and sharp, green eyes, rang up her groceries. The task was accomplished in a strained silence, until the woman narrowed her gaze and barked out a sharp demand. "Where are you from, young lady? You're lookin' awful familiar."

The question sounded more like an accusation. Jessie's eyes widened in surprise. Flustered, she blurted out a stilted response. "Atlanta...I'm from Atlanta, Georgia."

"Humph—I coulda sworn I'd seen you before," the woman said, her skepticism obvious. Then, with a dismissive shrug, she continued, "So, you're a tourist, eh? The resorts are on the other side of the island. What brings you clear over here?"

"My car. I, uh, sort of had an accident. It's being repaired."

The woman tsked loudly. "That's too bad. Not a good way to start a vacation. Some of the hotels have shuttle services. You might be able to get someone to pick you up while you're waiting."

"Well, actually, I'm not staying at any of the resorts."

"That right?" The woman raised one graying brow. "Where are you staying?"

Remembering the stranger on the highway and his reaction when she told him of her new residence, she hesitated. Another customer, a middle-aged, blond-haired woman, stepped up beside her, waiting her turn in line. Feeling uncomfortable, wishing the conversation to be over, Jessie murmured quietly, "Gull's Cottage."

She might as well have shouted her answer. Their reactions couldn't have been any more extreme. Both women appeared shocked by the news. They exchanged quick glances, their expressions guarded.

The blonde standing beside her was the first to recover. She gave a nervous laugh. "I didn't know Gull's Cottage was for rent this summer."

"It's not," Jessie said, still trying to understand the reason for their reactions. "I own it."

The gray-haired woman blinked, not bothering to hide her disbelief. "You bought Gull's Cottage?"

"No, I inherited it. It was my mother's."

Silence followed her announcement. The words hung in the air like a dark and ominous cloud. The gray-haired woman stared at her. Finally she said, "I thought I recognized you. You're Eve Pierce's daughter...little Jessie."

"Y-yes, I am. But how—"

"Lord, help us," the blonde murmured beside her. Her face paled; she looked as though she'd seen a ghost.

The gray-haired woman stared mutely.

Jessie glanced from one woman to the other, confusion building inside her. "I'm sorry. Should I know you?"

"No, you wouldn't," the gray-haired woman said finally, her searching eyes never leaving Jessie's face. "You were too young, just a little thing when it all happened."

Jessie's confusion turned to unease. "When what happened?"

"Don't you know, honey?" the blonde piped in.

She shook her head. "Know what?"

"About your mother," the blonde said, her tone matter-of-fact, as though she assumed Jessie had a clue as to what she was talking about.

"You mean, about Eve Pierce? I...I know she died here on the island..." Jessie hesitated. Just how much did she really want to tell these women? Was it wise to admit how little she knew of her past? But finding out about her mother and understanding her past was the reason she was here. Taking a chance, she drew in a breath and admitted, "The truth is, I was adopted when I was five. I really don't have any memory of my birth mother."

"Oh, honey, that's too bad," the blonde said. "Then you don't know about Gull's Cottage. About the way Eve was—"

"Sarah," the gray-haired woman said sharply. Disapproval laced her tone. "We've kept this young woman long enough. There's no need to fill her head with gossip."

Looking contrite, the blonde glanced away, refusing to meet Jessie's gaze.

What was going on here? What was it they weren't telling her?

Stiffly the gray-haired woman handed her the bag of groceries. "That'll be $18.50."

Her hands shook as Jessie fumbled in her purse for the money. She wanted to demand that they finish telling her about her mother. But her instincts were telling her not to ask...that whatever they had to say, it was bound to be bad news.

After the day she'd already had, she wasn't sure if she was ready to hear it.

Chiding herself for being such a coward, she handed the money to the gray-haired woman, mumbled a quick thank-you, then fled the store.

The sun was beginning to set by the time Jessie pulled her car into the lane leading to Gull's Cottage,

her new home for the summer. Still shaken by her encounter at the grocery store, she pushed the troubling
events from her mind, focusing her attention instead on
the narrow, rutted lane.

It looked as though it had been a long time since
anyone had traveled this way. From what she'd
learned, she would be the first to stay in the house in
nearly twenty-five years. She couldn't help but wonder
what kind of condition the cottage might be in. If the
lane were any indication, she expected the worst.

The lot was pie shaped, with the widest part of the
slice at the entrance. The tip was at the end of the lane,
where she assumed the property emptied out onto the
beach. In between, there was a thick tangle of towering
oaks, palmettos and untamed underbrush. The dense
mixture cast the grounds into a premature darkness,
giving the property a haunted, eerie feel.

Jessie shook off her discomfort, telling herself her
unease was nothing more than the wearing effects of a
growing headache and an empty stomach. Both of
which would be taken care of once she'd unpacked her
bags and had settled in for the night.

The trees thinned and the waning sunlight peeked
through, relieving her anxiety. The reprieve was brief,
however. Within moments the house came into view.

Jessie blinked once, twice, unable to believe her
eyes. She checked her map, making sure she had the
right address. But there was no question. This was
Gull's Cottage.

Cottage...a misnomer for sure. It was the most beautiful beach house she'd ever seen. A large, one-story
home, painted white, with a high, slanting roof and a
wraparound porch. There were floor-to-ceiling win-

dows on the sides she could see. The view of the ocean must be breathtaking, she thought.

It was much more than she'd expected. Obviously, over the years, someone had taken a great deal of care of the house. She wondered what other surprises awaited her.

Jessie parked the car in the circle drive, as close to the house as she could. As the sun began to sink into the horizon, she felt an urgency to hurry and unpack, to go inside where it was safe.

Frowning, she turned off the ignition and stepped out of the car, wondering where these feeling were coming from. Her only true fear was that of complete darkness. But she had ample time before the sun made its final descent. For now, there was plenty of lingering light in the dusky sky. So why was she suddenly so unnerved?

She grabbed the groceries from the front seat. Forcing herself not to hurry, she strode up the uneven brick walkway to the front porch. Unlocking the door, she let herself in.

The rooms, dark and thick with shadows, set her nerves even further on edge. Groping for a light switch, she said a quick prayer of thanks when the entryway emerged from the shadows, glowing warmly beneath the overhead light. Before leaving home, she'd checked to make sure the utilities were in service. The lawyer for her parents' estate had assured her that the cottage was being looked after by a caretaker, that its power and water were hooked up and that someone came in monthly to clean.

The heels of her sandals tapped against bare wood as she walked slowly through the house, her footsteps echoing loudly in the quiet rooms. The floors were golden, heart of pine planks. Even a thin coating of dust couldn't hide the richness of their patina. Sheets covered most of the furnishings, giving the place a ghostly ambiance.

As she continued to explore, she was struck by an uneasy feeling of déjà vu. It was as though she'd been there before...which she had, she reminded herself. After all, she was supposed to have spent the first five years of her life in this house.

The thought sent an unexpected shiver of apprehension down her spine.

Forcing herself to continue, she made her way to the back of the house, turning on more lights as she went. When the wooden floor gave way to a burnt-red flagstone, she knew she'd stepped into the kitchen.

She felt along the side of the wall until she found the electrical switch. A pair of twin lights over a large center island came to life. The cabinets were carved of oak, the countertops a snowy white ceramic. Though yellowed with age, a delicate floral-print paper covered the walls. The room appeared cozy and inviting. She glanced outside. Even in the growing darkness that pressed against the windows, the view of the ocean was amazing.

But the beauty of the room didn't matter, once she stepped farther into the kitchen.

Without warning, the room spun beneath her feet. A fist of anxiety squeezed her chest, making it impossible to draw a breath of air. Her heart pounded so quickly, so hard against her rib cage, she was afraid it was going to explode.

Suddenly her head felt light, as though it was floating. The room slowly darkened. Dropping the groceries, she reached out, flailing her arms for something, anything to support herself...because in another minute she was sure she was going to faint.

Somehow, through the sheer strength of willpower, she made it to the glass-paned door that led outside. Struggling with the lock, she stumbled out onto the porch that overlooked the beach. There was no furniture, nothing to collapse onto. Instead, she headed for the railing, leaning her weight against it for support.

Gulping in deep breaths of air, she willed her racing heart to slow. Never in her life had she experienced such a blind sense of fear. What in the world could have provoked such a panic attack?

Too overwhelmed to consider the possibilities, she closed her eyes and slowly slid downward, until she felt the solid wooden deck beneath her. How long she sat there, listening to the pounding of the surf against the shore, she wasn't sure. By the time she felt strong enough to open her eyes, the night had gotten a firm foothold in the sky.

Compared to the pounding fear that had gripped her earlier, the momentary flutter of apprehension at the unexpected darkness seemed insignificant. Besides, it wasn't completely black outside. There were stars twinkling overhead. And a full moon glowed in the night sky.

The air had grown colder, also. She was shivering— from the chill or from shock, she wasn't sure which. But her heartbeat was steady, and her breathing had returned to normal. The soothing night air had worked its magic. She felt calm enough to go back inside.

Pushing herself onto unsteady feet, she walked slowly to the door. Her hand on the doorknob, she hesitated. Once again her heart jackhammered in her chest, telling her she wasn't in complete control.

Unexpected anger surged deep inside her. All day long she'd backed down from one challenge after another. First she'd allowed the man on the highway to take advantage of her helplessness. Then, the women in the store. Because of her own timidity, she'd passed up an opportunity to find out more about her birth mother. She'd had enough of playing the part of a wilted Southern flower.

Forcing herself to face her fear, she threw open the door and stepped inside. While she didn't suffer another panic attack, she wasn't comfortable, either. Her appetite had fled, right along with her composure.

It had been a long day, she told herself. Perhaps the best thing would be to unpack her groceries and suitcases, then call it an early night. Right now all she wanted was a hot shower and a soft bed. Then she'd try to forget about what promised to be one of the worst days of her life.

"She's dead," a deep, male voice called out.

"No, she can't be," Samuel growled, refusing to accept the verdict. Stubbornly he turned the ignition one more time. Once again his attempt to start the engine of his shrimp boat was met with complete silence.

In the pilot house, he slammed his fist against the steering wheel. The sun was just a promise in the sky and already this morning he'd overslept his alarm clock, nor had he had time for his morning cup of coffee, and now the engine wasn't working.

Dammit, what else could go wrong today?

"Give it up, Samuel." A thin, wiry man clambered out of the hold, hoisting himself onto the deck. Scratching his salt-and-pepper beard, he shook his head in disgust. "The engine's busted. Looks like we won't be trawling for shrimp anytime soon."

"Thanks, Jacob. Tell me something I don't know," Samuel said sharply.

Jacob held up both hands in surrender. "Hey, don't shoot the messenger. I'm only doing my job."

Samuel sighed. There was no use alienating one of the few men on his crew he could always count on. Jacob was loyal and hardworking. More than that, he was a friend. In a town where memories were long and acceptance was short, friendships were hard to come by. Jacob didn't deserve any unnecessary grief dumped on his shoulders.

"Sorry," Samuel said. "Ignore me. I'm just in a bad mood."

Jacob eyed him curiously.

Self-consciously Samuel rubbed a hand along the stubble of his unshaved beard. Maybe he could have taken a little more time combing his hair, too. But all the primping in the world wouldn't hide the dark circles under his eyes.

Finally Jacob said, "Looks like you could have caught a few more zees last night."

"Nothing a little coffee can't fix," Samuel growled.

"I can take a hint." Jacob chuckled as he headed for the crew's quarters. "I'll fix us a pot of java before we tackle the engine."

"Thanks," Samuel called after him. Rising to his feet, he pushed himself from the pilothouse and stood outside on the empty deck. The boat swayed beneath his weight. Above him the heavy iron outriggers creaked in the morning breeze. Their raised arms formed a black vee, pointing toward the heavens. He lifted his face and let the growing sunlight warm the chill from his heart.

He blamed all of his troubles on Jessie Pierce.

Ever since he'd bumped into her yesterday, nothing seemed to be going right. As much as he hated to admit it, he hadn't been able to keep his mind on anything but her. Last night, when he'd tried to shut his eyes and sleep, her image had haunted him.

It was as though she were there with him in his bedroom. Her hair black and shiny. Her dark-blue eyes glittering with an inner light. Her skin so creamy and smooth he'd wanted to brush his fingers along it. Even the thought of her full red lips, curving slightly, as though she were ready to laugh at his foolish infatuation, only fanned the heat of his ill-advised fascination.

Samuel blew out a breath, releasing some of the pent-up tension building inside him. What was wrong with him? He had more important things to consider than his beguilement with a woman. Not just any woman, he reminded himself sternly, but Jessie Pierce, of all people.

He had to focus on his future. If he wanted to make the mortgage payments on his boat, he couldn't afford to lose another day's work. He had to get the engine fixed—now.

With a sigh he turned toward the hold, ready to tackle the engine. Out of the corner of his eye, he caught an approaching jogger on the beach.

At this time of day, there was always an occasional walker or jogger passing by. Summertime on the island brought the tourists out of the woodwork. They all seemed fascinated by the sight of shrimp boats, thinking of them as a novelty, not as a man's work, his lifeblood.

But this time there was something about the way the jogger moved—with a delicate, sure-footed grace—that held his attention. As she neared, he saw the dark hair and slender body in a red T-shirt and white shorts and knew it was the woman of his dreams.

Earlier he'd wondered if his day could get any worse. He'd just gotten his answer.

Jessie Pierce was headed his way.

Crossing paths with the woman who'd had such a devastating effect on his life twice in as many days was more than a man's patience could bear. He felt an unwarranted anger stirring deep inside him. She had no business being here. No business invading his private sanctuary.

This was *his* part of the island.

Her pace slowed as she neared the docks. Raising a hand against the brightening sun, she scanned the pier, her gaze traveling from one boat to the next. Her expression was rapt, curious.

The tension in Samuel's gut increased, tightening like a string on a bow, as her gaze closed in on him. He told himself to turn away before it was too late. But like a man caught in the path of an out-of-control vehicle, he couldn't move. All he could do was stand there and let it happen.

Her gaze faltered then stopped as she locked onto his face. Her lips parted; whether she was surprised or about to say something, he wasn't sure. Either way, her expression altered, the bloom fading from her eyes. Closing her mouth with a click, she stood staring at him, frozen by the chill of his gaze.

Slowly Samuel felt a tide of heat rise up inside him. A heat that had nothing to do with the sun or the warm summer morning. Heat that was born not only of an undeniable sensual awareness for the woman standing before him, but also of humiliation and anger…the very emotions he'd tried to put behind him all these years. That, and the hot frustration of knowing there wasn't a damned thing that he could do to stop the past from coming back to haunt him, once again.

Heavy footfalls sounded on the floor of the deck as Jacob neared. "Here's your coffee, Samuel."

Startled, Samuel glanced at the approaching man. In his hand, Jacob held two steaming mugs of coffee. Murmuring his thanks, Samuel accepted the offering.

By the time he turned his gaze back to the beach, Jessie was gone.

He stepped forward, moving starboard on the deck. It took him only a moment to single her out among the passersby. Spotting the red T-shirt and the white shorts, he watched as she disappeared from sight.

Jacob stood beside him, following the direction of his gaze. He whistled his approval. "Not bad for a tourist."

"She isn't a tourist," Samuel said without thinking, a lingering burr of irritation getting the better of his judgment.

Jacob glanced at him curiously. "You know her?"

"We ran into each other yesterday," he said with a shrug, trying his best to sound nonchalant.

Jacob grinned. "Well, now I understand your sleepless night. I wouldn't have been able to get a wink, either, not with such a pretty young thing on my mind."

"It's not what you think," Samuel said quickly, hiding his embarrassment behind a sip of coffee. He winced as the hot liquid scalded his tongue. Muttering a curse beneath his breath, he blamed Jessie for yet another of his tribulations.

Jacob's chin jutted upward and out. "Now, how do you know what I'm thinking?"

"Years of experience," Samuel said, with a sigh. Forcing a smile, he placed a hand on his friend's shoulder. "Come on, Jacob. We've got better things to do than to argue about a woman. Let's get back to work."

Reluctantly Jacob nodded.

With one last glance at the beach, Samuel turned his back on Jessie's disturbing image and headed for the familiar safety of the hold.

Chapter 3

Never before had she felt such animosity directed at her from another person.

Reeling from the impact of the exchange, Jessie could think of nothing but putting as much distance between her and the man on the dock as possible. In her haste she almost stumbled on a large shell half-buried in the sand. She caught herself as she tried vainly to concentrate on the strip of beach before her.

She'd sensed his presence even before she'd spotted him. There'd been a prickling of awareness, a buzz of anticipation in her chest, telling her that someone near was watching her. She'd recognized him immediately. There weren't many men blessed with that devastating combination of sun-streaked hair, pale blue eyes, high cheekbones and strong jawline.

Jessie couldn't believe her own foolishness. She'd been on the brink of saying hello, of letting bygones be bygones. And then she'd caught the look in his eye. That look of pure, unadulterated hatred.

What had she done to deserve his disdain? He didn't even know her.

Frustration churned inside her. She pushed herself, running faster, faster, willing the image of the man on the dock to fade from her mind. Her feet pounded the beach. Wet, hard-packed sand slid beneath her tennis shoes. The salty air whipped her skin, stinging her eyes. At least, that's the reason she allowed herself for the tears blurring her vision. All she wanted to do was to go back to the cottage, where she could hole up and wallow in privacy.

Breathless, her heart racing, she slowed to a walk when she finally came to the boardwalk that crossed the dunes to Gull's Cottage. Sea oats waved in the light breeze. A squirrel darted across the walkway, startling her. Pressing a hand to her breast, she laughed at her own skittishness.

Stepping back, she watched the reckless rodent scramble up a nearby oak tree. Once he'd disappeared beneath a thick canopy of leaves, she turned around and nearly collided with a woman blocking her path on the walkway.

Jessie gasped, her heart leapfrogging into her throat. She couldn't move, couldn't speak. Instead, she stood rooted to the spot with fear, staring into the face of the other woman.

She looked to be in her midfifties. She was short and squat. Her hair was brown and straight, cut in an unflattering pageboy. Her face was wide and square. She wore round glasses that glittered in the sunlight as she studied Jessie's face. When she spoke, her words were brisk and to the point, "So, you've come back, Jessie Pierce."

"How did you know—" The words caught in her throat.

The woman smiled, seeming amused by Jessie's flustered confusion. "Thelma from the grocery store called me this morning." She nodded toward the wood and stone house a few yards down the beach. "I'm your neighbor. The name's Dora Hawkins. I've been the caretaker of your house for over twenty years. Last night I noticed your lights on. Surprised me—I almost came over to check it out for myself. It's been a long time since anyone's stayed at Gull's Cottage."

"Yes, well...I've been living in Atlanta," Jessie said, finally recovering her voice.

Dora took a moment to digest the news, then said, "I also heard you couldn't remember anything about your mother, about Eve."

Bad news traveled fast on the island, Jessie mused to herself. Sighing, she said, "No, I can't. As a matter of fact, there's not much about the first five years of my life that I can remember."

"Nothing at all?" Dora asked, studying her curiously.

Jessie fought the urge to fidget beneath the woman's scrutiny. She felt like a schoolgirl about to be caught in a lie. The troubling memory of last night's panic attack flickered in her mind. Until she understood the cause of her fear, she could not share this information with anyone. She shook her head. "No, nothing at all."

Abruptly Dora changed the subject. "How long are you staying?"

The conversation felt more like an interrogation. Jessie bit back another sigh at the woman's tenacity. In the polite world where she'd been raised, Dora Hawkins would have been labeled as an eccentric. Which was a nice way of saying the woman was odd. Harmless undoubtedly, but still a kook.

Striving to be patient, Jessie said, "I'm not sure. Maybe for the summer. I need to get things settled here…decide what to do with the house."

"So, you're thinking of selling."

Jessie shrugged. "Possibly. I live and work in Atlanta. There's not much point in my keeping a house here on Prudence Island."

"Probably for the best," Dora said with a sniff. She cast a glance at Gull's Cottage. "The house is full of bad memories. No need for you to become mired down by them."

Uncomfortable with the conversation, Jessie searched for a quick way for it to end. She forced a smile. "I'd invite you inside for some coffee, but I forgot to buy any at the store yesterday."

"No matter, I've got work to do," Dora said, not seeming offended by Jessie's dismissal. With a nod goodbye, she turned, the rubber heels of her shoes scraping against the wooden walkway. Then, with an abruptness Jessie was fast becoming accustomed to, she stopped, wheeling around to look at her. "How does it feel to be back in Gull's Cottage?"

"I—I'm not sure," Jessie said once again, taken aback by the woman's brusqueness. "It's quiet, a little spooky. I guess it'll take a while for me to get comfortable."

The woman humphed. "I'm not so sure about that, considering…"

Jessie frowned. This was the second time in as many days that someone had alluded to something that had

happened in the house. After her panic attack of last
night, she couldn't allow another opportunity to answer
the questions of her past to pass her by. "Considering
what?"

Dora hesitated, seeming uncertain for the first time
since their conversation began. Finally, looking Jessie
straight in the eye, she dropped her bombshell. "Considering the fact that your mother was murdered in
Gull's Cottage."

Your mother was murdered in Gull's Cottage.
The words echoed hollowly in her mind as Jessie
shifted her car into gear and stomped on the gas pedal,
taking the rutted lane leading from the house much too
fast. Somehow, after her conversation with Dora Hawkins, she'd found the strength to return to Gull's Cottage, despite her instincts telling her to run…to run
from the cottage, from the island, to run all the way
back to Atlanta to her home where she belonged.

Home. Was there really such a place? It was as
though her entire life had been built on quicksand.
Everything that she'd thought was safe and solid was
slipping away, crumbling beneath her feet.

When she'd set out on this quest to learn of her past,
she'd never imagined just what she might uncover. Eugenia, her only remaining link with her parents, had
told her there'd been some sort of scandal surrounding
her birth mother's death. She'd thought it had to do
with Eve being so young. Never in her wildest dreams
had she believed she would stumble onto a murder.

The air felt close, pressing in around her. Jessie inhaled deeply of the salty scent. She'd been on Prudence
Island for only two days.

It seemed like a lifetime.

Now she understood the curious glances, the troubled reactions of the townspeople. Her mother had been murdered on their quiet island. In a community of this size, it must have caused quite a sensation. No wonder they weren't sure what to make of her presence.

But it still didn't explain the hatred she'd seen in the eyes of one of their residents—the stranger on the highway, the man on the docks. Why would her return evoke such a strong reaction from him?

The bottom of her car scraped the ground as she hit a deep rut. She slowed the car to a more manageable speed, forcing the troubling thoughts from her mind. She only hoped that she'd made the right choice.

Despite the shock, she'd decided to stay. Now more than ever she had to find out the truth. Her mother had been murdered…and she had no recollection of any of it happening. She was left with nothing but the dreams that haunted her and a crippling inability to trust others.

She needed to know why.

Turning onto the main road, she drove the short distance into town, slowing when she came to Main Street. She parked her car in a public lot near the city hall, then she strode across the town's square to the brick building housing the library.

Even in a small town there had to be a local newspaper, Jessie reasoned. Her best bet of researching her mother's murder was to check out the back issues. She climbed the steps to the entrance and pulled open the heavy wooden door. The library was small compared to the ones in Atlanta. But it held the same quiet hush, the same musty odor of old books. Her tennis shoes squeaked against the tile floor, unnerving her as she made her way to the front desk.

A young red-haired woman, looking to be close to

her own age, greeted her with a smile. "Good morning. You're up early."

Despite the emotions churning in her stomach, Jessie managed a smile in return. At last, a friendly face. Someone who was too young to remember the scandal that had rocked the community nearly twenty-five years ago. "I need to do some research on a project. I was wondering if you had any back issues of the local newspaper."

"We certainly do," the librarian said proudly. "All the papers have been transferred onto microfilm. What year were you looking for?"

Jessie hesitated, uncertain how far back to look. Deciding to be safe rather than sorry, she said, "Would it be possible to get a five-year span, say between twenty and twenty-five years ago?"

"That's a lot of research."

"It's a big project."

The librarian laughed. "Let's get you started."

After directing Jessie to the right machine, she showed her how it worked. "Normally we have a thirty-minute use limit. But since it's a quiet day, and no one else is here yet, I don't think we have to worry. Take your time."

"Thanks," she said. As soon as the clicking of the librarian's heels against the tile floor faded in the distance, Jessie loaded the first of the cartridges. Minutes passed slowly. Her head began to throb. Her eyes burned as the articles flew past in a blur. And still there was nothing in the newspapers about the murder.

Then, just as she was about to give up, a headline jumped out at her...Local Woman Murdered On Island.

Jessie stared at the picture of the woman who had

been her mother. Her hair was long, past her shoulders, and dark, like Jessie's. But her features were finer, her bone structure more slender. There was a delicateness about the woman, a fragility, that Jessie had never possessed.

Once over the initial shock, Jessie forced herself to read the accompanying article. It was a gold mine of information. Not only did it tell of her mother's death, but it also gave her a valuable insight into her mother's life. She was an artist, Jessie discovered—something they had in common. While Jessie chose a more commercial outlet for her talent, her mother apparently had been making a name for herself as a painter in the art world. A former resident of Charleston, she'd moved to Prudence Island shortly after the death of her husband, Jonathan Pierce. She had resided in Gull's Cottage with her daughter, Jessica.

The account of the murder was sketchy, yet, at the same time, shockingly blunt. Schooling her emotions, Jessie scanned the description. Her mother was killed by a blow to the head in the early evening hours of May twenty-first. Her body was discovered by a Deputy Sheriff Gilbert Broward, who'd gone to the cottage after calls by a concerned friend went unanswered. Mrs. Pierce's five-year-old daughter was found unharmed in the house. How much of the crime she had witnessed was unknown. Attempts to question her were unsuccessful.

For a long moment Jessie stared at the screen, forgetting to breathe. Her stomach roiled in protest. A bitter taste rose in her throat. She was afraid she might be sick.

Only now did she realize that the uneasy feeling of déjà vu, the terror that she'd felt entering Gull's Cot-

tage last night, had roots in reality. She'd been in the
house when her mother had been murdered.

No one knew how much she'd seen.

The panic attack…was it triggered by a forgotten
memory? Had she actually witnessed her mother's
murder? Or was her fear merely the result of the trauma
that she'd surely suffered at the loss of her only parent?
Frustrated, she realized there were still too many questions and not enough answers.

She still didn't know who had killed her mother.

Her hands shook as she forced herself to continue
her search, reading account after account of the progress of the investigation into her mother's death. Until
finally, a headline with an accompanying grainy photo
leaped out at her…Local Man Charged In The Murder
Of Evelyn Pierce.

With that single headline, the world dropped out beneath Jessie's feet. It was as though time had stopped.
He hadn't changed at all in nearly twenty-five years.

Her hands shook as she reached to press her fingers
against the grainy picture on the screen. She didn't
know how it was possible, but she'd met the man who
was accused of murdering her mother…yesterday on
the highway, this morning on the docks…the stranger,
the man with the hatred burning in his eyes.

Now she had a name to go with the face…Samuel
Conners.

Slowly, reason returned. No, it was impossible. The
man in the newspaper, if he were still alive, would have
to be nearly sixty years old. The man she'd met yesterday was in his early thirties. They couldn't be one
in the same.

But the resemblance was uncanny. The two men
must be related—perhaps a father or an uncle.

Still feeling numb with the shock, Jessie scanned the rest of the articles. Her search turned up more information regarding the trial and the conviction of the man accused of murdering her mother. Once she'd finished, she copied the articles she had found. Gathering up the cartridges, she returned to the front desk.

The librarian smiled as she approached. "That was quick." When she took a closer look at Jessie's face, her smile faltered. "Are you all right?"

"Yes, I'm fine," Jessie said, unable to stop the trembling in her voice. Clearing her throat, she asked, "Would you happen to have a phone book?"

"Sure, it's right here." She reached behind the desk, pulling out a thin yellow book. Her gaze lingered on Jessie's face. "Are you sure everything's all right?"

"Positive," Jessie said, forcing a quick smile. Her hands shook as she riffled through the pages, belying her claim. Aware of the other woman's hovering presence, she quickly flipped through the book until she came to the *C*s. Running her finger down the column, she froze when she found the name she sought.

There *was* a listing under the name of Samuel Conners.

She stared at the book, her suspicions confirmed. Fumbling in her purse for a pen and paper, she scribbled down the phone number and address. Thanking the librarian, she stumbled out of the building and into the brilliant sunlight. For a long moment she stood looking out at the town's square. A thick carpet of green grass covered the courtyard. Beds of pink begonias bordered the sidewalk. A flag whipped the air, dancing in a steady breeze. Everything seemed so normal.

Yet, her entire world had been turned upside down.

A gray-haired couple walking hand in hand passed her by, studying her curiously, reminding her that she hadn't moved. She descended the stone steps. The truth was that little by little she was uncovering a mystery. But the more she learned, the more uneasy she became.

As she strode across the square, she recounted her meeting yesterday on the highway with Samuel Conners. He'd seemed polite, almost friendly and ready to help her...until she'd told him that she was staying at Gull's Cottage. When she'd told him her name, he'd left abruptly, abandoning her without a word of explanation.

On shaking legs she crossed the street to the parking lot, ignoring the glances of passersby. At first she'd attributed Samuel's actions to rudeness. Now she believed recognition had played a role in his behavior. It would certainly explain his reaction to her identity— he'd been shocked.

Distractedly she unlocked the door of her car. Climbing inside, she started the engine and pulled out of the lot, not exactly sure where she was going. Then, as though the car had a mind of its own, she found herself searching the island for the address listed in the phone book.

Eventually she found Samuel's house on the outskirts of town, near the docks. She slowed her car to a stop, her curiosity getting the better of her. It was an older home, but well taken care of. It was painted a creamy yellow, with dark-green shutters. Bright, multi-colored flowers spilled out of the window boxes lining the front of the house. A rustic brick walkway led to the door.

The familiar red truck parked in the driveway surprised her. It was still early, barely twelve o'clock, the workday only half over.

There were no other signs of life. No car, no swing set, no bicycles, nothing to indicate anyone else was around. She wondered if he lived alone.

Suddenly the front door swung open, and Samuel Conners stepped outside. He stood on the front porch, glancing at the street. When he spotted her car, a stormy expression crossed his handsome face. Before she realized what was happening, he strode angrily toward her car, making short work of the distance between them.

His face dark with fury, he placed both hands on the frame of her window, blocking her escape. With a harshness that sent a chill down her spine, he snarled, "What the hell do you want, Jessie Pierce? Why did you have to come back to Prudence Island?"

Samuel had had enough. One chance encounter was unavoidable. He'd even believed that twice was a mere coincidence. But three times in less than twenty-four hours was more than any man could accept.

The woman was following him…and he was determined to find out why.

Jessie stared at him, her mouth dropping open. She looked scared, rightfully so. He supposed he appeared a little wild and dangerous. He certainly felt on the verge of losing control.

But he would never hurt a woman….

Not that she would know that.

Samuel's gaze remained hard, unwavering. Just what did she know? That was the million-dollar question, wasn't it? Everyone from the sheriff to the prosecutor to the defense attorneys had wanted to know exactly what young Jessie had seen the night her mother had died.

But no one had been able to discover the answer.

Unwanted memories flashed in his mind. He'd been ten years old when it had all happened. She couldn't have been more than four or five. Too shocked and upset, in the end, for anyone to press for her testimony. Protected by her family's wealth and standing in the community, she had disappeared from Prudence Island, leaving unanswered questions and more pain than she could have imagined.

Now she was back.

"What are you doing here?" he demanded, as the bitterness of his past threatened to overwhelm him.

"I found the article," she whispered, her voice so quiet he could barely hear her. She had the scared, petrified look of a cornered animal. Shrinking back against the seat, she leaned away from him, away from his anger. "The newspaper, the picture of the man who murdered my mother. I know it couldn't have been you, but it was your name, your picture...."

The words fell like a blow against his chest, knocking the breath from his lungs. Samuel bore the name and the face of his father. It had been his burden in life. He stepped away from the car, feeling sickened by this unwanted invasion from the past.

Resignation stole the heat from his anger. Still unable to accept the final verdict, he backed away from the car. "Samuel Conners was my father. He was a kind, gentle man. He couldn't have done anything so vile, so brutal. He died for a crime he didn't commit." He pointed a finger at Jessie, not caring that his hand shook. Or that his voice was nearly choked by a lump of overwhelming emotion. "If anyone should know that, it's you, Jessie Pierce."

With that he turned on his heel and strode back to the blessed sanctuary of his house.

Chapter 4

My father...a kind, gentle man...he couldn't have done anything so vile, so brutal.

Samuel's final words played over and over in her mind, as Jessie slammed the BMW into gear and sped away from his house. Her tires squealed in protest at her rough handling, spewing out dirt and crushed shell. Within seconds the house disappeared behind a cloud of dust and debris.

His father. Of course. She should have known he'd been the man in the newspaper article. Who else could have borne such a striking resemblance to this man than his own father?

He died for a crime he didn't commit. If anyone should know that, it's you, Jessie Pierce.

She gripped the steering wheel tightly, trying to still her trembling hands. The look on Samuel's face, the adamancy of his tone—he actually believed she knew his father to be innocent. That she'd allowed a wrong-fully convicted man to die in prison.

No wonder he held such animosity toward her.

Golden rays of the midday sun glinted off the road, turning the pavement up ahead into a shimmering mirage. Yet she felt none of its comforting warmth. Jessie drew in a shaky breath. She felt chilled by the elusive memories of her past.

Too soon she spotted the lane leading to her cottage. She slowed the car, carefully making her way over the deep ruts. Even at high noon the towering, moss-covered live oaks and the thick underbrush cast huge shadows, choking out any filtering light. The house, despite its brilliant coat of white paint, wore an ominous pall.

Unable to face the darkness that surrounded the house, Jessie parked her car in the driveway and walked the short distance to the beach. A few feet past the boardwalk, her strength gave out. She sat down hard on a cushion of soft, warm sand, her muscles shaking with relief. Blindly she stared at the undulating waves of the ocean.

Her mind still reeling, she forced herself to go over the events of her disturbing encounter with Samuel. He had said that his father had died for a crime he did not commit. Which meant Samuel believed someone else had murdered Eve Pierce.

Or did it?

Mixed in with the anger and the bitterness, Jessie had seen another emotion shadowing Samuel's eyes. An emotion so raw and painful, it had hurt for her to witness it. An emotion so intense, she had wanted to reach out and ease his suffering.

There had been a guilty uncertainty in his gaze.

Despite his protests to the contrary, Samuel was not completely sure of his father's innocence.

Jessie's breath caught painfully in her throat. More than anything else, her own reaction toward Samuel's anguish had disturbed her. Caring didn't come easy for her. Her protective instincts usually kept her aloof from others and their problems. Better to live an isolated life, she reminded herself, than to risk the pain of caring too much. Especially not for a stranger, a man whose father may very well have murdered her own mother.

That is, if the newspaper accounts of her mother's death had been accurate. She frowned. Could they have been wrong? Could the person who murdered her mother still be at large?

Jessie shuddered at the possibility that such a devastating mistake could have been made. Slowly she became aware of her surroundings. The foaming waves of the ocean formed a jigsaw pattern against the beach. The air was heavy with the scent of salt and the live fish of the sea. In the distance a mother and child laughed in delight as the winds carried their kite high into the sky.

Everything seemed so normal, so peaceful. It felt odd that the lives of others went unaffected while her life had undergone such a complete and staggering change.

Her mother had been murdered in Gull's Cottage. That much she knew for sure. The truth of whether or not she'd been a witness to the horrible crime was still buried deep inside her. According to the newspaper's account, Samuel's father was found guilty of the murder. But the little voice in the back of her mind told her that something wasn't quite right with the story.

That there was more to the events of the past that hadn't yet been revealed.

Unfortunately Samuel's father was dead, as was her mother. Did that mean the secret behind her mother's death would forever be buried?

She closed her eyes against the emotions roiling inside her. In Atlanta she'd learned to cope with her fears by distancing herself from her own emotions. Though her adoptive mother had constantly tried to bring her out of her shell, Jessie had stood firm in her belief that if she didn't allow herself to feel, to get close to others, then she would never be hurt.

In her own way she had become an island.

Until she'd returned to Gull's Cottage, she'd never realized how fragile her world had become, how successful she'd been at denying the truth. Clearly, the emotional problems of her adulthood were tied to the one traumatic event of her childhood—the event that she'd tried so hard to suppress—her mother's death.

Drawing in a steadying breath, Jessie slowly opened her eyes. She hadn't been the only one whose life had been changed by that violent act. Samuel had been deeply affected by his father's conviction of guilt.

Through the actions of their parents, her past and Samuel's were irrevocably connected. He was the key to the answers she sought. No one else would know as much about his own father as he did.

Whether she liked it or not, the path to the truth passed through Samuel Conners.

The next morning Jessie steeled herself for what lay ahead. She'd risen early, even before the sun. Now, with the dawn stretching ribbons of purple and pink throughout the lightening sky, she walked along the beach, heading for the one place where she knew she would find Samuel.

The docks brimmed with activity as she approached. Crews of fishermen called out to one another, laughing, joking as they prepared for their morning's work. Boats rocked against their moorings, the water slapping against their hulls. Gulls screamed overhead, as though impatient for their chance at scraps from the morning catch.

Despite the crush of activity, her appearance didn't go unnoticed. As she passed, she received curious glances from the sea of primarily male workers, some more blatant in their show of appreciation than others. Her step faltered, her face flushing with embarrassment, as catcalls followed her down the wooden dock. Quickening her step, she hurried to Samuel's shrimp boat.

The *Marianna* stood silent, oblivious to the frenetic activity of the surrounding fishermen. So quiet, in fact, that Jessie wondered if anyone was aboard. She hesitated, biting her lower lip as she studied the white boat with its blue trim, debating the wisdom of calling out and attracting any more unwanted attention.

Just as she was about to turn around and head back to Gull's Cottage in defeat, a familiar blond-haired figure emerged from the shadows of the hold. Samuel's powerful body dwarfed the boat as he stepped onto the deck. Like a magnet drawn to steel, his gaze flew to her. In stunned silence, he stared at her.

She froze, held by the force of his gaze. Dressed in a grease-stained T-shirt and faded jeans, he wore a harried expression on his face. The wind stroked his sun-streaked hair, blowing it across his forehead. Absently, rubbing his hands with a dingy white cloth, his gaze slid up and down the length of her body.

Jessie fought the urge to squirm beneath the touch of his assessing glance. Even without the censure that she saw reflected in his eyes, she felt out of place in her pristine white jeans, her black-and-white-striped shirt and her unscuffed tennis shoes. He didn't need to tell her what they both already knew.

That she didn't belong here.

Jessie was the first to break the silent standoff. Gathering her courage, she cleared her throat, then said, "I need to talk to you."

For one terrible moment she thought he might turn and walk away, ignoring her and her request. Instead, he slowly shook his head. "I don't think that'd be a good idea," he said, his tone a low warning.

Aware of the other nearby fishermen stopping to watch them, Jessie braced herself against the undisguised hostility in his stance and the anger which corded his muscles. Sternly she told herself she could not let him intimidate her. Lifting her chin, feigning a confidence she did not feel, she said, "Is that because you're too scared to talk to me?"

For the first time since she'd met him, Samuel actually smiled, seeming amused by the question. He drew himself up to his full six-foot-plus height and stepped forward, closing the distance between them. In a cool voice that sent a chill down her spine, he said, "I'm not the one who should be frightened."

Jessie's heart pounded against her breast. She fought the urge to turn and run. Despite the challenging look in his eyes, she sensed that his threat was harmless. That, no matter how daunting an image he tried to project, Samuel would never hurt her. Taking a gamble on

her instincts being correct, she stood her ground and
refused to budge.

Slowly his smile faded. Releasing an impatient
breath, he stepped down from the boat and landed with
a thud on the dock in front of her. For a long, resolve-
stealing moment, he stood within inches of touching
her. Close enough that she felt the heat of his sun-
kissed skin. So close that she grew lost in the pale
blueness of his eyes. Dizzied by his overwhelming
presence, she was tempted to rest a hand against the
anchoring strength of his wide shoulders.

"I don't have time to waste on chitchat," he said
finally, his curt tone snapping her out of her trance. He
jabbed a finger in the direction of his boat. "Right now
I've got to take a test run with my repaired motor. If
you want to talk to me, it'll have to be out on the
ocean."

Without another word, he stepped away from her and
began loosening the thick lines of rope that moored the
boat, leaving her to deal with a confusing rush of emotions.

He wanted her to turn and run. She'd heard the challenge in his voice. He was letting the decision to stay
or go fall squarely on her shoulders, gambling on the
chance that she'd be too scared to actually take him up
on the offer.

If she were smart she would run as fast as her feet
could carry her. Knowing how much he must resent
her, she told herself, she would be a fool to go anywhere alone with him. Once they were on the ocean,
there would be no one to protect her from his anger.

Despite what reason might be telling her, Jessie felt
as though she could trust the man standing before her.
As illogical as it might sound, deep in her heart she

believed that nothing bad would happen to her as long as she was with him.

Besides, she was tired of running away. Tired of crawling into her protective shell of isolation at the first sign of trouble. Never opening herself up to what the world had to offer, good or bad, had proved a very lonely way to live.

Oblivious to the battle raging inside her, Samuel tossed the last line onto the boat. With a wordless glance, he looked to her for an answer.

Surprising both of them, Jessie grabbed a piling for support and climbed aboard the *Marianna*.

He'd never thought she would accept his challenge. Clenching his jaw against a growing agitation, calling himself a fool for allowing her anywhere near him, he climbed onto the boat after her. He'd wanted her to run scared, to go back to where she came from and leave Prudence Island for good. And to take with her all of the memories that her presence promised to stir up.

But, as he was the last to find out, Jessie Pierce wasn't a woman who scared easily.

Now she stood on his deck in her expensive clothes, making him all the more aware of his grease-stained hands, his sweat-soaked T-shirt and his work-faded jeans. Her complexion glowed with the beginnings of a tan. The rising sun shimmered through the strands of her dark hair, tempting him to warm his fingers in their silky locks. Her dark eyes wide and uncertain, she glanced cautiously around the boat. She looked small and vulnerable, reminding him to be gentle.

Impatient with himself for feeling anything for Jessie but contempt, Samuel strode past her, making his way to the storage locker in the hold. Digging out a life jacket, he returned to the deck and held it out to her.

She hesitated, raising one finely sculpted brow in question.

"In case you fall overboard," he said, unable to keep the bite from his tone. In a streak of pure orneriness, he added, "If you drowned, I wouldn't want to be accused of murder."

She flinched at the blunt reminder of his words. Looking as though she'd sooner slap him than accept his offer, once again she surprised him. She took the jacket and slipped it over her slender shoulders. Fastening the belt around her waist, she glared at him, silently daring him to comment.

He declined the challenge. Instead he turned away, unwilling to admit, even to himself, an unexpected stirring of admiration. With her petite height and stature, Jessie might look fragile and helpless. He had no doubt, however, that she had the strength and the determination to put him in his place if need be.

Feeling the need to escape with his pride still intact, he headed for the pilothouse, taking his seat behind the wheel. Gunning the motor to life, he weighed anchor, then eased the *Marianna* from the dock.

Without waiting to be told, Jessie joined him in the pilothouse. Standing behind him, resting a hand against the back of his seat for support, she watched as he slowly made his way out to sea.

He ignored the prickling of gooseflesh her closeness brought him, attributing the reaction to unease, rather than awareness. Once they were safely away from the shore, he picked up speed, giving the newly repaired motor its head. The engines roared beneath their feet, drowning out any opportunity to speak.

He told himself his delaying actions had nothing to do with the woman standing so near to him that he could smell the sweet scent of her perfume. He'd have to be blind not to notice that she was beautiful, he reasoned. So what if he felt as though she'd just stepped out of the dream that had kept him awake for the past two nights? That didn't mean he'd become infatuated with her. *Tormented* would be a more appropriate description of his feelings.

Just what the hell did she want from him?

As soon as the shore was nothing more than a thin line on the horizon, Samuel cut the engine. Silence descended upon the pilothouse. A silence so utterly complete it served to emphasize the remoteness of their location, the solitude of their encounter. There wasn't another ship, not another living soul for miles.

Letting the boat drift, he slowly turned to face her. Not allowing the fragile delicacy of her features to sway him, he said gruffly, "You wanted to talk, now's your chance. I'm listening."

She hesitated, her glance wary. Finally she blurted out, "I need your help."

"My help? You must be crazy." The pilothouse reverberated with the shock waves of his voice. The walls felt as though they were closing in on him. Surging to his feet, he moved past her and stepped onto the deck. He stood beneath the clear, blue morning sky and took deep, calming breaths of air into his lungs.

She followed him out onto the deck. In a quiet rush she said, "If you'd just let me finish—"

"Lady, you've got some nerve," he said with a shake of his head. "After yesterday—"

"*Yesterday* was a mistake," she insisted. Her chin

lifted, she met his gaze straight on. "*I* made a mistake."

Her apology caught him by surprise. He wasn't sure what he'd thought she'd say next. But he would never have guessed her to admit she was wrong. Though his curiosity was piqued, he stared at her, letting her continue to flounder without his help.

Looking discomfited, she averted her eyes, focusing her gaze on the flat stretch of calm water. "I shouldn't have come to your house without calling first. Yesterday I—I'd been to the library. I'd just come across the articles in the newspaper about my mother's—" Her voice caught. Swallowing hard, she continued in a voice that was stronger, clearer, "About my mother's death. When I saw your father's picture in the paper, I—"

"You assumed, just like everyone else, that he was the man who murdered your mother."

"That he was the man who was *accused* of murdering my mother," she corrected, whipping her gaze around to face him. Without so much as a blink of an eye she added, "I'm not sure if that's true."

Winded by the impact of that simple statement, he refused to get his hopes up, refused to believe that after all this time, she was going to tell him that his father did not commit the crime for which he had been convicted. Nothing in this world came that easy. Almost afraid to hear her answer, he forced himself to ask, "What are you trying to say? That my father was innocent?"

She sighed. "No, I'm not."

Samuel leaned forward, gripping the railing as disappointment crashed in around him. "What do you want?" he whispered harshly, the words barely audible. "Why can't you just leave me and the past alone?"

"I can't," she said, her voice so soft he could barely hear her over the pounding of his own heart. She drew in a trembling breath. "You have to understand. I have no memory of my past, of the time I spent on Prudence Island. Until a few weeks ago, I didn't even know that Eve Pierce was my birth mother."

The admission stunned him. He wasn't sure whether to believe her or not. He looked at her, anger and bitterness churning inside him. Hadn't Jessie Pierce and her faulty memory caused enough damage to him and his family? After she'd left Prudence Island, it had taken him years to pick up the shattered pieces of his childhood. Surely she didn't expect him to sit back and let her destroy the rest of his life, too.

He gave a disgusted breath. "Even if I could help you, which I can't, what makes you think I'd want to do something so crazy?"

"Because my past is yours, as well," she said, bearing the weight of his anger without flinching. "I have to believe that you're the one person on this island who needs to know the truth as much as I do."

He stopped and stared at her, unable to find the words to argue. He did want to know the truth. More than anything else, he needed to close that chapter of his life for good.

"You say you don't remember the past," he said, narrowing a shrewd glance. "What makes you think there's still a chance to prove that my father is innocent?"

She searched his face as though trying to memorize each line and curve. "You bear an uncanny resemblance to your father."

"Tell me something I don't already know."

"You're not making this easy for me," she said with an irritated sigh, showing the first signs of losing her patience.

"I didn't know I was supposed to," he countered.

Annoyance glittered in her eyes. "Fine, then explain this. You admit that you look like your father. If he killed my mother, and I was a witness to her death, then why aren't I afraid of you?"

"You're not?" he asked, giving a harsh laugh.

"No, I'm not," she said, slowly shaking her head. Samuel winced inwardly at the unmistakable look of pity shadowing her expression. "When I look at you, it's not your face that I fear…it's the bitterness that I see in your eyes."

The admission cut him to the quick. He hadn't realized how easily she could read his emotions, how much he had revealed to her already. He wondered what else she knew about him.

"All I want is to find out the truth," she said, drawing him out of his troubled thoughts. "I want to know what really happened to my mother. If you feel the same way, couldn't we work together to find the answers?"

Samuel had lived his entire life with the shame of his father's past. For too many years he had hoped against hope, fighting in vain to find a way to prove his father's innocence.

Not once, in all those years, had anyone ever offered to help him.

Not until now.

Jessie seemed so earnest, so unbelievably innocent. While her intentions might be good, her naïveté was obvious. She had no idea of the battle that lay ahead.

No idea what sort of ugliness she would expose in her quest for the truth.

Although he had more reason than anyone to want to see her suffer, he didn't want to be the one to disillusion her.

Samuel sighed, deciding it best to delay his refusal. "It's time we headed back to port."

She nodded but remained on deck as he returned to the pilothouse. He restarted the motor, the roaring engine shattering the quiet of the ocean. Sensing her disappointment, he kept an eye on her as he guided the boat toward the shore.

The wind whipped her short hair into her eyes as she clung to the railing. Instead of fighting the rolling pitch of the boat, she let her body move with each rise and fall. Her legs were slender, as were her hips. At the sight of them, he felt an unwanted stirring of awareness deep in his belly.

No matter how ill-advised it might be, he couldn't deny the pull of attraction he felt whenever she was near.

Anxious to return to shore, he opened up the throttle, picking up speed. He didn't let up on the gas until the shore came into sharp focus. Slowing, he eased the boat across the bay, heading for the nearly deserted harbor.

A lone figure stood on the dock, leaning against a piling at the slip assigned to the *Marianna*.

Frowning, Samuel reached for the binoculars, unable to believe his bad luck. His gut tightened in agitation. From the moment she'd reappeared in his life, he knew it would be only a matter of time before Jessie's presence on the island would cause him problems.

It would seem that trouble was already beginning.

There was an unexpected visitor awaiting them... Prudence Island's sheriff.

Chapter 5

The man waiting for them on the dock looked to be in his mid to late fifties. He had a head of thick, reddish-blond hair, a broad, square face and a strong chin. Considering his age, he stood tall and erect, his large body trim and athletic. He wore the dark-brown uniform of the sheriff's department. The badge pinned to his shirt glittered, catching the morning sun.

Despite the differences in their ages, Jessie felt the heat of the lawman's appreciative gaze upon her. She shifted uncomfortably on the deck of the shrimp boat, looking to Samuel for a clue as to why the island's law enforcement might be present.

Samuel stared straight ahead, refusing to meet her gaze. Minutes ago his face had been a mirror of pain and anguish, the emotions he'd felt in his heart. Now he wore a stony expression, his feelings unreadable. The change in his demeanor set off warning bells in her head.

Something was wrong.

Her troubled gaze returned to the sheriff. Just what was the man doing here?

Samuel slid the *Marianna* alongside the dock. He cut the motor, and they bumped to an uneven stop. Without a word he stepped out onto the deck and tossed a line, securing the boat to a piling.

While relieved to be safely ashore, Jessie almost felt disappointed that their trip was over. Samuel hadn't given her his answer yet. She didn't know if he would help her in her quest for the truth about their past. For all she knew, this would be the last she saw of him. Pushing the disturbing thought from her mind, Jessie fumbled with the buckles of her life jacket.

"Miss Pierce?" The sheriff called out as he stepped toward the shrimp boat, demanding her attention. He focused his sharp gaze solely upon her, ignoring Samuel, who stood nearby on the deck.

"Y-yes, I'm Jessie Pierce," she stammered, feeling slightly bewildered. Prudence Island was a small community, but it still amazed her that so many people seemed to know of her. The fact that this instant notoriety might have something to do with her relationship to one of the island's few murder victims only added to her unease.

With his hands resting on his hips, his booted feet set wide apart, the sheriff gave the impression of a solid and immovable force. "My name's Sheriff Gilbert Broward."

Jessie's heart thumped unevenly in her chest as recognition jolted her. She knew the name. In the news articles about her mother's death, Deputy Gil Broward of the island's Sheriff's department had been the first

to arrive at the scene of the murder. The man standing
before her had discovered her mother's body.

"I had a call you might be in trouble," he drawled
with his thick Southern accent.

"Trouble?" Jessie frowned, confused by his assumption. Nervously she tugged at the last of the life
jacket's buckles, yanking it loose. She slipped the
jacket from her shoulders and suddenly felt exposed,
vulnerable.

"Yes, ma'am." The sheriff cast a pointed glance at
Samuel. The barest hint of an amused smile touched
his lips. "A few concerned citizens felt that you hadn't
left the island of your own accord. That you might be
in danger."

Stunned, her gaze flew to Samuel.

Samuel refused to look at her. Instead, he stood
stiffly on the deck, his muscles tense, as though fighting
an inner battle for self-control.

Empathy and anger billowed inside her. Jessie did
not understand how the sheriff—or the townspeople,
for that matter—had jumped to the wrong conclusion.
She was appalled by the man's attitude. By the blunt
and uncaring manner in which he was handling his inquiry. It seemed to her that he was intentionally goad-
ing Samuel into a confrontation.

As though to give credence to her concerns, Samuel
moved closer to the railing of the boat, looking ready
to leap down onto the dock. Given further provocation,
she had no doubt that he wouldn't let a uniform stand
in the way of defending his tarnished honor.

Jessie's chest tightened with frustration and with
fear. What had Samuel done to deserve this sort of
treatment? How could the sheriff and the citizens of
this island assume the worst of him?

But she already knew, didn't she?

It had to do with his father's past, with her mother's death. Samuel was still being punished for the sins of his father. And she'd been the catalyst to the harassment. By forcing herself into Samuel's life, she had brought on this unjust humiliation.

The heat went out of her anger. Tears of regret stung her eyes. She blinked away the emotion, knowing sympathy was the last thing Samuel would want. But still, if this was the way he'd been treated all of his life, then how could he have stayed on Prudence Island? Why hadn't he left years ago?

Brushing the unsettling thought aside, she concentrated on the problem at hand—how to ward off a confrontation. A confrontation which would only end badly for Samuel. The need to protect him nearly overwhelmed her.

Deciding it best to soothe ruffled tempers, she forced a pleasant smile. "There must be a misunderstanding, Sheriff. As you can see, I'm just fine."

The sheriff peered up at her, his expression doubtful.

"Samuel was kind enough to give me a tour of the island. We just returned." She looked to Samuel for support, her smile strained. "Isn't that right, Samuel?"

Samuel hesitated, then gave a grudging nod.

Jessie breathed a quiet sigh of relief.

"I didn't know the two of you were acquainted," the sheriff said, his gaze speculative.

Samuel did not answer. He remained mute, his expression hard and uncompromising. The air between the two men crackled with tension.

"Actually, we just met a few days ago, when I arrived on the island," Jessie said, taking up the slack, struggling to avoid a collision of wills. "Samuel helped me when I had car trouble."

"Well now, wasn't that convenient," the sheriff drawled. His good-ol'-boy smile didn't reach his eyes. The gesture seemed cold, calculating.

"Yes, it was," Jessie said, searching for a way to end this unnerving conversation. She brushed the wind-blown hair from her eyes, giving a self-deprecating grimace. "Well, it's certainly been a long morning. I must look a mess. Perhaps we could continue this conversation at another time, Sheriff. Right now, I'd like to go back to Gull's Cottage and take a hot bath."

"Yes, ma'am," the sheriff said, taking the hint. He stepped back, as though preparing to leave. Then, catching her off guard, he asked, "May I offer you a ride home?"

"No," she said, louder than she'd intended. Too loud, in fact. The sheriff raised an eyebrow in surprise. While she couldn't explain the reason, the last thing she wanted was to be alone with this man. Forcing herself to be cordial, she softened her refusal. "No, thank you, Sheriff. It's a beautiful morning. I'd rather walk. I could use the exercise."

The sheriff nodded, but didn't leave. He studied the two of them, waiting for their next move.

Slowly Jessie turned to Samuel, feeling the heat of uncertainty rise on her face. Samuel still had not told her of his decision. She didn't know whether he intended to help her or not. With the sheriff standing there watching, she didn't know how to broach the subject, how to get his answer.

"Thank you for the tour, Samuel," she said, handing

him the life jacket. Their fingers brushed as they made the exchange. Jessie drew in quick breath at the spark of awareness his touch brought her.

Samuel glanced at her sharply, his pale blue eyes searching her face.

She swallowed hard, forcing herself to continue, "We haven't settled our plans for...for dinner this evening. Will seven o'clock be all right?"

He stared at her for a moment, not saying a word.

More heat flushed her skin as she waited for his answer. Subterfuge wasn't her forte. She felt clumsy, inept. She knew her inexperience was showing. Most times she was scrambling to find an excuse to decline a man's invitation for dinner, not using her feminine wiles to trick him into seeing her again.

But she told herself this was no ordinary situation. Too much depended on his decision. If Samuel declined her invitation, then she would know he had no intention of helping her. If he said yes, then she wouldn't be alone in her quest for the truth behind her mother's death.

Finally Samuel nodded. His deep voice vibrated in her ears, giving her such sweet relief. "Seven o'clock will be fine."

"I'll see you then," she said, with a genuine, heartfelt smile.

Clambering down the ladder on the side of the boat, refusing both Samuel's and the sheriff's attempt to help, Jessie stepped down onto the dock. With the heavy measure of two separate gazes upon her she made her escape, hurrying to the beach and to Gull's Cottage.

* * *

Samuel was still reeling from the impact of Jessie's departure when Sheriff Gil Broward slowly turned his attention to him.

Any lingering civility disappeared from the man's eyes. His true feelings for Samuel surfaced with a look of pure contempt. Not one to mince words, he said, "Just what the hell do you think you're up to, Samuel?"

With a smile that was certain to annoy the pompous lawman, Samuel answered the question with one of his own. "What makes you think I'm up to something, Sheriff?"

"Years of experience." The sheriff's stare was steely, chilling. "You've got the look of a guilty man."

Samuel's smile faded, the words bringing him a sharp reminder of the past, of the helplessness he'd felt when his father had been unjustly convicted of murder. A conviction in which the man before him played a large role. Facing the condemnation in the other man's gaze, he said, "Seems to me I'm not the one who should have anything to feel guilty about."

The sheriff flinched.

Samuel took little comfort that his blow had hit its mark. He'd learned long ago that nothing would be accomplished in trading insults with this man.

"Listen to me, Samuel," the sheriff said as he stepped forward, straightening his shoulders, using his big body to intimidate. "You've been a thorn in my side since the day I arrested your daddy. You think I don't know that you blame me for everything bad that's ever happened to you and your family?"

Samuel did not answer. He stood on the deck, silently daring the man to continue.

"Dammit!" The sheriff released a whistling breath

of impatience. "I've had just about enough of you and your sanctimonious notions of persecution."

Samuel couldn't help himself. Knowing he was only fanning the fire of ill feelings, he said, "Wrong again, Sheriff. I'm not the one with the chip on his shoulder."

The sheriff stiffened, his hands balled at his sides. Like a snake coiled for action, he looked ready to strike. Instead, he jabbed an angry finger in his direction. "Your father's gone. So is that poor girl's mamma. There's no need to disturb the dead." His voice, as well as his hand, shook with emotion. "What's past is past. Don't you forget that."

Lowering the brim of his hat over his eyes, the sheriff pivoted on the ball of one foot, then strode the length of the dock. His booted feet pounded against the wooden boards, his long legs making short the distance to his patrol car. He slung himself into the front seat, gunning the engine to life. Spitting up dust and crushed shell, he peeled out of the dock's parking lot.

And Samuel realized he'd just been given a warning.

His chest burned with agitation. Slowly he released the breath he hadn't even realized he'd been holding. He and the sheriff went back a long way. They shared a dark history that had started with the arrest of his father for the murder of Eve Pierce. Thanks to his rebellious teenage years, their relationship had grown steadily worse as time had passed.

Samuel wasn't proud of the things he'd done as a youth. He had found a release for his pent-up anger in self-destructive ways. First by skipping school, then by hanging out with a bad crowd and roaming the streets at night and, finally, by vandalizing the town's courthouse. After that prank, only the intervention of his uncle had kept him from spending time in juvenile court. Considering their pasts, it wasn't surprising that the animosity between himself and the sheriff had continued on into adulthood.

Simply put, they rubbed each other the wrong way. Neither of them held much respect for the other.

Samuel raked both hands through his hair in frustration. He'd dealt with the sheriff and his narrow-minded views all of his life. Right now the man's opinion of him was the least of his concerns. At the moment Jessie Pierce promised to be a bigger problem.

What was he thinking, agreeing to meet her for dinner?

Sheriff Broward was right about one thing. His father was dead and buried. No one cared about him or his reputation. No one but his son, that is. Jessie wanted to find out the truth behind her mother's death. She didn't care whether that truth cleared his father's name or not.

Samuel shook his head. Just how much would dredging up the past really help?

If they were to uncover the truth and find that someone else had murdered Eve Pierce, then what? It was too late to change his father's fate. But it could shake a murderer from his hiding place. Jessie's good intentions could very well put both of them in danger.

Jessie. In his mind's eye, he saw her standing next to him on the deck. Once again he saw the stubborn tilt of her chin as she faced Sheriff Broward. The delicate slope of her neck as she raised her head in defiance. Her supple curves as the wind molded her clothes tight against her body. Samuel's blood warmed, his own body hardening at the memory. He drew in a deep breath, willing the untimely awakening of his libido under control. Jessie was a beautiful, strong-willed woman. But she was no match for a murderer.

Tonight he had no choice but to tell her to forget the past. To leave Prudence Island before it was too late.

If only she would listen.

She had never been this nervous, Jessie realized, as she prepared for Samuel's arrival.

After her encounter with him that morning on the shrimp boat, she'd felt the need to get rid of some restless energy. So she'd spent the entire day cleaning and inspecting the cottage, reacquainting herself with her only physical link to a forgotten past. She hadn't found any clues to her mother's death. Only a few pictures of herself as a child...and of her mother.

But the pictures were priceless. They showed a love that had been undeniable. In each photo her mother held her close. Whether they were walking hand in hand on the beach or building sand castles near the water or sharing an ice cream sundae on the porch, they wore carefree smiles. Heartfelt smiles that were impossible to feign.

The love she'd witnessed in these photos made her all the more confused. She didn't understand what had happened to her since her mother's death. How could she have forgotten this beautiful, loving woman?

Jessie shivered, glancing around the cottage's large kitchen. Now, with the lights shining brightly to ward off the night, Gull's Cottage sparkled beneath a clean coat of polish. But the superficial shine could not rid it of its hovering darkness. While she had settled into this house that had once been her home, she did not feel comfortable.

The dream that had haunted her in Atlanta was worse

here on Prudence Island. It was more vivid, more alarming. It was as though it had somehow found a source of strength, a terrifying life of its own on this beautiful, peaceful island.

Restlessly Jessie picked up a spoon and stirred the simmering pot of clam chowder. It was an old recipe, one that her adoptive mother had made often. She'd never asked Samuel his preference for dinner. Being a fisherman, she'd assumed he would like seafood. Perhaps she'd been presumptuous. After all, a baker faced with pastries all day long was known to tire of the taste of sugar.

Rolling her eyes at her own insecurities, she dropped the spoon on the counter and stepped outside to put the finishing touches on the patio table. That afternoon in the storage shed, she'd found a set of white wicker table and chairs. After a vigorous scrubbing, they were more than presentable. With pink and green floral cushions on the seats and matching place mats on the table, she was confident of the dinner's setting.

A gentle breeze stirred the warm night air. She took a box of matches from the pocket of her skirt. Cupping a hand to protect the flame, she lit the arrangement of candles beneath the hurricane glass. Light glimmered against the darkness, casting a soft glow upon the glass tabletop. She was glad that she'd decided to eat outdoors. No matter how much she wanted it to be different, she felt too uncomfortable inside the cottage.

The doorbell rang, shattering the quiet ambiance. Jessie's heart leaped into her throat. She gripped the back of a wicker chair, steadying herself, desperately trying to calm her nerves. While she told herself that it was just a dinner, she knew it was so much more.

Instinctively she knew Samuel was the key to her

future as well as her past. With his help she had a chance to finally find peace. A chance at a healthy and untroubled life.

Without him she didn't know what might happen to her.

Pushing the disturbing thought from her mind, Jessie smoothed imaginary wrinkles from the skirt of her cream-colored sundress as she strode to the front door. She checked her makeup in the hall mirror and finger combed her hair into place. Then, frowning, she stared at her reflection. If Samuel meant nothing more to her than a helpmate of sorts, then why was she primping?

Not allowing herself to consider the answer, she reached for the brass knob and pulled open the door. Her breath caught at the transformation of the man standing before her. Until now she'd only seen Samuel in work gear: worn jeans and sweat-stained T-shirts. Tonight he wore a pale blue polo shirt that matched his eyes and emphasized the dark hue of his skin. The knit fabric clung to his wide shoulders, molding his strong muscles. His khaki pants were carefully ironed with knife-sharp creases. On his feet he wore a pair of casual loafers. His blond hair was still damp from a recent shower, the strands of gold glistening beneath the overhead light. His face looked smooth, his stubble newly shaved.

She knew she was staring, but she couldn't help it. She'd never realized just how devastatingly handsome he was beneath that gritty layer of hard work. As her adoptive mother would have said, Samuel cleaned up nicely.

"Am I too early?" he asked, frowning slightly.

"E-early?" she stammered.

"You did say seven, didn't you?"

"Seven," she repeated, feeling like a parrot. A parrot with a very limited vocabulary. Blinking hard, she forced herself out of her trance. "You're just in time. Please, come in."

She stepped back, allowing him to enter.

The air stirred as he moved into the foyer, stroking her bare skin like a lover's caress. Jessie drew in a steadying breath and inhaled the heady combination of clean soap and spicy cologne. She felt dizzy with awareness. Oblivious to her battle for control, he glanced around the cottage, taking in the rich heart of pine woodwork, the floor-to-ceiling windows and the shimmering lights of the overhead chandelier.

Jessie closed the door, watching as he continued his inspection.

As though feeling the weight of her gaze, he turned to her, his expression unapologetic. "This is the first time I've ever been inside Gull's Cottage," he admitted. "Until now I've only been on the outside looking in."

Sympathy surged inside her as she realized Samuel had probably just summed up his entire life in a nutshell. In her mind's eye, she saw him standing alone on his shrimp boat, stoically bearing the stares of the nearby fishermen. And the way he'd suffered through the cool disdain of the town's sheriff, as though he'd been through the ordeal often. Whether it was by choice or by force, Samuel lived his life on the outside, always watching. Never being included. Never allowed to be a part of the community.

Samuel was as much a loner as she.

Knowing her sympathy was the last thing he would want, Jessie averted her eyes. She noticed for the first time that he held a bottle of wine in his hands.

Awkwardly he held the wine out to her. "I wasn't sure what you would be serving. I hope this will be all right."

She reached for the gift, and their fingers linked on the neck of the bottle. Her skin sizzled at his touch. A jolt of electricity traveled up the length of her arm. For a long moment, neither of them moved. They stared at their joined hands, unable to break the connection.

Samuel was the first to pull away. Reluctantly he dropped his hand.

Shaken by the exchange, Jessie tightened her grip on the bottle, afraid that she might drop it. The glass felt cool against her skin, so different from Samuel's warm touch. Her voice trembled as she said, "Chardonnay. It's perfect."

His fleeting smile set her heart racing.

She turned away, heading for the kitchen. Too nervous to look if he followed, she called over her shoulder, "I hope you like seafood. I'm making clam chowder."

"Sounds great," he said, his deep voice close.

She breathed a sigh of relief that he hadn't changed his mind and left. Her stomach lurched, as it did every time she stepped into the kitchen. Ignoring the queasy sensation, she hurried to the island, pulling open drawers. "I'm sure there's a corkscrew around here somewhere. Aha, here it is." Leaving the bottle safely on the counter, she handed him the corkscrew. "I'll let you open the wine while I finish the dinner."

Glad for the distraction, she scrounged through the kitchen cupboards looking for the wineglasses. Finding them, she placed them on the counter. By the time she'd sliced a loaf of bread and had filled the tureen

with the aromatic soup, Samuel had poured the wine
into the glasses.

"Dinner's ready," she said needlessly, as she picked
up the soup tureen.

Quietly he followed her out onto the porch, carrying
the wine and both of their glasses.

The softly lit night, with the candles glimmering
against the tabletop, seemed too obviously romantic.
Jessie blushed, wondering what sort of impression she
must be giving him. She resisted the urge to flip on the
overhead porch light and chase away the intimate
mood.

Instead, with shaking hands, she placed the tureen
on the center of the table. Then she excused herself,
using the bread as her reason to escape. She hurried
into the kitchen and leaned against the counter, feeling
breathless and confused.

She hadn't realized how difficult being this close to
him would be. Everything she did felt like a romantic
overture. She was as obvious as a love-starved, infatuated schoolgirl. Jessie closed her eyes and gave a soft
moan of frustration. How was she going to get through
the night without making a bumbling fool of herself?

Blaming her inexperience with men, she admitted
that she had underestimated the effect Samuel had upon
her, the strength of the attraction she felt toward him.
But she had invited him to her house. It was too late
to ask him to leave. Too late to turn back now.

Opening her eyes, she took a deep breath and told
herself to move. Purposefully she picked up the bread
and returned to the porch.

He stood at the railing with his back to her, facing
the view of the beach. As the heel of her shoe scraped

against the wooden floor, he turned to look at her. She saw the uncertainty in his eyes.

She forced a smile. "Sorry it took so long. Won't you sit down? The soup's getting cold."

He nodded, but waited until she'd taken her seat before joining her.

Jessie ladled the soup into the waiting bowls.

They ate in silence, listening to the surf pounding steadily against the beach. As the tension between them thickened, Jessie was barely able to taste the savory soup. Her mouth felt dry. She reached for her wineglass and nearly choked on a healthy swig. The liquid burned as it traveled down her throat, her muscles relaxing as the heat warmed her body.

"Tell me about yourself," Samuel said, breaking the strained silence.

She glanced at him, surprised. "Wh-why?"

He met her gaze without wavering. "You want me to help you uncover your past. I know who you *were,* when you used to live on this island. I'd like to know who you are *now,* the person you've become."

Jessie bit her lip, considering her answer. How much did she want to tell him? That she was haunted by dreams she couldn't explain? That she'd never been able to make a relationship last because of some defect in her persona that would not allow her to trust anyone? That she'd come to the island in search of a past because she was desperate to save herself from a dismal future?

No, she couldn't tell him the truth. No matter how much she might want to confide in him, she wasn't ready to reveal that much about herself to anyone.

She placed her spoon on the plate, sat back in her chair and said, "I'm an artist."

"Like your mother."

Jessie smiled. "Yes, but I didn't realize that until just a few days ago. In fact, the earliest memory I can recall is in Atlanta with my parents, Louise and Malcom Pierce. Of course, at the time I didn't know they were really my aunt and uncle, or that I'd been adopted. They were such loving people." She hesitated, letting the pain of remembrance pass. Then, gulping in a breath to gain confidence, she continued, "I was five or six at the time, and we'd spent the day at the art museum. I remember being fascinated by the beautiful pictures I'd seen, though I doubt if my parents knew just how much so. I'd always been a quiet child. It used to drive my adoptive mother crazy. She worried when I bottled up my feelings."

Jessie frowned at the memory. "Anyway, I came home and immediately went in search of a pencil and paper. My parents found me later in my bedroom sprawled out on the bed, filling up page after page of a notebook with drawings. They were quite good, actually." She reached for her glass, sipping the wine. "It was then my parents realized that I was gifted in art. From that moment on, it became the center of my life. When I wasn't in school, I was drawing or taking art lessons. I graduated from college with a degree in fine arts. Now I work as an illustrator, mostly for children's books. My parents were my biggest supporters...until now." Her voice caught. She shrugged off the emotion, trying to make light of the devastating event that had change her life. "Malcom died a year ago, Louise last month. Now I'm alone."

Samuel studied her, his eyes never leaving her face. Even in the dim light of the candles, she could see his thoughtful expression. This was the first time she'd ever shared memories of her past, good or bad, with anyone. For some reason she felt closer to him than she had to any other man.

"Your turn," she said, feeling uncomfortable with the personal bent of the conversation. She gave an encouraging smile. "It seems only fair that if we're going to be working together, that I should know more about you, too."

For a moment he didn't answer.

Jessie shivered as the silence lengthened. Goose bumps prickled her skin. She blamed her reaction on the cooling ocean breeze, refusing to attribute it to apprehension. While his face betrayed none of his emotions, she saw a storm brewing behind those expressive eyes of his.

"It can't be all that bad," she said, with a nervous laugh.

Slowly Samuel placed his napkin on the table next to his plate. His blue eyes shimmering in the candlelight, he said, "It's nothing but bad."

Her breath caught. She stared at him, a part of her wanting him to continue, a part wanting him to stop. She wasn't sure if she was ready to hear what he had to say, if she was strong enough to bear the burden of someone else's shattered life.

"I was ten when they arrested my father," he said, his voice flat, emotionless, as though he were speaking by rote. "Eleven by the time they convicted him to a life in prison. Less than a month after his sentencing, my mother committed suicide. She couldn't live with the shame the scandal had brought our family. My father died five years later. The official explanation was congestive heart failure brought on by viral pneumonia. But the truth is, he blamed himself for my mother's

death, and he simply lost the will to live. He wanted
to die.''

"Samuel, I—I'm so sorry," she said, the words
catching in her throat. She reached across the table,
placing her hand on his arm.

He glanced down at her hand. Slowly his gaze traveled upward to her face. Hesitating, he shifted his arm,
forcing her to drop her hand. The wicker chair scraped
loudly against the wooden floor as he surged to his feet.
He stumbled to the railing, leaning heavily against the
wooden bar.

Not letting herself reconsider, she rose to her feet.
She stood nearby, but did not touch him.

"I tried to stop all of it from happening, but no one
would listen to me," he said, the words echoing hollowly. "They said my father was having an affair with
your mother. That he was obsessed with her. And when
she tried to break it off, he'd killed her in a fit of
jealousy."

"But you don't think that's what happened," she
said softly, encouraging him to continue. She needed
to hear this, as much as he needed to tell her.

"No, none of it was true," he said harshly. His tone
so adamant she wondered who he was trying to con-
vince—her or himself. "My father might have been
infatuated with Eve. She was beautiful and exotic, different from any other woman on Prudence Island. But
he was a deeply moral man. He wouldn't have broken
his marriage vows."

"Then why would the prosecutors believe he was to
blame?"

"Because he was a convenient target," Samuel said,
still not facing her, his bitterness clear. "My father did
odd jobs for your mother, repairs on the house. Some-

times he'd bring her fresh shrimp from the morning's catch. It was a business relationship, never anything more."

"You were just a child," she murmured, wanting to reach out to him, to ease his pain. But she couldn't find the strength, or the courage to take that step. "How can you be so sure?"

"Because he brought me with him every time he paid a visit. He made sure he was never alone with your mother. My father told me that Prudence Island was a small community. He didn't want there to be any talk, any reason to shame my mother. I tried to tell that to the lawyers, but they wouldn't believe me."

Jessie's heart caught in her throat at the image his words conjured. In her mind's eye she saw Samuel as a young boy, trying desperately to plead his case, trying to get someone—anyone—to listen to him.

Now he shook his head, staring out onto the ocean. "They accused me of lying to protect my father."

Unable to stop herself, Jessie reached out to him once more. Tentatively she placed a hand on his arm and felt the tension thrumming through his body.

This time he didn't push her away. Instead he turned to look at her. His eyes were glazed with pain and something more…resignation.

"You shouldn't have come back, Jessie," he said, his voice so quiet she could barely hear him. He covered her hand with his, gripping it firmly. She couldn't have pulled away, even if she'd wanted to. Once again he said, "You shouldn't have come back. Why didn't you stay in Atlanta where it was safe?"

Jessie's heart slammed against her chest. Not with fear, but with anticipation. She couldn't move, couldn't think. She stood frozen to the spot, waiting for his next move.

She didn't have long to wait. One hand still gripping hers, his other found her waist. In a quick, fluid motion, with a growl of frustration low in his throat, he drew her snug against his hard body. Then, without warning, he lowered his mouth and kissed her.

Chapter 6

Before he had time to reconsider the wisdom of his actions, Samuel pulled Jessie into his arms, his lips hungrily seeking hers. He had never felt like this before. He'd never wanted, never needed a woman as much as he did her.

Her lips were warm, moist. They trembled beneath his. He heard the sharp inhalation of her breath, and a reckless thrill coursed through his veins, making him feel as though he'd just stepped out into the deep end of the ocean. Anchoring both hands at her waist, he pulled her close, needing the soft reassurance of her body against his.

For a breath-stealing moment she stiffened in his arms.

His heart thudded as he waited for her to push him away.

But she didn't. Instead, she dug her fingers into the knit fabric of his polo shirt, gripping it tightly.

Taking this as an assent, he deepened the kiss, slowly increasing the pressure of his lips against hers. With a quiet moan, her mouth opened to him. And a firestorm of desire ignited deep inside him, heating his blood, robbing him of all reason. He delved his tongue into her mouth, struggling with a need for urgency, tasting a sweetness he'd only imagined in his dreams.

With a sigh Jessie seemed to give up any pretense of fight. Her muscles went limp. She wrapped her arms around his neck and clung to him, pressing her slender body to his. Her velvety smooth skin felt hot to the touch; her breasts full and heavy against his chest. Her belly nudged his manhood.

Samuel groaned. Irrational though it may be, he wanted her. He wanted to forget about the past, forget about the future and lose himself in the pleasure of her embrace. But in his heart he knew it wasn't possible. No matter how pliant or how willing she might be now, neither of them could hide from the real world forever.

He had no doubt there would come a time for regrets.

Reluctantly he ended the kiss. Needing a moment to recover, he buried his face against the curving slope of her throat, brushing his lips against the side of her neck. Breathing deeply, he inhaled the delicate fragrance of her skin, catching the scent of jasmine.

Jessie shivered in his arms. With a choppy breath she raked her fingers through his hair and pulled his face up to hers.

He looked into her eyes and saw the reflection of his own desire. Growling with resignation, he took her mouth once again. This time he allowed himself all the urgency he felt in his body and his soul.

Jessie met his demands with a lusty need of her own,

matching each thrust of his tongue, letting her fingers slide down the length of his spine, resting her hands on his hips and drawing him close.

Just as he was about to lose himself in the softness of her body, the sweetness of her lips, the tenderness of her touch, an unwanted image from the past flickered in his mind. An image so vivid, so acute, it pained him to remember.

The image of his father kissing Eve Pierce.

Samuel froze at the memory. He hadn't been completely honest with Jessie. He hadn't told her of the time he'd walked into the storage shed in the back of Gull's Cottage and found his father kissing her mother. Only ten years old, he'd been shocked and confused by what he'd seen. He'd run, run all the way to the docks and had hidden. His father had found him eventually. He'd told Samuel he couldn't help himself. That he'd made a mistake. He had promised him that it would never happen again.

At the time Samuel didn't believe him. He didn't understand why a man as big and powerful as his father couldn't resist a woman as small and fragile as Mrs. Pierce. How could her will be stronger than his?

But now he understood.

Samuel knew how weak Jessie made him feel. When he was in her arms, his muscles trembled with the strain of self-control. His knees threatened to buckle beneath him. He felt as though his willpower had melted in a heat of passion as quick and strong as any brushfire.

He was repeating the sins of his father.

"No," he rasped, tearing his lips from hers. Before he could change his mind, he stepped back, pushing her away. Without the comforting heat of her body next to his, the cool night air swept his passion-heated skin, chilling him.

Jessie stared up at him, blinking in confusion. She swayed and placed a hand on the railing to steady herself. Her dark hair was disheveled, her lips red and swollen. She had the look of a woman who'd been thoroughly kissed.

A woman he still wanted to kiss.

"This isn't what I came for," he said, the words sounding harsher than he'd meant.

She moved toward him. "Samuel, I—"

"No," he said, backstepping, putting a much-needed distance between them. "This...this has to stop, now, before it goes any further."

Jessie's dark brow furrowed with uncertainty. "I...I don't understand. You don't think I planned for any of this to happen, do you?"

He felt winded, his breathing strained. He raked a hand through his hair. "I don't know what to think," he admitted.

"Samuel, please," she said, stepping forward, reaching out to him.

He shrugged off her embrace, not giving himself the chance to be lost in her touch.

Jessie flinched as though she'd been slapped by his rebuff. Looking numb, she let her hand fall heavily to her side. Her voice sounded brittle as she said, "No matter what just happened between us, Samuel, I still need your help."

He shook his head slowly. "I'm no hero, Jessie. I can't help you...I can't even help myself. I want no part of this obsession of yours with your mother's death." His voice echoed in the quiet night. He hardened his heart against the pain and confusion he saw in her eyes. He couldn't allow his emotions to stand in the way of doing what was right, of protecting her. "Rooting up the past will cause both of us unnecessary pain and trouble. There's nothing you can do to change my mind, not even using your powers of seduction."

With that final, cutting remark, he sealed his own fate. Knowing she would never be able to forgive him for such callousness, he turned and left.

For a long moment Jessie stared after him, watching as he strode off the porch and rounded the house to the front driveway. As he disappeared around the corner, she drew in a sharp, painful breath. It hurt so badly, she felt as though a dagger had lodged in her heart.

She didn't understand what had just happened. One minute Samuel was a tender, gentle lover, holding her in his arms, evoking in her such an intense reaction. The next minute he was cold and angry, pushing her away, making her feel as though she were to blame for everything that had happened between them. As though she were some sort of Mata Hari, bending his will to suit her own.

What had she done to cause him to think so little of her?

Her eyes filled with unwanted tears. She stumbled to the table, sitting down hard in a chair. Staring down at their unfinished dinner, she struggled to understand why the evening had ended so badly.

When she'd talked about her childhood in Atlanta, he'd listened with what seemed like genuine interest. She truly believed he had cared. In turn, he had trusted her enough to reveal the painful secrets of his own past, of his mother's suicide, of his father's death in prison. A tear spilled down her cheek. Compared to Samuel

she had lived a fairy-tale life, virtually devoid of
trauma.

Before he'd kissed her, she could have sworn they'd
grown closer, that a connection had been formed between them. She'd felt the change in her heart. They
had broken through the initial defenses of mistrust and
had carved out a new, albeit tentative, relationship. For
the first time she had felt as though she'd finally found
someone who understood her. Someone who'd shared
the bond of a troubled childhood.

Another tear escaped, then another. Jessie swiped
impatiently at her damp cheek. How could everything
have gone so wrong so quickly?

But she already knew the answer. She'd allowed her
heart to rule her judgment. She'd allowed a physical
need to overshadow her quest for the truth behind her
past. She'd mistaken Samuel's compassion for something more than he'd intended.

Because of her own lack of control, she'd turned the
one person she needed most against her.

On trembling legs Jessie stood. The chair scraped
against the wooden porch floor, sounding too loud in
the silent night. It was over. Samuel was gone. There
was nothing she could do to take back her mistake.

With a determination she did not feel, she picked up
the napkins and the bowls of soup and began to clear
the table. Samuel had told her it was time to leave
Prudence Island. Time to go back home to Atlanta. But
she knew she couldn't live with herself if she ran away
now.

She had to know the reason for her nightmare. Or
she would never find her chance at peace.

Samuel told her he was no hero. That he couldn't
help himself...let alone help her. So be it. With or

without his help, she was going to stay on the island and continue her search for clues to her past.

If there was a dragon to slay, then she would have to slay it on her own.

In the shadows of the trees a solitary figure stood on the beach, watching as Jessie moved about on the porch.

It's happening again.

Like mother, like daughter. Attracting men like bees to nectar. One just as much a whore as the other.

A person would have thought Samuel Conners would have more sense, that he'd have been immune to the whore's charms. But he's fallen under Jessie's spell, just like his father fell for Eve.

The palmettos rattled on the ocean breeze, sounding like the clucking of a disapproving tongue. Hands clenched, the figure trembled with bottled-up rage.

With Jessie back on the island, questions will be asked. Once again speculation will be raised. It won't be long before everyone will wonder if the right person was tried and convicted of Eve Pierce's death.

And all because the whore returned.

Jessie, her hands laden with dishes, turned away from view and disappeared into the house. The figure stared at the empty porch and waited, too overwhelmed with emotion to move.

It cannot happen again. All my carefully laid plans will be ruined.

Someone has to stop the whore before it's too late.

Voices.

Loud, angry voices.

Confused and uncertain, she climbed out of bed.

Stumbling, she followed the night-darkened hallway and hurried toward the sound of shouting. Her feet leaden, she felt as though she were moving in slow motion. She was disoriented, but did not stop. Her heart raced, fluttering in her chest like a butterfly's wings.

The voices grew louder. Emotion distorted their timbre, making it hard for her to identify them.

Then, suddenly, there was silence. A heart-stuttering silence.

A beam of light sliced through the inky night, blinding her, paralyzing her with fear....

A shape emerged from the shadows.

A shape large and frightening, coming closer, closer...

Her heart leaping in her chest, she stumbled back, one step, two, until she couldn't go any farther....

And then there was nothing but darkness. All-encompassing darkness.

Jessie jerked awake, her heart thumping against her ribs. The bedsheets were tangled about her legs. Perspiration drenched her skin. The light cotton fabric of her oversize T-shirt clung to her body. For a panic-seizing moment, she didn't know where she was.

The light from the hallway spilled into the bedroom. Rubbing the sleep from her eyes with the back of one hand, Jessie quickly reacquainted herself with her surroundings.

She was in Gull's Cottage in the bedroom that had once belonged to her mother. She knew this to be true, not because of any lingering memories or comforting images the room had brought her. Rather, because of the articles of a woman's clothing in the closet. A forgotten straw hat, a pair of size five, flipflop sandals, a long, colorful scarf…articles that had been forgotten in someone's haste to remove all traces of the former occupant.

Jessie shuddered as the cool night air seeped into her overheated senses. Tonight the dream had been worse than usual. She'd felt as though she'd been trapped, unable to pull out, to wake up, until it was almost too late….

She released a breath on a soft cry of frustration. Too late for what?

To stop the argument? To save herself?

She twisted the rumpled bedsheet in her hands. She didn't know what to think, how to interpret the nightmare. So much of the dream was just a blur.

But not everything was hazy, she reminded herself. The dream had finally revealed something important. Something even more frightening than a childhood fear. Slowly Jessie rose from the white wrought-iron bed. Her legs trembling, she walked to the door of the bedroom, then hesitated before stepping into the hallway. Her heart pounded in her chest as she stared down the long, narrow corridor.

It was the hallway in her dream.

Even in the shadowy images of sleep, she recognized the telltale landmarks. The high ceiling, the tall, carved baseboards, the row of watercolors on the wall, all signed by the artist, Eve Pierce.

This was the hall she had traveled for years in her sleep. The long, unfamiliar hallway that had led her into her worst nightmare.

The floor beneath her feet shifted. The room began to spin. She felt dizzy, sick to her stomach at the realization. If the hallway was real, then the shouting voices must be real, too. Her dream wasn't a dream, after all.

It was a memory from her past.

Jessie turned from the door and stumbled to the bathroom. She clung to the edge of the marble sink and fought a bitter wave of nausea. Turning on the faucet, she splashed handful after handful of cold water onto her face. Her fingers shook as she reached for a towel.

Pressing the soft terry cloth to her cheeks, she stared at her reflection in the mirror. She looked pale, her face gaunt, her eyes wild with fear. Jessie shuddered. If this was how she reacted to retrieving just a small part of her memory, what would happen when she remembered everything?

Would she survive the ordeal?

Carefully she replaced the towel on the rack. Once again Samuel's warning to leave Gull's Cottage and Prudence Island flitted through her mind. Perhaps he was right. But how could she return to Atlanta, knowing that the past was still buried in the recesses of her mind, ticking like a time bomb, waiting to explode? Even if she did run away, the dream would still be there, still haunting her, never giving her a moment's peace.

Jessie drew in a ragged breath and turned away from the mirror. She moved into the bedroom and crossed to the wall of windows. Pulling back the curtains, she stared out onto the expanse of silvery beach.

If she hadn't known it before, she knew now that recovering her memory would not be an easy task. Unlocking the secrets of her mind would be the most difficult job she'd ever had to face. She had to be strong. She couldn't lose her courage.

Not when she was getting so close to the truth.

The graying sky told her it soon would be dawn. Just like the birth of a new day, she, too, needed a fresh start. But before she could begin anew, she had unfinished business to take care of.

Jessie set her shoulders in a determined line. Today, before she lost her nerve, she would tie up the most pressing of those loose strings.

It was still early when Samuel returned from his morning of shrimping. The day's catch filled the boat's cargo hold. Despite the dull ache that throbbed in his head from lack of sleep, Samuel was pleased with the morning's results. They'd had a good run. A few more days like today, and he'd make up for the money lost when he'd been waylaid by a broken motor.

The engines whined as he eased the *Marianna,* the boat named for his mother, alongside the dock at an empty space near the shrimp company. He coasted to a smooth stop, then cut the motor. Jacob and Billie, the junior member of Samuel's crew, scrambled to secure the boat, tying the thick lines to the pilings. Samuel climbed down from the pilothouse, moving toward the hold to help his men transfer the iced-down shrimp onto the waiting conveyor belt.

As he strode onto the deck, he took two steps, then stumbled to an abrupt halt. Blinking hard, he couldn't believe his own eyes as he stared at the woman standing on the dock.

It was Jessie.

She was the sole reason why he had not slept last night. Guilt had kept him awake. After returning home from their disastrous dinner, he'd tossed and turned in his bed, unable to relax. Over and over in his mind he'd replayed the events that had led to their fateful embrace.

He didn't think he'd ever forget how perfectly she'd fitted in his arms. Or how sweet her lips had tasted. Or the fire that had ignited in his belly at her touch. Or the pain and confusion he'd seen in her eyes when he'd pushed her away.

Now she stood waiting for him on the dock, a bittersweet reminder of what a fool he'd made of himself.

His gaze narrowed as he fought his own battle of indecision. A part of him wanted to turn around, to join his crew and lose himself in the mind-numbing bliss of hard labor. He wanted to deny himself the temptation of being anywhere near her.

But the illogical part of him, the part that ruled his heart and not his brain, wanted a second chance. He wanted to tell her that he hadn't meant the harsh words he'd spoken, that he hadn't wanted to push her away or to hurt her.

Samuel groaned inwardly. From the prohibitive expression on her face, he doubted if she were in the mood to forgive and forget.

"Looks like we've got company," Jacob said, startling Samuel out of his troubled musings. The wiry man stood beside him, squinting down at Jessie. Grinning, he sidled a curious glance at Samuel. "As much as I wish it were true, I don't think the pretty lady's here to see me."

Samuel scowled, embarrassed heat rushing to his face. "Don't you have some shrimp to unload?"

"I suppose I do," Jacob said. His grin widened. He didn't appear at all intimidated by Samuel's foul mood. "You know, Samuel, if you wanted a little privacy, all you had to do was say so."

Samuel glared at his friend.

With a wink Jacob headed for the hold. "Don't you worry none. We'll get that catch unloaded. You just take care of the pretty lady, ya hear?"

The sound of chuckling followed Jacob down the steps into the hold.

Samuel set his jaw against a prickly burr of irritation. Telling himself he was a fool for bothering, he slung himself off the side of the boat. His boots thumped against the wooden dock as he landed a few feet in front of Jessie.

She flinched, shifting in surprise. But to his disappointment she wasn't nearly scared enough to hightail it back to where she came from. Instead, swallowing hard, she smoothed a trembling hand down the length of her blue-jean clad thighs and stood her ground.

"I thought you were leaving town," he growled, in lieu of a greeting. He stepped toward her, unmindful of the raw scent of shrimp and sweat that permeated his clothes.

"Well, you thought wrong," she said, raising her chin in a stubborn show of defiance. He had to hand it to her, she was a lady through and through. No matter how strong the odor, not once did she wrinkle her sculpted nose at him in disdain. She met his stern gaze without wincing. "I have no intention of leaving Prudence Island. Not now or anytime soon."

Samuel bit back a curse. Feigning an impatience that he didn't really feel, he demanded, "Is that it? Is that all you came out here to tell me?"

"No," she said, nervously licking her lips. His pulse quickened at the sight of her tongue gliding over her lips. Desire stirred as he remembered how sweet those lips had tasted, how much he'd like to sample them again. "I've come here to tell you that I'm going to find out what really happened to my mother...with or without your help."

"You're wasting your time."

"No, I'm not," she said, refusing to back down. "There *is* something to accomplish by rooting up the past. It'll bring peace of mind. That and an answer to the question that's nearly destroyed both of our lives..." Her voice broke. "I need to know the truth, Samuel. I need to know what really happened to my mother."

"And what if the truth isn't something you expected to hear?"

"Then I'll have to deal with that when the time comes."

Samuel stared at her, not sure what to say to change her mind. Silence strained between them. The only sound to be heard was the lapping of the water against the hull of the *Marianna*. That and the call of the sea-gulls overhead, voicing their disapproval at his lack of courage.

If he trusted himself enough to touch her, he would take her in his arms and try to shake some sense into that stubborn head of hers. Couldn't she see how much danger she was putting herself in?

Dammit, why did he have to feel so responsible for her?

His silence proved more effective than a hundred discouraging words. Finally growing impatient with him, she blew out an exasperated breath. "I don't know why I bothered coming here. I should have known you wouldn't care."

She started to leave. Then suddenly she changed her mind. Whipping around to glare at him, she said, "Just one more thing, Samuel. I never have and I never will seduce a man to get my way.''

With that she turned on her heel and stomped away.

She got about three feet down the dock before he stopped her. Grabbing her arm, he wheeled her around to face him. She opened her mouth to speak, but the words would not form. Instead, she stared at him in mute surprise.

''There's something I need to tell you,'' he said quietly.

''Now? You want to talk now?'' she asked, finding her voice. Indignation flashed in her dark eyes. She tugged her arm, vainly trying to loosen his hold. ''Let go of me.''

''Not until you hear me out,'' he said calmly, in the wake of her rising anger.

''You had your chance,'' she snapped, still trying to jerk her arm free. ''It's too late. There's nothing more I want to hear from you now.''

''Not even an apology?''

She stopped struggling. She frowned, uncertainty shadowing her eyes.

''About last night...'' The words caught in his throat. Samuel cursed softly beneath his breath, wondering what in the world had possessed him to stop her. He should have let her walk off the dock, walk out of his life forever. Admitting he was wrong, about anything, just wasn't in his nature. Unable to face her, he averted his gaze. Staring at the hull of his boat, he forced himself to continue, ''I'm sorry, Jessie. I don't blame you. If I hadn't wanted to kiss you, it would never have happened.''

Still she didn't say a word. He looked to see her studying him, her expression wary. Samuel clenched his jaw in annoyance. She wasn't going to make this easy for him, he realized. He was going to have to do more than ply her with the right words to make amends. He was going to have to prove that he was sincere.

Sighing, he said, "If you want to know about your mother, then you need to talk to someone who knew her best—Dora Hawkins."

"Dora Hawkins?" she repeated, flinching at the name.

He raised a brow. "Do you know her?"

"We've met. She introduced herself to me on my second day on the island," she admitted with a troubled frown.

Seeing her reaction, he said, "I take it your meeting didn't go well."

"Let's just say the encounter was a little disturbing," she said with a dismissive shrug that failed. Choosing her words carefully, she added, "Dora seemed a bit on the eccentric side."

He laughed, amused for the first time that day. "Dora isn't eccentric. She's out-and-out odd. But she's also a good friend of mine. One of the few friends who've stuck by me throughout the scandal involving my father."

Jessie nodded, still looking uncertain.

Knowing he was asking for trouble, Samuel ventured another suggestion. "If you'd like, I could come with you when you talk to her. You might feel more comfortable with someone else there."

Jessie looked up at him, her eyes searching his face, as though trying to judge the depth of his sincerity. Apparently he passed muster. With a hesitant smile she said, "I'd like that."

Samuel's lips twitched. Unable to stop himself, he grinned in return. "Give me a minute. I need to shower and change and tell my crew that I'm leaving."

She nodded.

He felt her gaze upon him as he clambered up the side of the boat. Once on board, he looked back one last time. The wind whipped her dark hair into her eyes. She brushed the lock away with her long, tapering fingers. Her jeans fit her curves snugly, emphasizing her slender legs. She looked just as beautiful today as she had last night.

Samuel forced himself to look away. He must be crazy to think he could spend time alone with her and not be tempted.

Dammit, what the hell did he think he was doing?

Chapter 7

"Tell me about the island."

Samuel shot her a quick look across the front seat of his truck. Since Jessie had walked to the docks, Samuel had offered to drive her to Dora Hawkins's house. She had agreed.

Now she sat just an arm's length away, wishing she could see his eyes—those pale blue eyes that revealed so much emotion—that were hidden behind the dark frames of his sunglasses. Since leaving the docks, Samuel hadn't said a word. Jessie didn't have a clue as to what he was thinking.

His brow creasing into a frown, he turned his attention back to the highway. "What do you want to know?"

"Everything." A breeze drifting in from the open wind lifted a strand of her hair across her face. Tucking the stray lock behind her ear, she looked out at the live oaks with their gossamer ropes of spanish moss. Flow-ering bushes lined the roadside. She breathed deeply the rich scent of magnolia. "It's so beautiful here. You must love living on the island."

"Looks can be deceiving," he said quietly.

Jessie glanced at him sharply. "Is there something about the island that you haven't told me?"

"No dark secrets, no curses, if that's what you mean," he said with a brief smile. Sobering, his grip tightened on the steering wheel, cording the muscles of his arms. "But there's more to a community than the land it's sitting on. There's the people who live on the island."

"I take it you haven't found the residents to be as pleasant as the island itself."

He hesitated before answering. Then, with a resigned breath he said, "Let's just say that memories are long in a small town. And they aren't always forgiving."

His curt tone encouraged no further discussion. Silently Jessie wondered who clung to the memories of the past more, the residents of Prudence Island or Samuel. While she didn't yet know him as well as she would like, Samuel seemed to carry a heavy burden on his shoulders. One that may or may not be of his own making. Perhaps the residents of Prudence Island weren't the only ones unwilling to give someone a second chance.

Just past Gull's Cottage, Samuel turned off the highway onto a narrow lane. Unlike her own driveway, the road was paved and well maintained. Like hers, however, the underbrush along the roadside was thick and wild. So thick, Jessie couldn't see Gull's Cottage, even though she knew it was nearby.

The sound of the ocean grew louder, its salty scent stronger. Gradually the thicket cleared and a large, gray, wood and stone house came into view. Surprised, Jessie did a double take. In sharp contrast to the home's dull exterior, brightly colored flowers were everywhere, sparkling like jewels in the sunlight. From the boxes beneath the windows, to the beds lining the stone walkway, flowers spilled out in every direction, occupying every nook and cranny of available garden space.

"Goodness, this must take hours to tend," she said, her voice filled with wonderment. "How does Dora find the time?"

"She doesn't have much else to do," Samuel said, with a shrug. He pulled the truck to a stop in front of the house and turned off the ignition. An eerie silence descended between them as they both studied the house. "Dora's never been married. She doesn't have children. No brothers, no sisters. Her father was a lumber baron. He owned a large mill up in the northern part of the state. When he died he left Dora with enough money to do with as she pleased. She's all alone in the world. I suppose gardening fills a void."

Quietly Jessie digested this insight into her eccentric neighbor's life. She scanned the property, not seeing anyone stirring. "Do you think she's home?"

"There's only one way to find out." With his hand on the door handle, he hesitated. He turned to look at her, his eyes still hidden from view. "It's not too late to change your mind. Are you sure you want to go through with this?"

Jessie's tummy quivered with trepidation. A chill of foreboding swept her body. It wasn't the first time Samuel had tried to discourage her from digging into the past. What was it he wasn't telling her?

"I'm sure," she said, with more determination than she actually felt.

"Right. Then, let's go." The battered door of the old truck sighed in protest as he pushed it open.

Reluctantly Jessie opened her own door and stepped down onto the paved driveway. The sun felt warm against her skin. Thanks to the multitude of flowers, a deliciously sweet aroma filled the air, mingling with the salty scent of the ocean. Seagulls flew into patterns in the sky, swooping down toward the beach in search of their day's meal. It seemed odd that a woman as abrasive as Dora Hawkins chose to live in such a calm and peaceful setting.

Jessie followed Samuel up the stone pathway to the front door. He lifted the antique pewter knocker and rapped sharply. Seconds ticked by like hours as they waited for someone to answer.

"She must not be home," Jessie said after a few moments, stating the obvious. Disappointment and relief warred inside her. While she was anxious to learn more about her mother, the thought of facing the eccentric woman once again sent shivers down her spine. Wanly she hazarded a suggestion, "We could try again later."

"Let's check around back first," Samuel said, nodding toward the oceanside. "There are more gardens facing the beach."

Midway around the house, the view of the ocean opened up before them. Wide stretches of white sand and blue water played a breathtaking background to Dora's rainbow-colored garden. For the first time, Jessie spotted Gull's Cottage in the distance. Even with its brilliant white siding, the house looked forlorn and empty.

"Dora's not back here, either," Samuel said, glancing around the grounds. He shook his head in disgust. "Looks as though we've wasted a trip."

A movement on the path leading to the beach caught her eye. Jessie held a hand over her brow and squinted into the sunlight. "No, wait. Someone's coming."

Gravel crunched beneath his feet as Samuel turned, following the direction of her gaze.

Sunlight blinked off a pair of round glasses. Jessie recognized the short, squat figure with the brown hair and the square face. It was Dora.

The older woman strode quickly up the path, with her head bent down, her eyes focused on the ground before her. Her expression distracted, she tucked a pair of work gloves into the pocket of her loose-fitting khaki pants. She didn't notice their presence until she was almost upon them.

When she finally saw them, she stopped so quickly she nearly slipped on the gravel path. Her mouth dropped open in surprise. A hand fluttered to her throat. She stared at them, unable to say a word.

"Dora?" Samuel said, his expression full of concern as he moved toward her. "Are you all right? We didn't mean to scare you."

"Samuel," Dora managed, on a strangled breath. Her sharp gaze flew to Jessie. "I wasn't expecting company."

Jessie fought the urge to squirm beneath the accusing measure of the other woman's stare. There was something about Dora's reaction that unnerved her. It went beyond mere surprise. The woman seemed flustered, disconcerted by their appearance.

Not that Jessie blamed her. Seeing her and Samuel together would make for quite a shock. After all, considering their families' mutual history, they were an unlikely couple.

"We didn't call before coming over," he admitted, his tone apologetic. "We thought we'd take our chances that you'd be here."

"That's quite all right," Dora said crisply, recovering her aplomb, though her smile seemed forced. "Now that you're here, why don't you have a seat? I'll fetch us some lemonade and we can visit."

"Actually, we're here for more than just a visit," Samuel explained quietly.

Dora's smile faded. Her troubled gaze darted from Samuel to Jessie, then back again. "Maybe you'd better tell me exactly what it is you want."

Slowly Samuel took off his sunglasses and slipped them into his shirt pocket. He looked at Jessie, his blue eyes warm and encouraging. "It's about Eve. Jessie wants to know about her mother. I thought it best she heard from someone who knew her…as a friend."

"I see," Dora said, her eyes traveling once again to Jessie. For a long moment she didn't say a word. Then "You sure you're ready to open that can of worms?"

Jessie blinked in surprise.

Samuel shifted uncomfortably beside her. Frowning, he said, "Dora—"

"No, Samuel," Jessie said, stopping him from protecting her. She faced the other woman, determined not to let her see how much she intimidated her. "Whatever it is you have to say, I want to hear it. All of it."

Dora's gaze narrowed assessingly. "I was wrong. You have more spunk than I gave you credit for. You *are* your mother's daughter." With a sweep of her hand she motioned to the cedar bench and chairs.

"You'd better make yourselves comfortable. I'll get the lemonade."

With that dubious show of Southern gentility, she disappeared into the house.

Samuel waited for Jessie to make the next move. She stood stiffly in the garden, her back to the house, looking out at the ocean. A pensive frown marred her beautiful face. Her dark lashes fluttered as though staving off unwanted tears.

A part of him wished she would change her mind. That she'd ask him to take her back to Gull's Cottage...before it was too late. He fought the tension thrumming through his body, tension born of guilt.

For the life of him, he couldn't be the one to tell Jessie the truth. He didn't even know if he could stay and witness her inevitable disillusionment. He had no doubt that what Dora was about to tell Jessie would crush her.

"I'm my mother's daughter?" Jessie asked, drawing him from his troubled thoughts. "What does that mean?"

"Jessie, maybe this was a bad idea." He took a step closer, wishing he trusted himself enough to give in to his wants and touch her. "Why don't I take you back to Gull's Cottage? It's not too late to forget about all of this—"

"No," she said, shaking her head. "If I want to learn about the past, then I have to face the good as well as the bad." She looked at him, a plea for honesty in her dark eyes. "What Dora has to say...it is bad, isn't it?"

Samuel's breath caught painfully in his chest. He wasn't sure what to tell her, how to cushion the blow.

Her smile trembled. "That's all right, Samuel. You don't have to say anything. I can see it in your eyes."

The screen door squeaked on its hinges, alerting them to the fact that they were no longer alone. Gravel crunched beneath approaching footsteps. Samuel turned to see Dora heading toward them with a tray of tall glasses of lemonade.

"Sit down," Dora said, in her usual brusque manner. "I've been working all morning and my bones are tired. I refuse to be the only one seated for this conversation."

Wordlessly Jessie complied. She took a seat on the cedar bench, crossing one slender leg over the other. Looking nervous, she waited for the others to join her.

Experiencing an unfamiliar need to protect, Samuel sat down next to her. On the small bench their bodies touched, thigh brushing thigh, hip against hip, shoulder to shoulder. The warmth of her body reassured him. It felt almost as good as holding her in his arms...almost.

"What I remember best about your mother was her beauty. But she was also very lonely. Beauty and loneliness can be a dangerous combination," Dora mused, handing them moist glasses of icy lemonade. She sat down in a chair opposite them, placing the empty tray on a nearby table. "I suppose she was still grieving over your father's death. At least, that would explain—"

Dora hesitated, frowning as she sipped her drink.

Jessie leaned forward in her seat. "Please, Dora, whatever it is, I need to know the truth."

Dora exchanged a cautious glance with Samuel.

Samuel's muscles tightened reflexively, as though preparing himself to ward off a blow.

"Well, the truth is, Eve had a lot of men friends,"

Dora said finally. "Not that she could help it. Like I said, she was such a pretty little thing. Men just naturally flocked to her. Though I have to admit, all that attention made quite a few of the women in town upset…jealous, mostly." Dora's sly smile of amusement seemed out of place, grating against Samuel's overwrought nerves. "I guess they couldn't handle the competition."

Jessie stiffened beside him. Giving in to his instincts, he slipped an arm over the back of the bench, letting its reassuring weight rest across her shoulders. She relaxed slightly beneath his touch.

"It didn't take long for the womenfolk to clamp down on their wayward husbands. And things got a little quieter on this side of the cove," Dora said, oblivious to Jessie's rising distress. "But there were a few men who wouldn't give up. They still came around often enough. It didn't matter if they were married or not." Dora looked directly at Samuel. It took all of his strength to meet her gaze without flinching. "Your daddy was one of those admirers, Samuel. I had to testify to that at his trial."

Samuel nodded. "I know."

Dora shook her head, as though trying to rid herself of the unpleasant memory. "Your father and I were friends. As much as I wanted to help him, I think I did more harm than good at the trial. I couldn't tell those lawyers anything useful, not really. I had heard shouting that afternoon, coming from Gull's Cottage. But I never saw who it was that Eve was arguing with. She had so many men coming around, it could have been anyone. Not that the sheriff or his deputies paid any mind to what I said. They already had their suspect."

My father, Samuel silently reminded himself, his stomach knotting with tension.

"Was Sheriff Broward one of the men who came to see my mother?" Jessie asked suddenly.

Samuel looked at her, surprised by the question.

"You do remember some of that summer," Dora said, her tone almost accusing, her glance shrewd.

"No," Jessie insisted, her expression calm and unreadable. "I don't remember anything. It's just a hunch."

"Well, your hunches are pretty good, child." Dora chuckled, her eyes twinkling with amusement. "Let's just say there was a lot more patrolling on this side of the island that summer. And yes, I do believe our Sheriff Broward was smitten by the young, grieving widow."

Anger and confusion billowed inside Samuel. His grip tightened around his untouched glass of lemonade. He was stunned by the news. He had no idea that Sheriff Broward's interest in Eve Pierce was anything but professional.

Dora sipped more of her drink, her gaze darting curiously between the two of them. Then, heaving a breathy sigh, she said, "Of course, all of these questions might have been answered, if only they'd found Eve's diary."

"Diary?" Jessie repeated.

Samuel froze. "What diary?"

"You didn't know?" Even with one brow raised innocently in question, Dora had the smug look of the cat that had swallowed the canary. If he didn't know better, he'd have thought she enjoyed catching them off guard.

He pushed the unkind thought from his mind, reminding himself of the countless times Dora had defended him and his family in the public eye. No one had been kinder to his father during his stay in prison than Dora. And after his mother's death, she hadn't shunned him as the others on the island had. Dora had stood by him during the worst of his stormy youth.

"Well, I'm not surprised you didn't hear about the diary," she said, jarring him out of his memories. "The sheriff's department kept it all hush-hush. But I know for a fact they practically tore the house down looking for it." She sniffed the air disdainfully. "They never did find it...which was too bad. Eve might have been tight-lipped when it came to confiding in others. But I'll bet dollars to doughnuts she wrote everything down in that journal of hers, including all the men who came to visit."

An uncomfortable silence fell upon the garden as they considered the news. Butterflies hovered in the air. The cloying scent of flowers made his stomach roil in protest. Samuel had a sick feeling that they'd stumbled onto a dangerous bit of information.

"I wish I could be of more help," Dora said with another sigh. She rose to her feet. "But that's all I can remember."

Taking this as their cue to leave, Samuel stood.

Reluctantly Jessie followed his lead.

They placed their untouched drinks on the table and politely said their goodbyes. Samuel felt the heavy measure of Dora's watchful gaze as they left her standing in her beautiful garden.

Mulling over this new insight into Eve's life, he barely noticed Jessie's own silence. Over and over in his mind he considered what they had learned. Sheriff Broward had had a personal interest in Eve Pierce.

Whether or not that interest was returned was anyone's guess.

Or perhaps not.

Eve had kept a diary, a diary that was never found. A daily journal which very well could contain Eve's own account of the events leading to her last, fateful day. If it was found, it could prove to be a silent but lethal witness.

Samuel reined in his runaway hopes. He had to remember that while the diary could be the key to clearing his father's name, it could also be the tool to damning him forever.

The gravel path gave way to pavement as they neared his pickup truck. Heat radiated upward from the blacktopped drive, warming the sudden chill in his heart. He strode around to the passenger side to open the door for Jessie.

It wasn't until he held the door for her that he noticed the emotion burning in her eyes.

Jessie looked devastated.

"Talk to me, Jessie," Samuel said.

Jessie didn't answer. She turned her head and stared unseeingly out the window of his truck, refusing to look at him. She couldn't face him, not now. Not after what she'd just learned. She didn't know how she could face anyone on this island again.

Now that she knew the truth about her mother.

The truck bounced over a rut in the lane leading to Gull's Cottage, rocking her from side to side. Instinctively she placed a steadying hand on the dashboard. For once she was glad for the darkness that blanketed the property of Gull's Cottage. Glad that Samuel couldn't see the shame written on her face.

"We've come too far to have you shut me out now," Samuel said, impatience edging his voice. "I know you're upset. Please, Jessie, talk to me."

Tears pressed against her eyes, blurring her vision. She drew in a choppy breath. Then, unable to stop herself, she whispered, "Why didn't you tell me?"

"Tell you what?" he asked, his confusion obvious.

"About my mother—" Her voice broke. Swallowing hard at the lump of emotion in her throat, she forced herself to continue, "Why did I have to find out from that woman that my mother was the town slut?"

Samuel winced. Instead of answering, he muttered a soft oath beneath his breath.

Needing the truth, she persisted, "Did you know?"

Still he didn't answer.

Blinking hard, fighting the tears, she looked at him and saw the guilt in his eyes. She nearly cried out as a new wave of pain washed over her. "Is that why you brought me to Dora's? So that I could be humiliated?"

"No, dammit," he said harshly. "That's not the reason at all."

She shook her head, trying to make sense of what had happened. "Then why didn't you tell me yourself? Why did I have to find out from Dora, of all people?"

The trees thinned. Sunlight poured into the truck, stinging her eyes, as Gull's Cottage appeared in the clearing. Samuel pulled to a lurching stop in front of the house. Switching off the engine, he turned to face her.

Regret clouded his face. "I didn't tell you myself because you wouldn't have believed me if I had."

"How can you say that?"

"Because no one has ever believed me," he said in a flat tone. A vein pulsed at his temple. "No one be-

lieved me when my father was on trial. You didn't
believe me, either...not when I warned you about looking into the past. I told you it would cause both of us
unnecessary pain.''

She stared at him, not sure what to say.

A brittle silence lengthened between them. Tension
choked the air, making it hard to breathe. No matter
what excuse he might give, it didn't change the fact
that she had trusted him. Nothing he could say—not
now, perhaps not ever—could ease the pain of betrayal
she felt in her heart.

Fumbling with the handle, she pushed open the door.
She scrambled out of the truck, needing to put a distance between them. Her legs trembling, her feet slipping on the rocks, she hurried up the uneven stone
walkway.

Even without the sound of his heavy footsteps, she
knew he was close. A prickling awareness skittered up
her spine, raising the hairs on the back of her neck. He
was right behind her. She quickened her step.

But not quickly enough.

He grabbed her arm, spinning her around to face
him.

Jessie's breath caught at the anger she saw in his
eyes.

''Don't you understand?'' he ground out. ''It's too
late to change the past. Nothing good will ever come
of this. If you keep digging up things that have been
long buried, you're only going to be hurt.''

''That's my problem,'' she said, twisting her arm,
trying to loosen his viselike grip.

''No, it's mine,'' he said, slowly shaking his head.
''Don't you get it? Whatever you do affects me, also.
It's my life...my father's life that's being opened up

for public scrutiny. Do you really think I want to relive
the events that destroyed my family?''

Fresh tears filled her eyes. He was the last person
she wanted to hurt. But she didn't know any other way
to find out the truth. ''I—I'm sorry, Samuel. But I
can't…'' The words caught painfully in her throat. She
swallowed hard. ''I just can't quit now.''

Suddenly the fight seemed to leave him. Samuel let
go of her arm. Looking numb, he stared at her. His
silence unnerved her more than anything he could possibly have said.

At that moment Jessie knew she wasn't the only one
who felt betrayed.

Frustration and regret welled up inside her. They
were at a deadlock. There was nothing either of them
could say to change the other's mind. Knowing it was
hopeless, she whirled around, making her escape to the
cottage.

With key in hand, two feet away from the door, she
stumbled to a stop, confused at first by what she saw:
the door stood ajar, one of its windowpanes broken.
Shards of glass lay on the floor. It took her a moment
to register these facts. A chill swept her body as she
finally understood.

Someone had broken into her house.

Chapter 8

Something was wrong.

He sensed it, even before Jessie turned to look at him. Her face was ashen, her expression alarmed. She swayed, looking as though she might faint.

A fist of fear gripped Samuel's heart.

Forgetting the disagreement that had just passed between them, in three quick steps he was at her side. He placed a steadying hand on her shoulder and felt the trembling of her body. "Jessie, what is it?"

She opened her mouth to speak, but the words would not form.

By then it wasn't necessary for her to explain.

Samuel already saw what she couldn't tell him. The door stood open. Jagged teeth of glass were all that remained of one window. The cottage had been broken into.

"Wait here," he said, pushing her gently but firmly behind him.

"No," she said, finding her voice. "I'm going with you."

"Whoever broke in might still be here. You'll be safer outside," he insisted, keeping his own voice low.

"I don't care. I'm not staying behind."

Samuel recognized the stubborn look on her face. He'd seen it often enough these past few days. Giving up the fight, he nodded. Then he stepped ahead of her, taking the lead.

Thankfully, this time she didn't argue. Instead, she followed close behind, their bodies bumping as they moved slowly into the foyer. Another time, another place, he wouldn't have minded the intimate contact. But right now he feared more for Jessie's safety than the stirring of his libido.

After only a few steps into the house he froze. Samuel sucked in a quick breath, feeling as though he'd been sucker punched as he stared at the carnage wreaked upon the rooms.

Someone had trashed Gull's Cottage.

He heard a soft gasp behind him and knew Jessie had seen the damage. Turning, he saw the shocked look on her face and felt his heart plummet. He placed both of his large hands on her shoulders and looked into her eyes. "Are you all right?"

She nodded, swallowing hard.

"You don't have to go any farther. You can stay right here and wait."

"No," she said, shaking her head with that same stubborn adamancy. "This is *my* house. I want to see what they've done to it."

"Then, you'd better stay close," he said, with a resigned sigh and took Jessie's hand in his.

The viciousness of the attack appalled him. Books

had been pulled from the shelves in the living room, the pages torn from their spine. Cushions were tossed from the couch, their fabric ripped as though with a knife. Dining room chairs were upended. Quilts and sheets were stripped from the beds and puddled in heaps on the bedroom floors. In the kitchen, dishes were broken, pans battered. The refrigerator door stood open, with milk and bottles of juice spilling out onto the floor.

This was no ordinary break-in, Samuel realized, after searching the house and finding it empty. There wasn't a room that hadn't been touched. It was as though whoever did this had gone through the house in a rage.

"We need to notify the sheriff," Samuel said, struggling to keep his voice calm while fruitless anger churned inside him. He wished he could have kept her from such malicious destruction.

"Yes, of course," Jessie murmured, still looking dazed, but holding her own.

"If you want, I'll call."

"I'd appreciate that."

Wanting to do more to take away her pain, he strode to the wall phone in the kitchen and dialed the number for the sheriff's department. As he waited for an answer, Jessie wandered out of the room, moving out of his line of sight. After three rings, the dispatcher picked up. Identifying himself, Samuel kept the call brief and to the point. Giving as many details as possible, he stressed the urgency of the situation. Once finished, he hung up the phone and went in search of Jessie.

She stood at one end of the empty hallway, staring at the mutilated artwork. Deep gashes tore at the watercolors, destroying the beautiful paintings. He stepped closer and saw the name at the bottom of one picture...Eve Pierce. The paintings had been her mother's work. No wonder Jessie looked so upset.

He reached out a hand, intent on consoling her, when he heard the high-pitched whine of a distant siren. The sheriff's department was about to make an entrance. Dropping his hand to his side, he sighed. "I'll go outside and meet them."

Jessie nodded, averting her gaze, unwilling for him to see the emotion filling her eyes.

Reluctantly Samuel strode to the front door, steeling himself for yet another confrontation with Sheriff Broward. To his relief the sheriff was nowhere in sight. Instead, two of his deputies answered the call.

The men worked efficiently and professionally. The younger of the two, a baby-faced deputy named Purty, took pictures of the scene. He chatted incessantly as he worked, smiling an apology each time he was forced to ask them to move out of his way.

The older deputy, Jeff, a hard-faced, middle-aged man with glints of silver in his military-style haircut, wasn't quite as cordial. After dusting the front door for fingerprints and taking samples of their own for the process of elimination, he questioned them more thoroughly. "What time did you say you left the house this morning, Miss Pierce?"

"Around ten-thirty," Jessie said.

The deputy glanced at his watch. "It's one o'clock, now. That's a little over two hours, plenty of time for someone to break in." Raising a brow, his gaze slid to Samuel. "If you don't mind me asking, Samuel...where were you this morning?"

Samuel wasn't surprised by the question. His only surprise was that it hadn't come sooner. Since his youthful days of indiscretion, whenever there was trouble in town, he continued to make the sheriff department's short list of suspects. As he'd told Jessie earlier, memories were long in a small town...and they were far from forgiving.

Tamping down his anger, he said, "I was on the *Marianna* until half past eleven. After that—"

"He was with me," Jessie interrupted, her voice filled with indignation. While he'd learned to school his emotions around those he didn't trust, Jessie felt no such compunction. Her dark eyes flashed with anger. "We've been together ever since the *Marianna* docked. Samuel isn't the one who broke into my house, deputy. He's been a good friend and a great help to me." She stepped forward, jabbing a finger at the badge pinned to the surprised deputy's shirt. "Furthermore, I resent any implications to the contrary—"

"Now, hold on there, miss." The deputy held up both hands in mock surrender. "I was just doing my job. I had to ask. Samuel knows that. Don't you, Samuel?"

Samuel stared hard at the man, wishing he could say what he really felt in his heart. But he knew it wasn't the time or the place to stir up further trouble. Now was the time for a cool head and an open mind. "Sure," he said, his tone flat, emotionless. "I understand."

Looking uncomfortable, the deputy adjusted his gun belt. He riffled through his notes, giving himself a moment to recover his composure. "Now, you say you didn't see anyone. Not when you drove up? Or when you first looked around?"

"No," Jessie said, still looking as though she'd like to continue the fight where she'd left off.

Samuel shook his head, not trusting himself to speak.

The deputy frowned. "And there's nothing missing?"

"Not that I can tell," Jessie said with a frustrated sigh. "Everything's such a mess."

"Yeah, it sure is." Appearing puzzled, the deputy glanced around the shattered living room. Shifting from one foot to the other, his troubled gaze returned to Jessie. "It almost seems as though someone was trying to make a point. You haven't done anything lately to make somebody mad, have ya?"

Jessie hesitated, glancing at Samuel.

In that single exchange, Samuel knew what she was thinking. The investigation into her mother's death. Jessie had been asking questions, digging into the past, looking for the truth behind the murder. It would seem that Samuel hadn't been the only one disturbed by her actions.

Was it possible that Jessie had shaken a murderer out of hiding?

Jessie cleared her throat. Her gaze drifted over the room, purposefully not meeting the deputy's eyes. "I have no idea who would have done such a thing. I'm new to the island. I've only been here a few days. That's not nearly long enough to make any enemies."

A lie of omission. Yet still a lie. Samuel tensed, but remained silent at her side.

Purty, the baby-faced deputy, joined them, signaling to his older partner that he was finished.

The older man said, "Well, there's not much more we can do here. We'll be sure to beef up patrols in the area." His frown deepened as he glanced, once again, around the rooms. "If I were you, Miss Pierce, I'd change the locks. Maybe add a keyed dead bolt to the front door."

Play the

"LAS VEGAS"

GAME

GET 3 FREE GIFTS!

FREE GIFTS!

FREE GIFTS!

FREE GIFTS!

TURN THE PAGE TO PLAY! **Details inside!**

Play the
"LAS VEGA
and get
3 FREE GIFT:

FREE GIFTS!

1. Pull back all 3 tabs on the card at right. Then check the
   see what we have for you — 2 FREE BOOKS and a gift —
   FREE!

2. Send back this card and you'll receive brand-new Silhou
   Moments® novels. These books have a cover price of $4.
   U.S. and $5.25 each in Canada, but they are yours to keep

3. There's no catch. You're under no obligation to buy anyth
   nothing — ZERO — for your first shipment. And you do
   any minimum number of purchases — not even one!

4. The fact is thousands of readers enjoy receiving books by
   Silhouette Reader Service™. They like the convenience of h
   they like getting the best new novels BEFORE they're availal
   and they love our discount prices!

5. We hope that after receiving your free books you'll want to
   subscriber. But the choice is yours — to continue or cance
   all! So why not take us up on our invitation, with no risk of
   You'll be glad you did!

Visit us onli
www.eHarle

FREE!
No Obligation to Buy!
No Purchase Necessary!

Play the
"LAS VEGAS" Game

PEEL BACK HERE ▶
PEEL BACK HERE ▶
PEEL BACK HERE ▶

YES! I have pulled back the 3 tabs. Please send me all the free Silhouette Intimate Moments® books and the gift for which I qualify. I understand that I am under no obligation to purchase any books, as explained on the back and opposite page.

345 SDL C23Z

245 SDL C23V

NAME   (PLEASE PRINT CLEARLY)

ADDRESS

APT.#   CITY

STATE/PROV.   ZIP/POSTAL CODE

7 7 7	**GET 2 FREE BOOKS & A FREE MYSTERY GIFT!**
♣ ♣ ♣	**GET 2 FREE BOOKS!**
🍒 🍒 🍒	**GET 1 FREE BOOK!**
🔔 🔔 🔔	**TRY AGAIN!**

▼ DETACH AND MAIL TODAY ▼

The Silhouette Reader Service™ —Here's how it works:

BUSINESS REPLY MAIL

FIRST-CLASS MAIL   PERMIT NO. 717   BUFFALO, NY

POSTAGE WILL BE PAID BY ADDRESSEE

SILHOUETTE READER SERVICE
3010 WALDEN AVE
PO BOX 1867
BUFFALO NY 14240-9952

NO POSTAGE
NECESSARY
IF MAILED
IN THE
UNITED STATES

Jessie nodded.

The older deputy shot an uncertain glance at Samuel. Then with a curt nod he turned to leave. With his younger partner close on his heels, he strode to the front door, closing it behind them. Silence echoed hollowly in the cottage.

Once again Samuel found himself alone with Jessie.

Feeling awkward, not sure what to do next, he reached for an upended chair and put it back in its place. He stooped to pick up a cushion. Fingering the cotton stuffing that oozed from a tear in the fabric, he slid it onto the couch. Just as he was about to reach for another cushion, he noticed that Jessie wasn't moving.

She stood with her back to him, facing the bank of windows overlooking the overgrown treeline of the property. Even with the length of the room between them, he saw her body shaking.

Slowly he walked toward her. Hesitating, he placed a hand on her shoulder and turned her toward him.

Tears spilled down her cheeks. Her eyes were red, her breath choppy. She was crying—silent, jerking sobs of despair.

Without thinking of the consequences, he gave in to his wants and pulled her into his arms.

With a soft cry she melted against him. She turned her face into his shoulder and curled her arms around his waist. Holding on tight, she allowed him to support her fragile weight, letting the tears flow unchecked.

He wasn't sure how much time passed. He didn't care. His shirt grew damp with her tears. His heart felt heavy with her pain. Still he rocked her in his arms, holding her until her tears were spent, all the while trying not to think about how much he was beginning to care about her.

They'd known each other for such a short time. But that hadn't stopped a bond from forming between them. A bond born of a troubled past. Samuel tightened his hold upon her. He didn't want to see her suffer anymore.

After a moment he pushed away. Just far enough so he could look into her eyes. Brushing damp locks of hair from her face, he whispered, ''No more.''

Jessie's brow furrowed. She looked up at him, confused.

''I don't want anything to happen to you, Jessie,'' he said, feeling a thickness in his throat. ''This search for your mother's killer…it has to stop.''

''No,'' she said, shaking her head. She stepped back out of his arms, letting cold air rush up to meet him. ''Don't you see what this means? Someone is running scared.''

''Someone who might be a killer,'' he reminded her, the words sterner than he'd meant. He was agitated. The walls felt as though they were about to close in around him. The damage seemed more threatening without the reassuring warmth of her body next to his. He swept a hand around the living room. ''Take a good look, Jessie. Whoever did this was mad enough to cause a hell of a lot of damage. The next time they might not take their anger out on the house. Next time they might be looking for you.''

She cringed, but refused to back down. ''I'm not what they were after. They were looking for my mother's diary.''

He frowned. ''The diary?''

''Of course. What else could it have been?''

"A warning," he said bluntly. "Someone wants you to leave Prudence Island."

"Well, I'm not going anywhere," she said, straightening her shoulders. She lifted her chin in defiance. "I refuse to be intimidated. I'm not leaving until I've found out everything there is to know."

Samuel closed his eyes. They'd had this disagreement before. He could argue with her until he was blue in the face, and still she would not change her mind.

Slowly opening his eyes, he looked around the vandalized room and knew he could not abandon her. Like it or not, they were partners in this dangerous search for the truth. Aloud he said, "Then I have no choice but to help you...God help us both."

"It's getting late," Samuel mused.

Startled, Jessie looked up from the torn book of poems that she'd been skimming. A book of love poems, with verses that someone—her mother, she assumed—had highlighted with a yellow marker. Finding a touchstone, a connection to her mother, was the one good thing to come out of the horrors of the day's events. This unexpected glimpse into her mother's life somehow reassured her that her decision to continue her search into her mother's death was the right one. Slowly she rose to her feet, rubbing an aching spot in small of her back.

Samuel stood in the doorway, examining the keyed dead bolt he'd just finished installing in the front door. A small square of plywood temporarily covered the missing pane of glass.

Jessie glanced at the bank of windows facing the beach. Wind pummeled the coastline, kicking up sand and dust, bending the tall sea oats that lined the dunes.

Black, ominous clouds scudded across the horizon. A late-day storm was brewing.

They'd spent the last several hours sifting through the damaged rooms, setting aside articles that could be salvaged, stuffing into trash bags items that were beyond repair. The house wore the vacant, empty look of a wounded soul. While Jessie told herself the damage was only superficial, she knew in her heart that the spirit of the house had been dealt yet another serious blow.

A blow from which she doubted it would ever recover.

Her stomach growled, interrupting her thoughts, reminding her that she hadn't eaten since early this morning. Embarrassed, she placed a quieting hand on her tummy.

Samuel's face eased into a half smile.

"I don't know about you, but I'm starving," she admitted, with a sheepish grin. "How would you like some dinner?"

"I don't want you to go to any trouble," he said, closing the door and bolting the lock.

"Samuel," she said, sighing her impatience, "after all you've done for me today, a meal is the least I can offer you." Then, remembering all the tainted food they'd thrown out, she added, "At least, I think I can offer you a meal. I'd better check to see what I've still got in the pantry."

"Do you need some help?"

She waved away the offer. "No, I'll be fine. Why don't you have a seat and relax for a while? I won't be long."

Samuel didn't answer. Instead, he stood in the foyer,

frowning thoughtfully as he glanced around the devastated rooms.

She hesitated, following his gaze. There was still so much to do. The ruined couch would have to be replaced or recovered. She would need someone to come in and smooth out the gouges in the wooden floors and clean the stains from carpets. Even more daunting, her mother's paintings were torn beyond repair. But she hadn't found the strength to take them down from the wall and throw them away.

Jessie shivered at the thought of how much there was still to do. And yet she just wasn't sure how much time or money she wanted to spend on repairing the damage. While Gull's Cottage was a beautiful house, she'd yet to feel comfortable inside its doors. She hugged her waist, rubbing her arms to ward off a sudden chill. She was beginning to think this house could never feel as though it were a home.

Awareness stirred as she felt Samuel's gaze upon her. She turned to see him watching her, a concerned look on his face. Forcing a smile, she said, "It's still a bit overwhelming."

"You mean the break-in?"

"Not just that," she murmured. "It's the fact that someone hated me enough to do so much damage." She looked into his eyes, challenging him to disagree. "That is what this is all about, isn't it? Hatred? I can feel it every time I step into a room and see something else that's been destroyed. Whoever did this was filled with so much anger, so much bitterness."

He didn't answer. But the troubled expression on his face and the pity in his eyes told her she was right. He had come to the same conclusion.

''Dinner won't be long,'' Jessie said with a sigh, and turned away.

Earlier, they'd thrown out the spoiled food and spilled drinks. The floors had been washed and the counters cleaned. But the kitchen still felt sullied. And while she couldn't explain the reaction, every time she stepped into the room her stomach clenched with apprehension.

Jessie pushed aside her unease and strode to the pantry to see what the shelves held in way of a meal. Snapping on the light, she opened the wooden door and stepped inside.

Despite the overhead bulb that lit the small room, darkness seemed to reach out and engulf her. One step more and the floor began to spin beneath her feet. Her chest tightened. Her stomach roiled in revulsion as another paralyzing panic attack struck her.

Voices, loud, angry voices.

Jessie drew in a strangled breath. It was the nightmare of her youth coming to her in the middle of the day while she was wide-awake. She closed her eyes and tried to blot out the horrible images.

The night-darkened hallway...hurrying toward the sound of shouting...the voices, louder...

No matter how hard she fought them, the images kept coming. Unable to move or to scream out, Jessie stood panic-stricken, shuddering in the center of the small pantry. There was nothing she could do to stop the nightmare from happening again.

Then, suddenly, there was silence. A heart-stuttering silence.

A beam of light sliced through the inky darkness, blinding her, paralyzing her with fear....

A shape emerged from the shadows of the kitchen.

A shape large and frightening, coming closer, closer...

Her heart leaping in her chest, she stumbled back, one step, two, until she couldn't go any farther...

And then there was nothing but darkness. All-encompassing darkness.

A scream tore from her throat, unlocking her frozen limbs. She reached out, flailing her arms against invisible hands that tried to hold her. Stumbling forward, she fell against the pantry shelves. Cans and bottles toppled from their perches onto the floor, the crash echoing in the small room.

A glass jar of spaghetti sauce splattered against the tiled floor, looking like spilled blood. Spinning around in a blind panic, once again she felt hands reaching for her, arms surrounding her, binding her.

Their grip was tight, too tight. She couldn't breathe. Her lungs burned. Pushing and shoving, she fought the hold they had upon her.

Until she heard a voice...

Samuel's worried voice. "Jessie!"

She stopped struggling.

His iron grip loosened, giving her room to breathe.

She gulped in cooling drafts of air, and the spinning room slowed. Slowly the tight feeling of panic in her chest eased. Her heart still thudding, she looked up into a pair of familiar, blue eyes. Her muscles went lax, and relief flooded her body as she allowed herself to be calmed by Samuel's reassuring presence.

"What is it, Jessie? What's wrong?"

"Where was I found?" she demanded, barely able to muster more than a whisper.

He shook his head, looking confused. "I...I don't understand."

"The night of the murder…the newspapers said I was found in the house." She drew in a choppy breath, trying to slow her racing heart. "Where was I found?"

"I'm not sure. I…I thought someone said in a closet—"

"Could it have been in here?" Jessie couldn't stop the tremors from shaking her body as she glanced around the small room. "In the pantry?"

"I don't know. I suppose—"

"Well, I do know," she said, her voice echoing hollowly against the walls of the pantry. "I saw it. I saw the kitchen in my dream."

"Dream?" His expression grew more puzzled. "What dream?"

Jessie wanted to cry out her impatience. Of course he wouldn't know about her dreams. No one knew of them. Tears of frustration welled up in her eyes. She blinked hard, fighting the show of weakness. All these years, she'd been too embarrassed to admit to anyone that she was still haunted by a childhood dream. She'd never trusted anyone enough to share her secret.

Now she tried to explain. "Since my mother's death, I've had nightmares." She shook her head, impatient with her own clumsy efforts. "No, that's not right…I've had only one nightmare…but now, I know it's more than just a dream. It's a memory."

She looked up at him, eyes wide. "Samuel, I'm remembering my mother's murder."

Chapter 9

An hour later the storm that had threatened finally found its release. Rain pelted the glass windows of the Sassy Seagull restaurant, turning the sky and ocean a dirty gray. The beach looked almost deserted. Tourists, carrying umbrellas and wearing raincoats, hurried along the boardwalk, heading for dry places to settle for the evening.

Samuel sat across the table from Jessie, still feeling too on edge to speak. Considering the events of the past few hours, neither of them had felt comfortable staying at Gull's Cottage. Needing a break, they'd decided it was best to eat out. Now, as the silence strained between them, the implications of what had been revealed seemed even more foreboding.

Jessie's memory was returning. She was beginning to recall the events of the past. The events leading to her mother's murder.

Samuel sipped his beer, then glanced at Jessie's pale

face. He wasn't sure whether to be pleased with the news, or to consider it just one more reason to worry.

"Here you go," the waitress announced, interrupting his troubled thoughts. The young girl slid two platters onto the table before them. For Jessie she brought a sizzling plate of delicately broiled shrimp and rice pilaf. For Samuel, a stick-to-your-ribs steak and fries. With a wink and a grin, she thumped a bottle of ketchup on the table before leaving. "Enjoy your meal."

His appetite abandoning him, Samuel forced himself to pick up his fork. He stared at the food, trying to muster the desire to eat.

"Maybe this wasn't such a good idea," Jessie said, echoing his own thoughts. He glanced across the table to find her studying him pensively. "I'm not really that hungry. We probably should have just skipped dinner."

"We've got to eat sometime," Samuel insisted. He jabbed a French fry and forked it into his mouth. Around a mouthful of the food, he said, "Try your shrimp. The restaurant's known for their seafood."

Sighing, she picked up a shrimp by its tail and nibbled on the succulent shellfish. Nodding, she said, "You're right. It is good."

"I told ya." Samuel smiled. He skewered another fry. "You know what they say, everything looks better on a full stomach."

"I wish that were true," she murmured.

Hearing the uncertainty in her voice, he lowered his fork. "Listen, Jessie. You're getting your memory back. That's good news, not bad."

"Are you sure?"

He sighed. "No, I'm not sure. But it has to be better than this limbo you've been in." He studied her face.

"I thought you were the one who wanted to know the truth?"

"I *need* to know the truth...I'm not sure if I really *want* to know. There is a difference."

He hesitated, considering his answer. With the return of Jessie's memory, there was always the possibility that she could help him clear his father's name. He'd never given up hope that someday this might happen. But in doing so, Jessie could be putting her own life at risk.

A risk he wasn't sure he wanted her to take.

Samuel shifted uncomfortably at his unexpected change of attitude. For most of his life, he'd been a loner. The shame and bitterness he'd felt over the past had never allowed him to get close to anyone. Though he and Jessie were working together now, the arrangement was temporary. They came from two different worlds. Jessie was a woman of culture, used to the comforts wealth could afford. He was a shrimper, a simple man living a simple life. A life in which he struggled daily through hardships. Despite their differences, somehow she had been the one to break through his self-imposed wall of isolation. She had made him realize just how destructive his solitude had become. In caring for her, even if it was just for this brief moment in time, a weight had been lifted from his heart.

It was as though he were free for the first time to feel again.

Not caring what the other patrons in the restaurant might think, he reached across the table and took her hand in his. It was the hand of an artist, strong, yet delicate. Her skin was soft and smooth, making him all the more aware of his callused fingers, of the differences that would always shape their lives.

"Jessie," he said carefully. "I'd be lying if I said I wasn't concerned. The more you remember, the more you're putting yourself in danger. I don't like the idea of you making yourself a target for a killer."

"No one else knows that I'm regaining my memory," she reminded him.

"Not yet. But what happens when you do remember everything? Once you start opening the door to the past, you can't always shut it behind you." He met her eyes, holding them with his. "Are you sure you're ready to face the demons that might come out of the closet?"

Jessie shivered, slipping her hand from his grasp. "I don't have a choice, do I? Like you said, I can't go on living halfway between the past and the present. It's too late to turn back now."

Samuel pushed his plate away, his appetite abandoning him for good. "I'm not really that hungry, after all."

"Neither am I," she said, her tone resigned.

Samuel motioned for the waitress. When the young girl returned to their table, he asked for the bill.

"Is everything all right?" the waitress asked, frowning as she eyed their untouched plates.

"Everything's fine," he assured her. "We just forgot about a prior engagement. If you wouldn't mind, we're in a hurry to leave."

"Sure," the waitress said, flipping through her notebook for their check. Finding it, she tore off the page and handed it to him. "You can pay up front. I could get a doggy bag for you, if you want—"

"No, thank you," Samuel murmured, anxious to be alone. Once the girl left, he looked at Jessie. "I don't want to take you to Gull's Cottage. There are plenty of empty rooms at my house. Why don't stay the night and be my guest?''

''Thank you, but no.'' She straightened her shoulders in what was fast becoming a familiar gesture of determination. Lifting her chin, she said, ''I'm not running away. I'm getting too close to the truth to let anyone stop me now.''

Shaking his head, unable to stop a smile, Samuel said, ''Did anyone ever tell you you were stubborn?''

A fleeting smile touched her lips. ''I believe my adoptive mother might have mentioned something to that effect.''

''She must have been a very astute lady.''

''Yes, she was,'' Jessie said quietly. Her face softened as her gaze drifted to the rain-washed view outside. ''Sometimes I think she knew me better than I know myself. There isn't a minute that goes by that I don't wish she was still here.''

''I know the feeling,'' he said, thinking of his own parents. More than anything he wished he could take away the guilt and the uncertainty those memories brought him. Though he'd never admitted it to anyone else, after all these years a part of him questioned his father's innocence. What if he were putting Jessie through this turmoil for nothing? What if, when all was said and done, they discovered that his father had been responsible for Eve Pierce's death, after all? What would he do then?

He pushed the unspeakable thought from his mind. Placing the money for a tip on the table, he pushed his chair back. ''Are you ready?''

She nodded, then rose to her feet. Standing barely up to his chin, she seemed so small, so fragile. The delicacy was an illusion, he reminded himself. As he had witnessed firsthand, Jessie was a woman of immense strength and willpower.

But that didn't stop him from playing the part of her protector. Their departure brought curious glances from local patrons. He could see the speculative look in the eyes that followed their progress through the restaurant. Samuel stayed close, keeping a hand at the small of Jessie back, mentally and physically warding off the unwanted attention.

Once he'd settled the bill, they stepped outside and made their way to his truck. The worst of the storm had passed; a fine mist was all that remained. Dusk had given way to nightfall. The vapor lights in the parking lot scattered the darkness.

Opening the door for Jessie, he was struck once again by how mismatched they really were. With her designer clothes and refined features, she looked out of place sliding onto the patched vinyl seat of his beat-up pickup truck. Samuel slammed the door shut harder than necessary, angry with himself for thinking there could be anything more between them than a mutual need for cleaning the slate of their pasts.

The differences in their worlds were too great. Once they'd found out the truth behind the death of Eve Pierce, there would be no need for their paths to cross ever again. Jessie would return to Atlanta, and he would remain here on Prudence Island. It would be best if he kept that in mind and guarded his heart.

A feat easier said than done, Samuel realized as he drove in strained silence to Gull's Cottage. The delicate scent of jasmine, her perfume, filled the cab of the truck, wreaking havoc on his good intentions. By the dashboard lights, he could see the sculpted lines of her face, the smoothness of her complexion. She shifted her legs, drawing his attention to their shapeliness.

Muttering a quiet oath beneath his breath, Samuel pressed his foot down on the accelerator, picking up speed. As far as he was concerned, the sooner they were out of the close confines of the truck, the better.

Rain had slickened Jessie's driveway, making the ruts even more hazardous. He slowed the truck, trying not to jar his passenger. Pulling to a stop in front of the house, he stared at the dark, uninviting cottage. "Are you sure you want to stay here tonight?"

"Of course I do," she said, not sounding at all that confident.

Samuel sighed. "Then, I'm going in to check on the house first. I'm not leaving until I know you'll be safe."

She didn't argue. Instead, she scrambled out of the truck and followed him to the front door. She stayed close as he walked through the house, turning on lights and chasing away the shadows. The house appeared just as they'd left it, empty and looking even more depressing.

While he hated the thought of leaving her, he didn't see that he had much choice. He forced himself to return to the front door and step outside. Jessie followed him onto the porch. Moths batted themselves against the overhead light. Palmettos clicked in the soft breeze. The air felt heavy with the salty scent of the ocean.

For a long moment neither of them said a word. They simply looked at each other, their gazes uncertain, waiting for the other to make the first move.

Samuel wasn't surprised when he lost his battle for control. The need to hold her close overwhelmed any lingering doubts. With a sigh of resignation, he pulled her into his arms and kissed her.

There was a tenderness in the embrace that hadn't been there before. An undeniable connection had grown between them. Samuel slid his hands to her waist, pressing her soft body to his. Her lips tasted of wine, buttery shrimp and a flavor that was uniquely Jessie's. With all his blustering about keeping his heart out of harm's way, he knew it was already too late.

He could no longer deny the truth.

That he already cared too much for Jessie.

Knowing neither of them were ready to take this fledgling relationship a step further, reluctantly he ended the kiss. Pulling back, with Jessie still in his arms, he looked down into her beautiful face and lost himself in the depths of her dark eyes.

In that moment he knew he had never felt this way about any other woman. That he would never feel this way again. With Jessie he had found what he'd been yearning for…a reason to hope, a reason to live again.

Before he could put into words what he felt in his heart, he heard the *phhht* of something small and quick passing nearby. At first he'd thought it was a pesky moth, attracted to the glow. Then the light exploded over their heads, casting them in instant darkness, showering them with shards of glass.

Instinct told him what his mind refused to believe.

Someone was shooting at them.

Before Jessie realized what was happening, Samuel shoved her down onto the ground, covering her with his big body. The uneven stone floor bit into her chest and legs. A cold dampness seeped through her clothes, chilling her.

She had little time to think of her discomfort before another shot rang out. Followed by yet another. The shots thudded against the siding, sending splinters of wood falling about their heads.

Suddenly there was silence, a breath-stealing silence. She shifted beneath his weight. "Samuel—"

"Shhh…" he whispered in her ear.

She strained to listen, but all she could hear was the sound of her own heart pounding in her ears. Then, in the distance, she heard footsteps. Someone was running toward the road, crashing through the trees and thick underbrush.

Before she could stop him, Samuel rolled his weight off her. He scrambled to his feet, heading toward the shooter and certain danger.

"Samuel, wait," she called after him, clumsily struggling to her own feet.

"Stay here, Jessie," he ordered, half turning to look at her as he continued to sprint away. "Go inside and call the sheriff…now."

For a moment Jessie stood frozen, too stunned to move. She watched until Samuel disappeared from sight. Then, with a jerk, she snapped herself out of her trance. Spinning around, she did as Samuel had asked.

Leaving the front door open, she ran into the house, nearly tripping over bags of trash, knocking her knee painfully against a misplaced chair. The carnage of the house seemed minor in comparison to the danger Samuel now faced. He was out there, alone, trying to chase down someone with a gun.

Tears stung Jessie's eyes. She raised a trembling hand to her mouth to stop a sob from escaping. Now wasn't the time to lose control, she told herself. She needed to be strong. For her own sake as well as Samuel's she had to call for help.

Her fingers felt clumsy as she picked up the phone and punched in the number for the sheriff's office. It seemed like an eternity before her call was answered.

"Sheriff's Department."

"I need help," Jessie said in a rush. The words sounded breathless, as though she'd just run five miles. "There's been a shooting. Please, send someone right away."

"Slow down," the woman at the other end of the line commanded, her voice calm in the wake of Jessie's frenzy. "Tell me your name and where you are."

Jessie forced herself to take a breath, willing her pounding heart to slow. "I'm Jessie Pierce. I'm at Gull's Cottage, on the north side of town—"

"I know where Gull's Cottage is, Ms. Pierce," the woman said. "You said there was a shooting. Is anyone injured?"

"No…not that I know of," Jessie stammered, feeling the tension build inside her, wishing she knew if Samuel were safe.

"Is anyone else with you at the scene?"

"Samuel…Samuel Conners." She felt as though she were about to explode with impatience. She'd never been this worried, this keyed-up before in her life. "Could you please hurry? Samuel went out looking for the shooter. I don't know what's happened to him."

"A patrol car is on its way, ma'am. They should be there shortly."

Footsteps sounded in the foyer. Footsteps, quick and heavy, running into the house. A scream welled up in Jessie's throat. Numbly she turned toward the intruder.

And nearly collapsed with relief when she saw Samuel coming toward her.

"He's here," she blurted out. "Samuel's back. And he's all right."

"Yes, ma'am. That's good to hear."

She heard the sound of a siren approaching.

So did the dispatcher. "I hear the patrol car. You can hang up the phone now, Ms. Pierce."

"Thank you," Jessie said, her voice thick with emotion. Returning the receiver to its cradle, she watched as Samuel moved toward her. She saw the disappointment in his eyes.

"Whoever it was got away," he said, reaching out to touch her. But she slapped his hand away as anger and relief warred inside her.

"Don't you ever do that to me again," she said, trembling with pent-up emotion. "You had me scared to death. What were you thinking, running after a man with a gun? You could have been shot."

"You were worried," he said, having the gall to smile. He seemed pleased by her reaction.

"Of course I was worried," she snapped, moving back as he stepped toward her. "If you'd gotten yourself shot, it would have been my fault. Even if it was your own fool idea to put yourself in danger."

"I'm sorry, Jessie," he said, not sounding in the least bit contrite. He continued to close the gap between them. "Next time I won't play the part of a hero."

"N-next time?" Her voice broke on the words. "For Pete's sake, there'd better not be a next time."

This time, when he reached for her, she didn't push him away. Instead, she collapsed against him, letting him gather her into his arms. It felt so good to have him close, to know that he was safe. She didn't know what she would have done if he'd been harmed.

Samuel rocked her, holding her tight, murmuring words she could barely hear. She pressed her ear against his chest and listened to the steady, reassuring beat of his heart. All that mattered for now was that they were together.

Footsteps pounded in the hallway. Before either of them had time to react, the sheriff burst into the room, with his gun drawn and ready to fire. The look of concern in his eyes turned quickly to disgust when he spotted her in Samuel's arms.

"What's this about a shooting?" Sheriff Broward demanded, as he holstered his gun, impatience clearly written across his belligerent face. "Dammit, Conners. If you called me out here on a wild-goose chase, I swear—"

"This isn't a joke, Sheriff." Samuel released her, stepping away to face the irate man. "Someone shot at us while we were standing outside on the front porch."

"Standing?" The sheriff snorted his disbelief. His knowing gaze traveled from Samuel to Jessie, then back again. The smirk on his face was unmistakable. "Are you sure that's all the two of you were doing?"

Jessie drew in a sharp breath, appalled by the insinuation and by the man's unprofessionalism.

Beside her, Samuel tensed. A vein pulsed at his temple, and his hands fisted at his sides. He had the look of a man struggling to control his temper.

Thankfully, a deputy strode into the room before Samuel could act on his emotions. Tall, with the body of a weightlifter, the deputy glanced at them, his gaze curious, before directing his attention to his boss.

"Sheriff, I think you'd better come see this. We've found some bullet holes on the front porch."

Looking almost disappointed, the sheriff irritably turned away. His booted feet pounded against the hardwood floor as he followed his man through the disheveled rooms of the house.

Samuel stood stiffly in the doorway of the kitchen, watching them leave. "I shouldn't be here. I'm only making it worse."

"Samuel, please. Don't let him bother you." Refusing to let him blame himself for the pompous sheriff's behavior, Jessie laced her fingers with his. "You can't leave now. I need your help."

He hesitated. Then, with an uncertain nod, he led her to the front porch.

The baby-faced deputy, Purty, who'd answered their call this afternoon was shining a flashlight on the ground, searching through the shattered pieces of glass. He looked up and smiled a greeting when he saw them step onto the porch. "Evening, Miss Pierce. Y'all have been having a bad day, today, haven't ya?

An understatement for certain. Jessie managed a strained smile. "I can't recall a worse one."

The other deputy shone his light above their heads, directing the beam at the holes pocking the wood siding. "Looks as though there were at least three shots. I'm betting the bullets are still in there, too."

"Dig 'em out," the sheriff said, his voice gruff. He narrowed a glance at Samuel. "Either of you two see who might have done this?"

Samuel shook his head. "I tried to follow them. But whoever it was got away. They must have had a car or truck parked nearby. They just ran into the underbrush and disappeared."

"Purty," the sheriff snapped, pointing a finger at the woods. "Take a look out there. Stay along the treeline. See if you can find any spent casings."

With a nod, Purty hurried off the porch.

"I've got 'em, Sheriff," the other deputy called out. He snapped his penknife closed and held up a plastic bag with three misshapen bullets inside. "Looks like our shooter was totin' a .22."

The sheriff took the bag, turning it over in his hands. Without looking up, he said, "Charlie, help Purty look for those casings. And see if there's any foot-prints...besides Conner's."

"Yes, sir." The deputy turned, leaving them alone with the sheriff.

For a long moment, Sheriff Broward did not speak. He studied the bullets in his hands, as though consid-ering what to do next. With a sigh, he pushed his hat back on his head and scratched his thick shock of red hair. Fixing Samuel with a stony gaze, he said, "You just couldn't listen to me, could ya?"

Samuel shifted beside her, his foot scraping against the uneven ground. She felt the muscles of his body tauten.

"I warned you something like this might happen. But you couldn't leave things alone. You just had to stir up trouble, didn't ya?"

"You're blaming this on me?" Samuel asked, his voice deceptively calm. Jessie felt the anger thrumming through his body.

"Why shouldn't I?" the sheriff growled. "Trouble always has had a way of following your family around."

Samuel started, looking as though he'd been struck by the insult.

"Sheriff, you're not being fair," Jessie said, unable to stand back and allow the unjust accusations to continue. "Samuel had nothing to do with this. He's been trying to help me find out who really killed my mother."

"Who killed your mother?" the sheriff scoffed, with a short, unamused bark of a laugh. His brows knit into a deep scowl. Turning cold eyes upon Samuel, he demanded, "What kind of lies have you been telling this girl?"

"They're not lies, Sheriff," Jessie insisted. "My house was vandalized today. Just minutes ago shots were fired at me while I stood on my porch. Can't you see what's happening? Someone is trying to stop me. They don't want me to know what really happened to my mother."

Slowly shaking his head from side to side, the sheriff muttered a string of curses beneath his breath. "Now, you listen to me, young lady. If there was some sort of secret, don't you think I'd know about it? I was the one who worked that murder investigation."

Jessie sighed. "Sheriff, you don't understand—"

"No, I understand perfectly. You two think I made a mistake. That I botched the investigation. Well, you're wrong." Stepping closer, he jabbed a finger at Samuel's chest. "No matter what he might have told you, the right man was charged and convicted of Eve Pierce's murder."

Samuel's face hardened. His eyes glinted with undisguised hatred.

Without flinching, the sheriff met his bitter gaze. His jaw jutted out in challenge. The look in his eyes dared Samuel to argue.

Jessie's grip tightened around Samuel's hand,

squeezing it gently, willing him not to be goaded into a fight he could not win.

Thankfully, beams of light washed against the walls of the porch, heralding the return of both deputies. Boots clomped along the stone walkway. Charlie stepped up to join them. "We found some casings. They were about a hundred yards away. Not a bad shot, considering—"

"Considering they missed," Samuel finished, grinding out the words through clenched teeth.

"Samuel," Jessie murmured, her voice a subtle warning.

"We're finished here," the sheriff said, slapping a hand against his thigh.

"That's it? That's all you're going to do?" Samuel demanded.

"What more do you want? Someone to hold your hand?" the sheriff asked, with a disgusted breath. "The gunman's gone. There is nothing more we can do."

"Let them go, Samuel," Jessie pleaded. "They can't help us now."

"No one can help you," the sheriff said with a pointed glance. "Not until you stop snooping into business where you don't belong."

With that warning, he pivoted and strode from the porch. His deputies tagged along after him, like puppies following their master. Folding his tall frame into the front seat of his cruiser, he gunned the motor to life. Slamming it into gear, the car lurched forward, spitting out mud and rocks from beneath his tires.

Jessie stared numbly at the angry display. At that moment she knew it was hopeless. There would be no help from the island's law enforcement. She and Samuel were alone in their quest for the truth.

"I'm sorry, Jessie," Samuel said, his voice barely a gruff whisper. "Damn. If I hadn't been here, he would have listened to you."

"Stop it, Samuel," she said, surprising both of them with the anger shaking her voice. "I won't let you blame yourself for everything that goes wrong. This isn't your fault. The sheriff is the one to blame—him and his narrow mind." She growled, venting her frustration. "If this is the way you've always been treated, then why do you stay here? Why don't you just leave Prudence Island?"

"Because it's my home," Samuel said, his vehemence startling her. "This is where I belong. My family has lived on this island for generations. I'm not going to let anyone, not even a jackass of a sheriff, run me off."

A stunned silence followed his declaration.

Jessie blinked. She almost laughed, despite the tension filling the air—or perhaps, because of it. With a hesitant smile she said, "'So, I'm not the only one who's stubborn."

"I guess not," he said, his own smile slower in coming. Cautiously he scanned the grounds. "We'd better not stand out here. There's no need to make an easy target for someone."

Nodding, she stepped inside.

Samuel followed, closing the door and bolting it behind him. "Are you sure I can't talk you out of staying here tonight?"

"Not a chance."

"After all that's happened, you shouldn't be here by yourself." The determined look in his eye sent a shiver down Jessie's spine. "You can argue all you want, but I'm not leaving. Whether you like it or not, I'm staying the night."

Chapter 10

The air conditioner clicked before turning itself on. A gentle stream of cool air from the vents in the floor stirred the curtains in the living room windows. The floorboards creaked as they adjusted to the shifting flow. Samuel listened to the house settling itself in the quiet darkness of the night.

Earlier Jessie had wanted to fix a bed for him in one of the guest rooms. Afraid he might not hear an intruder if they broke in, he'd refused, telling her he would prefer sleeping on the couch. Now, nestled in the heart of the house, he felt restless, unable to sleep.

His insomnia was caused by more than just his concern for Jessie or being in a strange house, he realized. There was something about Gull's Cottage that made him uneasy. Despite its beauty, the house felt dark, forbidding. It was as though the ghosts of the past still walked its floors.

Samuel frowned. Impatiently he shook off the morbid thought. He'd be of no help to Jessie if he became mired down in the events of the past. He had to distance himself from his own feelings. He had to remain objective. Closing his eyes, he tried to empty his mind, willing his body to relax and, hopefully, give in to sleep.

Until a cry startled him.

His eyes flew open. Abruptly he sat up from his place on the couch, tossing the sheet aside. He heard it again, a soft mewling sound of pain. A sound that caused an icy finger of fear to stroke his spine. It took him a moment to register where the cry had come from…Jessie's bedroom.

Wearing only a pair of jeans, no shirt and no shoes, he scrambled off the couch and hurried down the hall. His bare feet padded against the smooth pine floor. He nearly slipped in his haste as he turned the corner to her room.

The door was partially open. Pale light shone from the adjoining bathroom, casting a soft glow across the room. He pushed the door open and saw no movement, except for Jessie tossing and turning in her bed.

She was having a nightmare.

Hesitating, he watched from the doorway, uncertain what to do next. Jessie had told him of her dreams. She'd said she believed them to be memories, her subconscious retrieving the past. But she hadn't told him of the force with which these dreams struck. He had no idea how deeply they affected her.

Jessie moaned and jerked in her sleep. But still she did not come fully awake. Her face was etched in so much pain, so much fear, it hurt him to watch.

Quietly he stepped into the room as he debated what to do. If he woke her, he would feel as though he was

invading her privacy. Earlier Jessie had been reluctant
to allow him to stay the night. He'd seen the hesitancy
in her eyes and knew its cause. There was a sensual
attraction that sizzled between them whenever they
were close. With such volatile feelings brewing beneath the surface, he knew he and Jessie were skirting
temptation by spending an entire night alone. It was
only at his insistence that she had finally relented. Now
he had no intention of taking advantage of her trust in
him.

Jessie flailed an arm, splaying her fingers in front of
her face, as though trying to ward off an invisible attack. Samuel fisted his hands at his sides, clenching
and unclenching them in frustration. How in the hell
could he turn around and leave her, knowing she was
in trouble?

When she cried out in her sleep, a cry of pure terror,
his decision was made. He had no choice but to help
her. Samuel closed the distance between them. Before
he could reach her, however, she sat up in bed and
screamed.

He froze. His heart stuttering, he called out her
name. "Jessie…"

Breathing heavily, her breasts rose and fell against
the knit fabric of her nightshirt. Her eyes were wide
open, but he wasn't sure she could really see him. She
looked dazed, as though her thoughts were somewhere
else, not in this room.

Moving closer, he started to reach out to her, then
stopped. He was too afraid of startling her. Once again
he said her name. "Jessie…"

Her eyelashes fluttered. She blinked as though trying
to bring her surroundings into focus. When she spotted
him standing in the center of the shadowy room, she

flinched. Cowering in fear, she scrambled to the opposite side of the bed. Her bare legs became tangled in the bedsheets. In her panic she nearly fell to the floor.

"No, Jessie, don't…it's me, Samuel," he said, his tone desperate. Dammit, he'd wanted to help her. But he'd only made things worse.

At the sound of his voice she stopped fighting, her body momentarily relaxing. Then, clutching the sheet in her hand, she turned and stared at him. "Samuel?"

"Yes, it's me." Slowly he approached the bed. "You were having a dream."

Drawing in a choppy breath, she shook her head. "No, not a dream…a nightmare. The same nightmare that I've had all of my life."

In the soft glow of the light from the bathroom, he saw her trembling. Her dark hair was mussed. Her eyes were wild with fear. He wanted to take her in his arms and protect her from the demons that haunted her. Instead he stood awkwardly at her bedside, not allowing himself the pleasure of holding her.

"You want to tell me about it?"

"No, n-not yet." She shuddered. "I just need a moment."

He nodded, then glanced around the room, searching for something to do, some way to help alleviate her distress. "Can I get you anything? A drink of water, maybe?"

"No…no, thank you." Self-consciously she glanced down at herself. Tugging on the hem of her nightshirt, she covered her exposed thighs, looking embarrassed at being caught in such a state of disarray. "I—I'm sorry I scared you. With you in the house, I didn't think I'd—"

She stopped, letting the words drift.

"That you'd have the nightmare?" Samuel finished. Cautiously he sat down on the edge of the bed. To his relief she didn't object to his closeness. "You told me it was the same dream you've had since you were a child. That you think it's a memory from your past. If you talk about it, maybe it'll make it easier to understand."

"I don't know," she said, looking as though the mere thought terrified her. "It's so jumbled...so confusing."

"Start at the beginning. Tell me what triggers the dream."

She was quiet for such a long time Samuel thought she'd decided not to answer. But then, in a tone so soft he had to strain to hear, she said, "Voices."

"Voices? Whose voices?"

She shook her head, her brows furrowing in frustration. "I don't know. They're so loud and angry, I— I'm not sure who they belong to."

"But you hear the voices," he prompted her.

"Yes, I'm asleep, but they wake me. I'm scared, but I still get out of bed and go toward the sound." She paused to raise a trembling hand, brushing the disheveled locks of hair from her eyes.

Samuel didn't say a word, too afraid to push her. He waited, letting her continue at her own pace.

She stared straight ahead, as though looking at an image which only she could see. "I'm in the hallway, here, in Gull's Cottage."

He frowned. "Gull's Cottage? Are you sure?"

"I'm positive. The pictures, my mother's watercolors. They're in my dream, just like they are now. Only everything seems different, the proportions are off. The rooms seem bigger, more threatening."

"Could it be because you're smaller in your dream?"

She glanced at him, looking surprised.

"Jessie, if it is a memory," he reminded her, "then you would have only been five years old when it happened."

A long shiver shook her body. She folded her arms around her waist, hugging herself tight. "I...I suppose it's possible."

"What else do you remember?" he said softly, encouraging her to continue.

She hesitated, considering her answer. "I remember being scared as I walked down the hall. More scared than I've ever been in my life. The farther I go, the louder the voices get...and they're so angry. Then I'm in the kitchen. It's dark, very dark. But I know it's the kitchen, because I see the outline of the cabinets and the pans hanging from the ceiling. Suddenly there's a light...a bright beam of light. It blinds me, and I...I can't move."

The pitch of her voice rose with each word she spoke. Samuel saw the fear in her eyes, and he allowed himself to reach out to her. Taking her hand, he squeezed it gently. "It's okay, Jessie. I'm right here."

Clinging to him, she drew in a shallow breath, struggling to calm herself. "I see a shape behind the light. It's stepping out of the shadows. It's large and frightening, and it keeps coming closer and closer. I try to move back, but I can't go any farther. And then—then everything goes dark...." Her grip tightened. He felt the tremors racking her body. In a weak voice she whispered, "That's it, that's all I can remember."

He gave her a moment to collect herself before pressing her for details. When she was calmer, he said,

"You said the shape stepped out of the shadows. Was it a person?"

"I—I'm not sure." She stared at the wall, straining to see something that wasn't there. "It would almost have to be. It was too big for an animal."

"Can you see anything else? A face? A hand? Anything that might help identify the person?"

"No, nothing," she said, shaking her head in frustration. She was trembling so hard Samuel was afraid she'd reached the breaking point. "I'm trying, Samuel. But I just can't remember."

"It's okay, Jessie. We've gone far enough for one night." Samuel rose to his feet. Plumping the pillows at the head of the bed, he said, "Just sit back and try to relax. I'll get you a drink."

Jessie scooted back against the pillows. She looked pale and fragile, smaller somehow in the big wrought-iron bed, as though she were pulling protectively inside herself.

Wondering if he'd pushed her too far, he strode into the bathroom. A glass was by the sink. He filled it with cold water and returned to the bedroom. Holding her shaking hand in his until he knew she had a firm grip, he stood by her bed and watched as she sipped the cool drink.

After a moment she placed the glass on the bedside table. With a strained smile she said, "Don't look so worried, Samuel. I'll be fine."

He nodded, shifting restlessly. Not ready to leave, but knowing he must. "Well, then…I'd better get back to the living room, let you try to get some sleep."

Turning, he took two steps toward the door.

But Jessie stopped him.

"Samuel, wait," she said quietly.

He swung around to look at her, his brows raised in a silent question.

Jessie hesitated. She sat up, the bedcovers slipping to her waist. Guiltily he caught a glimpse of the slender curves outlined beneath the soft fabric of her nightshirt and felt his pulse quicken. She licked her lips, looking nervous. Such an innocent gesture, and yet...

Awareness struck like a sledgehammer to his gut. Samuel felt winded, pulled under by an unexpected wave of desire. Ill-advised or not, he wanted her. He'd never needed to feel the closeness of a woman as much as he did Jessie.

Oblivious to his battle with desire, she said, "I know this sounds presumptuous...but would you mind staying? Just for a little while, until I fall asleep?"

He stared at her for a long moment, not trusting himself to speak, wondering if she knew what it was she was asking of him. Finally, swallowing hard, he said, "Of course I don't mind."

She scooted over, making room for him in the bed. And Samuel nearly moaned out loud.

Gritting his teeth, he struggled with his flagging will-power. Jessie was asking for comfort, not romance, he warned himself. Instead of thinking of his own needs, he should be thinking of hers. Instead of lusting after her body, he should be considering ways to protect it.

Reluctantly he forced himself to move. The box springs creaked a protest as he lowered himself onto the mattress beside her. The sheets still felt warm from her body. He drew in a quick breath, and jasmine, Jessie's scent, wafted up to greet him. Samuel set his jaw as he was hit by another ill-timed surge of desire.

"Thank you, Samuel," Jessie whispered, breaking into his troubled thoughts. She looked up at him, her

dark eyes wide and luminous in the shadowy light,
holding such innocence, such naïveté in their depths.
"The dreams…they keep getting worse. I…I just don't
think I could be alone right now."

Then, catching him completely off guard, she rested
her head against his shoulder and snuggled her soft
curves against him.

Samuel tensed, not allowing himself to savor the
contact, too afraid of how his unpredictable body might
react. Jessie trusted him. She had had enough shocks
this evening. The last thing she needed was to deal with
a fully aroused man in her bed.

Having her this close was such sweet torture. But he
forced himself to lie quietly beside her, listening until
her breath became even, watching until her beautiful
face softened with sleep. Only then did he allow himself to put a protective arm around her waist and pull
her close against him.

Jessie awoke feeling rested for the first time in
weeks. It was still early. Moonlight filtered in through
the drawn curtains of her bedroom windows. Not a
sound could be heard in the house. Nothing but the
sound of Samuel breathing softly next to her.

She shivered. Not from the cold, for the combined
heat of their bodies wrapped her in a cocoon of warmth
and security. But rather because his closeness brought
an unexpected quiver of anticipation traveling through
her body. Slowly, careful not to disturb him, she turned
to look at him.

The lines of tension that had marred his handsome
face earlier were gone. In sleep he looked relaxed and
comfortable. His blond hair was tousled, spilling across
his forehead. Her fingers itched to brush the errant lock

from his face, but she kept her hands pressed firmly to her sides. An early morning beard bristled his strong jawline. The sheet rode low at his waist, revealing wide shoulders, a matting of blond hair across his tanned chest and a flat, washboard stomach.

A warm flush of awareness flowed through her veins, pooling in the pit of her stomach. Though she had dated other men, the relationships had been brief and deliberately casual. Never before had she woken with a man in bed beside her. Though she had craved the tenderness of a man's touch—a temporary end to her loneliness—something had always stopped her from taking that step.

She had never felt strong enough to handle an intimate relationship. At times events in her life seemed beyond her control, her future uncertain. The unexplained dreams had always haunted her…a secret she had guarded with her heart. She'd never wanted to let anyone see her in such a vulnerable light. Besides, what man would want to get involved with a woman whose life seemed so unstable?

But with Samuel it was different. Not only did he seem to understand her, but with him beside her, she felt safe, secure. For the first time, she wasn't frightened of the future. Somehow he made her life simpler. He made her feel that everything would be all right.

She trusted him.

As though sensing that he was being watched, Samuel's eyelids twitched. Slowly his pale blue eyes opened. His sleepy gaze locked on to hers.

Embarrassed heat flushed her skin as she realized she'd been caught staring. Then the previous night's events tumbled back into her mind, and she felt guilty. Someone had shot at them. Because of her obsession

with the past, she had put Samuel in danger. Instead
of being angry, he'd been concerned. He'd insisted on
staying the night. But in doing so he'd been witness to
her own private hell...her nightmare.

Samuel had seen her at her worst, and he hadn't
abandoned her. He had comforted her and had tried to
make an unbearable situation bearable. For that she
would always be grateful.

But it was more than gratitude that she craved, she
admitted to herself. More than anything she wanted to
feel his body close to hers. She wanted to touch him,
to make love to him. She wanted him with such longing that it frightened her.

In her heart she knew he felt the same.

"Good morning." His deep voice rumbled in her
ears.

Suddenly shy—a reaction that seemed silly, considering the fact that she'd shared her bed with him—she
said, "Good morning."

"Feeling better?" he asked, with a smile that set her
heart pounding.

She nodded. "Much. I don't remember the last time
I slept so solidly. It helped...having you here." Her
flush deepening, she added, "I don't know how to
thank you."

"Jessie, you don't need to thank me," he said, looking her straight in the eye, holding her gaze. "Trust
me, staying the night with you was no hardship."

She stared mutely at him, not sure how to answer.

Samuel was the first to look away. Rubbing the sleep
from his eyes, he asked, "What time is it?"

She raised herself on one elbow to glance at the bedside clock. Lying back down on the pillows, she
sighed. "It's early, only five-thirty."

"I should leave soon. Or my crew will wonder what happened to me," he said, but didn't make an effort to leave. He shifted his weight, settling himself more comfortably in the bed, his movements bringing them even closer.

Jessie held herself rigid as his warm breath fanned her skin. Goose bumps skittered up and down the length of her body. Every fiber of her being came to an instant alert.

"You have to go to the boat now?" she asked, her voice sounding strained. Self-consciously she cleared her throat. "I mean…it's so early."

"The earlier the better," he said, his tone patient. "The best time to catch shrimp is before the sun rises."

"Oh, well, of course…" She stopped, heat scorching her face. What was wrong with her? Why was he making her feel like a tongue-tied schoolgirl? "I just didn't know—"

Smiling, he brought a finger to her lips, quieting her. "It's okay, Jessie. You're a city girl. You wouldn't know the ways of the island."

She drew in a sharp breath at his touch.

Slowly his smile faded. He stared down at her, studying her face with an intensity that made her tummy flutter. She trembled as he traced the outline of her mouth with the tip of his work-roughened finger. He lifted her chin. Then, with infinite care, he placed a light, tentative kiss upon her sensitive lips.

Jessie gasped beneath the tender onslaught. She slid her hands behind his neck, burying her fingers into the thick strands of hair. Feeling bold, she tugged him closer, impatient with the fleeting caress.

With a moan of frustration Samuel brushed his tongue against her mouth. Obligingly she opened up to him. And the kiss deepened, building with a mutual need.

Too soon Samuel pulled away. The bedcovers rustled as he shifted onto one elbow, turning his body to face her. He slid one jeans-clad leg between her thighs, the worn fabric feeling soft against her bare skin. Relief poured through her when he resumed his gentle exploration. He pressed butterfly kisses against her lips, her chin, her throat, he slipped his hands downward, tracing the curves of her body, sliding them beneath the hem of her nightshirt.

Jessie's breath caught in her throat. Her body quickened as heat pulsed at the center of her womanhood. She was dizzy with longing. Gripping his shoulders, she felt the breadth and strength of his muscles. Her hands moved restlessly, molding them to the contours of his back, fitting them around his narrow waist, stopping at the band of his jeans.

Impatiently Samuel pushed her nightshirt up and over her head. Cool air rushed to meet her, fanning her heated skin. For a long moment he didn't move to touch her. Instead, he raked an intimate gaze over her body. Jessie shivered. Her breasts swelled in sweet anticipation. A soft moan escaped her lips when his fingertips finally grazed the ripe crests, cupping them in his hands, weighing their fullness.

Her nipples contracted, hardening in response. Lowering his head, he brought his mouth to one, teasing it with his tongue, tugging gently. Jessie nearly cried out as shock waves of desire rippled through her body. She closed her eyes and bit down on her lower lip, her inexperience making her cautious.

Oblivious to her innocence, he found her mouth once again, taking it with an impatience matching her own.

With their lips sealed, he slipped his hand into her panties, finding her warm and moist.

At the intimate touch her reaction was immediate, intense. Jessie dug her fingers into the small of his back as a fireball of heat exploded deep inside her. Never before had she felt such exquisite pleasure, such throbbing need. She felt as though she might die from wanting him.

All logic, all fear abandoned her. She forgot about their troubled past, her lack of experience, all the reasons why they shouldn't be doing this. All that mattered was now, the present. The two of them together. The fulfillment which only they could give to each other.

Needing to remove all barriers, clumsily, she fumbled with the top button of his jeans. He sucked in a breath as her fingers brushed the hardness of his arousal. Pulling away, he rolled onto his back and unsnapped the fly of his pants. Jessie shivered at the erotic sound of each pop. He shimmied out of his jeans and briefs, until he lay naked beside her.

Curiosity winning out over any lingering inhibitions, she raised herself up far enough to stare down at him in innocent fascination. Never before had she seen a fully aroused man. Samuel was an overwhelming combination of strength and power, of raw beauty and pure maleness. Unable to stop herself, she touched him, closing her hand around him. And felt an illicit thrill course through her body.

Drawing in a sharp breath, he pushed her gently down onto the bed. He rubbed his chin against her tender breasts, his early morning beard chafing her sensitive skin. Burying his fingers in her moist heat, he tested her, readied her. Overwhelmed, Jessie threw back her head and drew in a shuddering breath. Her heart pounded in her ears, as she gave herself to the building urgency of his caress.

A confusing mix of emotions threatened. She felt nervous and anxious, all at once. She was afraid of disappointing him, yet intrigued by the challenge of pleasing him.

"Jessie..." he whispered.

Her breath caught at the raw sound of his voice. Panic stirred at her breast, afraid he'd changed his mind. "Samuel, what's wrong?"

"Are you sure this is what you want?" he asked, looking at her intently. "Because if it isn't—"

She answered him with a kiss. A hot, steamy mating of their lips that brought a tingling sensation from the roots of her hair to the tips of her toes. She left little doubt of her wants or her needs.

Groaning, he ended the kiss. Reaching for his jeans, he took out a foil packet and readied himself. Hovering above her, he paused, looking down into her eyes. Then, finally, he slipped inside her.

Jessie winced, drawing in a quick breath, as she experienced a moment of discomfort. Reflexively her body tightened around him as he nudged deeper, his unexpected fullness bringing her a pinch of pain. But overriding the pain was a shiver of excitement that sent tremors throughout her body.

At the first sign of resistance, however, Samuel froze, staring at her in surprise. To her dismay he began to pull away.

But she wouldn't allow him to stop. Clasping his hips, she drew him closer, unwilling to let him go.

For a moment he looked uncertain. Then, swearing softly beneath his breath, he closed his eyes and plunged deeper. Slowly, he moved inside her, stretching and filling her.

The initial soreness soon gave way to a more primal emotion…the seeking of pleasure, of fulfillment. She'd never felt such longing, such abandon. Her body moved with a mind of its own, rising up to meet each of his thrusts.

He slid his hands beneath her bottom, lifting her, driving himself deeper into her. Slow at first, then faster and faster. He rocked her, bringing her higher and higher, until she could stand it no more.

She called out his name on a burst of light and a flood of warmth. As her body exploded beneath him, he reached his own trembling climax. Seconds later she felt his pulsing release deep inside her.

Samuel buried his head against her shoulder, giving himself a moment to recover. His breathing was ragged; his chest rose and fell heavily against her breast. With their bodies still pressed together, she felt the rapid beat of his heart. Tenderly she stroked the strong curves of his back.

Finally he lifted his head and looked at her. In his eyes she saw a worrisome mix of emotions: satisfaction, wonderment and an undeniable annoyance.

She had no doubt that keeping her innocence from him until it was too late had made him angry. But she had no regrets, not now, not ever. Being with Samuel was even more special than she'd dreamed possible.

For just a moment, in his arms, she had felt loved.

Chapter 11

"You should have told me," Samuel said, his expression stern.

Jessie swallowed hard at the lump of guilt in her throat. She looked away, suddenly too embarrassed to face him. "Does it really matter?"

"Of course it matters. I could have hurt you." He caught a thumb beneath her chin, turning her to look at him. Frowning, he studied her face as though searching for the truth. "Did I...hurt you? Are you sure you're all right?"

Heat blossomed on her face. "I'm fine, Samuel."

Looking unconvinced, he disentangled himself from her embrace. Rolling to one side, he swung his feet off the bed and sat up. He paused before standing, staring down at the floor.

She felt his withdrawal like a slap on the face. Jessie shivered as cool air swept her passion-heated skin. She missed the reassuring warmth of his body next to hers, the closeness she'd felt in his arms. Clutching the forgotten sheet to her breasts in a belated show of modesty, she sat up and watched him.

Samuel, as she was still learning, was a man who took a great deal of responsibility upon his shoulders. He seemed to blame himself for whatever wrong was committed. Since the day she'd met him, she had sensed the guilt that was his constant companion.

When she'd first arrived on Prudence Island, he'd been rude and unfriendly, going out of his way to make her unwelcome. As time passed and they'd gotten to know each other, she truly believed he regretted his initial behavior and, perhaps, that was why he felt so guilty.

But now she wasn't so sure.

Whenever he spoke of his past, she saw a sadness in his eyes, a remorse so obvious that she had wondered at its cause. It was as though he held himself accountable for his parents' fate.

Yesterday, after the break-in and the shooting, when the sheriff and his men had tried to accuse Samuel of being the cause of her troubles, she'd watched as he took their condemnation in silence. He hadn't defended himself; he'd defended her need to be protected. It was as though he, too, blamed himself for what had happened.

Now, he wanted to blame himself for taking her virginity.

But this was one responsibility she couldn't allow him to assume. Not when her innocence was a gift she had willingly given.

"Samuel," she said, reaching out to him, placing the palm of her hand on his back.

He stiffened beneath her touch.

"Please, Samuel," she whispered. "Don't be angry."

"I'm not angry with you," he said, his tone flat, emotionless.

"No, you're angry with yourself," she said, her voice heating in frustration.

He flinched at the words, but didn't answer. Nor did he meet her gaze.

"Samuel, look at me."

Reluctantly he raised his eyes to hers, and she saw the telltale guilt shimmering in their depths.

"Oh, Samuel," she said, on a sigh. Her vision blurred as unwanted tears threatened. Goodness only knew, she'd made such a mess of things. She wondered if she'd lost him even before she really had him. "If anyone's to blame, it's me. I'm the one who wasn't completely honest. What happened between us—" Her voice broke beneath the weight of uncertainty. Swallowing hard, she whispered, "It happened because I wanted it as much as you did."

Slowly he shook his head. "I don't understand, Jessie. If you'd waited this long, then why did you let me—"

"Because I trusted you."

"You trust me?" Pressing a finger to his chest, he gave a hollow-sounding laugh. "You barely know me."

"I do know you," she insisted, refusing to let him brush away the feelings that had grown between them. "I know you well enough to know that you could never hurt me."

"Not intentionally," he admitted grimly. Closing his eyes, he said in a voice that sounded hoarse with emotion, "Things have a way of turning out badly in my life. People seem to get hurt whenever they get too close to me.''

''Not this time, Samuel,'' Jessie said, with more confidence than she felt in her heart. ''This time everything will be all right. You'll see.''

Slowly he opened his eyes and stared at her, looking as though he'd like to argue. She shivered beneath the intensity of his gaze, waiting for what seemed like an eternity for him to answer. Just when she thought she'd lost him for good, he gave a resigned breath and pulled her into his arms.

Holding her tight, he buried his face in her hair. His breath tickled her ear, sending a tremor down her spine as he whispered, ''I hope you're right, Jessie. I hope you're right.''

''You're sure about this?'' Samuel said, glancing at Jessie, wondering if he looked as doubtful as he felt.

''Of course I'm sure.'' A smile teased her lips. ''Don't you think I can handle it?''

''*You're* not the one I'm worried about,'' he muttered beneath his breath, scowling.

''It's not as though we have much choice, do we?'' she continued, ignoring his bout of bad temper. ''You're the one who insisted I couldn't stay at Gull's Cottage alone.''

''And I'm right, too,'' he said as he pulled his truck into the dock's parking lot. Angling into an empty slot, he cut the motor and flicked off the lights. Even at the predawn hour, the sky looked darker than usual. The wind gusted, driving its force against the truck as thick clouds scudded past. Fair-weather clouds, he told himself. Though he wouldn't be surprised if a storm was headed their way.

The thought left Samuel with an unexpected quiver of foreboding, an omen of dread. His frown deepened. He'd had enough bad luck in his lifetime; he didn't need more. Especially not now.

Too much was at stake, too much depended upon him.

Along with her virginity, Jessie had given him an even more precious gift—her complete and unwavering faith. Never before had anyone shown such confidence in him.

Whether he deserved it or not, she trusted him.

He could not fail her.

With the weight of responsibility resting uneasily upon his shoulders, he turned to Jessie and said, "Until we know who and what we're up against, there's no way I'm letting you out of my sight."

"Fine," she said with a stubborn tilt to her chin. "Then, unless you plan to miss work indefinitely, I don't see that we have any other alternative. I'm spending the day with you on the *Marianna.*"

Taking the determined look for what it was, Samuel heaved a sigh. "All right, then. Let's go. Time's awasting. It'll be dawn soon enough."

He popped open the truck door and stepped outside. The morning air felt cool against his skin. Jessie's door slammed shut; crushed seashell crunched beneath her feet as she joined him. He glanced at her and felt a hot flush of awareness warm the chill from his blood.

Before leaving Gull's Cottage, he'd told her to dress in something old, something she wouldn't mind getting dirty. The bright lemon-yellow tank top and the curve-hugging blue jean cutoffs weren't exactly what he'd had in mind. With Jessie onboard, he would have enough trouble keeping his thoughts on his work. Wearing that eye-catching getup, he'd be lucky if she didn't distract him so much that he'd run the *Marianna* onto a sand bar. Samuel gritted his teeth in frustration.

Bracing himself against temptation, he led her toward the dock. With each step he took, his doubts grew. He had no idea how his crew would react to having a woman onboard. They were fishermen. They lived simple lives, nothing fancy, with little show. He doubted if they had ever come across a woman as refined or as genteel as Jessie. It was anyone's guess how they would treat her.

Despite the early hour, the dock was brimming with activity. Other fishermen were readying their boats, checking their lines and testing their engines. With Samuel at her side, no one dared to remark at Jessie's presence. But many a man stopped what they were doing to ogle the newcomer.

A burr of irritation settled in Samuel's chest at the unwelcome attention. Refusing to attribute his reaction to jealousy, he still placed a possessive hand at the small of her back and urged her forward. The sooner he got Jessie aboard the *Marianna,* the better he'd feel.

With one booted foot hooked on the top rail of the boat, Jacob leaned forward and watched as they approached. "Samuel," he said with a welcoming nod. He cast a curious glance at Jessie.

"Jacob," Samuel said curtly.

"I see we've got a guest this morning," Jacob noted, keeping his tone neutral.

Samuel narrowed his gaze as he steadied the ladder for Jessie to climb aboard. "Is there a problem with that?"

"No, sir. No problem at all," Jacob said with an amused chuckle. Thoughtfully he stroked his salt-and-pepper beard. "It'll make for an interesting day, that's all."

"Well, I'm glad you won't be bored," Samuel growled as he pulled himself onto the boat.

Jessie watched the exchange with quiet interest, but she didn't comment.

He stepped onto the deck. Turning to Jessie, he said, "Jessie, I'd like you to meet Jacob Winters. Jacob, Jessie Pierce."

Surprised recognition flitted across the older man's face at the mention of her name. A slight frown creased his brow as he studied Jessie a bit closer. Thankfully Jacob had the good manners not to question her unexpected presence or her connection to Samuel's ill-fated past. "It's good to meet you, Miss Pierce."

"Jessie, please," she said, extending her hand in greeting.

With a smitten smile, Jacob accepted the gesture, holding her hand a tad too long.

Annoyed, Samuel cleared his throat. "Is Billy here?"

Reluctantly Jacob dropped Jessie's hand and returned his attention to Samuel. "He's down in the hold, checking on the ice."

"Good. Then, it's time we got started. Let's shove off." He moved toward the pilothouse. Pausing, he looked at Jessie. "Would you like to join me? Or would you rather stay out here on the deck?"

She hesitated, glancing self-consciously from him to Jacob. "I'll join you."

Samuel studied her for a long moment, sensing her awkwardness. Then, with a nod, he turned abruptly to hide his disappointment. His jaw tightened against a rising tide of unexpected emotion. She could try to charm his crew as much as she wanted, but the truth was undeniable: Jessie wasn't going to fit in. She was as different from him and his world as night was from day. He'd been fooling himself if he thought that just because they'd found magic in their lovemaking, they would find compatibility outside of the bedroom.

Taking his seat at the wheel in the pilothouse, he gunned the motor. He carefully steered the boat away from the glow of the shore and toward the darkness of the open sea. Running lights lined the edges of the boat, marking their way as the *Marianna* sliced through the black water. Jessie stood next to him, watching in silence. Goose bumps of awareness stroked his skin at her proximity. Samuel shivered, feeling her presence as intimately as though he were still holding her in his arms.

Gripping the wheel tightly, he stared at the endless stretch of sea before him. In taking Jessie with him on this outing, he'd taken on more than he'd expected. While having her beside him meant he would have peace of mind—after all, this was the only way in which he could guarantee she would be safe from harm—it also meant he'd be constantly reminded of the night they'd just spent together. Of their bodies moving in perfect harmony as he made sweet love to her. Of the flushed, breathless look on her face when she'd reached the point of release. Of the purely carnal pleasure that he'd found in her innocent body.

In fact, he still wanted her. Now more than ever. If it weren't for the presence of Jacob and Billy, he'd be tempted to shun his duties. Given the chance, he'd drop anchor, take her in his arms and make slow, tender love to her right now, here on the deck. But desire aside, that didn't change the depth of the differences that loomed between them. If he'd had any doubts before, he was certain now. This alliance of theirs was only temporary. Once they'd found the key that unlocked the secret to their pasts, they would both have to admit the truth: they had little, if anything, in common. No matter what his heart might be telling him, common sense assured him they did not belong together.

Samuel's heart thumped painfully in his chest. Stubbornly he set his jaw against the dull ache. Jessie was wrong: everything would not be all right. It would never be all right again.

Other than to call out orders to his crew, Samuel had not said a word to her since they'd gotten under way. The farther out they rode, the deeper the silence grew between them. Jessie knew something was wrong; she'd sensed a difference in Samuel's mood the moment they'd stepped aboard the *Marianna*. She hadn't a clue what it might be. Or how to fix it.

"Looking good," Jacob called out, interrupting her thoughts. He lifted a thumb in approval after retrieving a small, funnel-shaped net from the sea. She saw that at least ten or twelve good-size shrimp lay caught in the net's mesh.

"It's about time," Samuel growled. He slowed the boat, and Jacob tossed a buoy out onto the ocean, marking the spot. Shifting gears, Samuel began to steer the boat in a circle around the buoy.

"What's happening?" Jessie asked, raising her voice above a rumbling noise that suddenly shook the deck beneath her feet.

"Jacob's operating the winches," Samuel called out. "He's lowering the booms and dropping the nets."

"Do you think…" She stopped and shook her head.

"No, never mind." She bit her lip as she looked anxiously out the window of the pilothouse.

"Would you like to go out on deck and watch?"

Shrugging, she said, "I don't want to be in the way."

"Don't worry. Jacob will tell you if you are." His curt tone told her he didn't care whether she went or stayed. His brusqueness made her feel as though her presence was nothing more than an inconvenience.

"All right, then. I'll go," she announced. Straightening her shoulders, she turned to leave. She told herself grumpily, anything had to be better than sitting inside the pilothouse, listening to the brooding silence.

"Wait, I almost forgot," Samuel said, stopping her. He snapped open the doors of a storage bin and pulled out a pair of rubber boots. Handing them to her, he explained, "You'll be needing these."

She held the black boots at arm's length, glancing at them skeptically. They looked too large and clumsy, hardly her size. If she wore these, she'd be swimming inside them. "I suppose you don't have anything smaller?"

"Nope," Samuel said, his expression giving nothing away.

And yet there was something reflected in his eyes, a hint of challenge. Jessie's gaze narrowed. If she didn't know better, she'd swear Samuel was testing her. It felt as though he was going out of his way to make her first time out shrimping as difficult an experience as possible. It was as though he wanted her to fail. Hurt and confusion churned inside her. What was happening to them? Why was it the closer they became, the harder he seemed to push her away?

Biting back the urge to demand an answer, she

stepped into the boots, leaving her tennis shoes on, and stomped out of the pilothouse. The boots made a loud slapping noise against the wooden deck. Her feet wobbled inside the cavernous interior. With Samuel's watchful gaze upon her, she felt as graceful as an elephant plodding through a flower patch.

Jacob glanced up at her as she approached the stern. He smiled. "Come to help?"

"Just tell me what to do," she said, lifting her chin, daring him to refuse her offer.

"Well, until we fill our nets, there's not much to do." He pointed to two large iron beams jutting out on both sides of the boat. She had noticed the tall beams earlier, when they'd hovered in the air above them. Now they were lowered until they lay almost horizontal to the ocean. "Those are the outriggers. The trawling nets are attached to them. Once they're filled, we'll lift them on board."

"How long does it usually take to fill the nets?" she asked, fascinated by the new experience.

"Depends on how good the catch'll be," he said, reaching out to check the tautness of the lines. "Some mornings they fill up right away. Others, we have to wait a while. I don't think it'll be long today."

Jessie nodded, glancing out at the lightening sky. The wind ruffled her hair. The fishy, salty scent of the sea clung to the air. The ocean was quiet, the nearest boat a mere dot on the horizon. She'd never felt such peace, such solitude. She envied Samuel and his crew, savoring such an experience every day.

"Have you been a shrimper long?" she asked, filling the gap of silence.

"Nearly all my life. I started as a boy, not much older than our Billy over there," he said, thumbing her attention to the tall, skinny teenager sitting with his backside against the side of the boat, a sleepy look on his face. "In my younger days, I worked with a lot of crews, but I never stayed long with any of them."

"Why was that?"

With a wink and a grin, he tipped his head back, mocking a drinking motion. "Liked the spirits too much."

"Oh!" Her cheeks warmed. "I'm sorry, I shouldn't have—"

"Don't you worry none," he said, chuckling. "That's all behind me now. Thanks to Samuel and his family."

"Samuel?" she asked, frowning in confusion.

"Aye, it was Samuel's daddy who first took me under his wing. And none too soon. It was past time for me to give up the bottle. I worked with his daddy until—" He stopped abruptly. Jacob glanced at her uncertainly, his thick brows knitting into a frown. "Well, until his brother, Samuel's uncle, took over the business. Once he was gone, Samuel stepped in. Samuel and I, we've been working together ever since. Nigh on twelve years."

"You must know Samuel well," she murmured, her curiosity getting the better of her.

"Well as anyone, I suppose." He hesitated. Silence fell between them. Jessie shifted beneath the weight of his measuring gaze. It seemed as though he was considering how much to say, whether he would be overstepping the boundaries of Samuel's privacy. Finally he said, "Samuel hasn't had an easy life. But I suppose you already know that." She nodded, not trusting herself to speak.

"His parents' deaths hit him hard. It took a long time for him to get over it."

"I don't think he's gotten over it," she said quietly, meeting his gaze, defying him to argue.

Jacob studied her for a long moment, then nodded. "Aye, I suppose you're right. Some things a man never forgets."

"Not without help," she said with a fierceness that surprised even herself.

"Maybe, maybe not," he said thoughtfully. With a meaningful glance he added, "Once a person's allowed bitterness into their life, it's hard to make room for anything else."

A fist of apprehension tightened around Jessie's heart at Jacob's warning. Jacob had been with Samuel since he was just a child. He knew him better than anyone. If he had his doubts as to Samuel's ability to forgive and forget the past, then surely he couldn't be wrong.

Perhaps it was time for her to admit the truth. She was hanging her hopes on a pipe dream.

There never would be a future for her and Samuel together.

"The nets are full up," Jacob shouted, jolting her back to the present. "Let's haul 'em in."

Samuel cut the engine and the *Marianna* slowed to a stop. Once again the deck vibrated beneath her feet as Jacob worked the winches. The outriggers hoisted the bulging, dripping nets from the sea and lowered their loads to the deck near the stern. The overpowering smell of fresh fish filled the air. Water streamed from the nets, dousing everything and everyone in its path. Jessie wiped the drops from her face and raked her fingers through her damp hair.

When the catch was released, hundreds of trans-
lucent shrimp fell to the deck, slipping and sliding
about her feet. Jessie said a silent prayer of thanks for
the ugly, oversize boots she'd been forced to wear. The
winches whined, as Jacob lowered the nets once again
into the ocean. Samuel restarted the engines, easing the
Marianna through the waters in an ever-widening circle.

Jacob handed her a long-handled shovel. "Time to
throw out the trash."

"Trash?"

"We only want the shrimp," he explained, digging
his shovel into the slippery mass. "Everything else has
to go."

Jessie watched as Jacob and young Billy leveled the
mound of shrimp and began scooping up fish and debris she hadn't noticed before. A conch here, a yellow-
fish there, any number of sea creatures that had gotten
themselves caught up in the shrimp nets. Carefully she
jabbed at the pile. Until something long and black slith-
ered out across her boot. With a yelp of surprise, she
jumped back.

Jacob and Billy hooted with laughter.

Jessie's face burned with embarrassment.

"It's just a snakefish," Jacob told her, as he scooped
up the squirming creature and heaved it overboard.
Winking, he said, "There now, it can't hurt you none."

Self-consciously she glanced toward the pilothouse,
and her heart fell when she saw Samuel's unsmiling
expression. He didn't bother to hide his true feelings.
She knew her skittishness had disappointed him.

Self-righteous anger surged inside her. What did he
expect from her? She wasn't a shrimper. She was an
artist. She had no experience in this sort of work.

Setting her chin in a stubborn line, she turned away and forced her attention back to the mound of squirming shrimp. There was more at stake here than saving her reputation, she realized. Samuel was looking for an excuse to push her farther away, even if that meant placing impossible expectations upon her shoulders.

After everything they'd been through these past few days, she couldn't allow him to do this to her, to them.

If she wanted a place in his life, then she would have to fight for it.

Samuel watched from the pilothouse as Jacob washed down the shrimp with water. Once finished, he thumped a metal bucket down in front of Jessie, up-ending another for her to sit on. Then, with a patience that Samuel remembered from his own youth, he listened as Jacob instructed her on how to head a shrimp.

"Hold it in one hand. Like this," he said, as he picked up a shrimp. "Then with your thumb and fore-finger, snap the head off."

Hesitantly Jessie followed his lead. She picked up a shrimp and cautiously removed its head. Glancing up at Jacob, a pleased smile lit her face. With the early rays of the morning sun glimmering through her dark hair, she looked so beautiful, so innocent she stole Samuel's breath away.

"That's it," Jacob said, his grin encouraging. "You're doing fine."

Squaring her shoulders, she reached for another shrimp. The work was slow and tedious. Jacob and Billy headed at least six shrimp to her every one, but she never stopped. Knowing that her neck must be aching, her fingers sore and her muscles strained to their limits, Samuel couldn't help but feel a glint of admiration.

Confusion roiled inside him as he steered the boat in its slow circle. After he'd seen her shriek in fear at the sight of a snakefish, he'd thought his assumption had been proven correct. Jessie was a proverbial fish out of water, hopelessly lost when it came to the ways of the sea, as unsuited to the hard life of a shrimper as his own mother had been.

His father had named this boat the *Marianna* in tribute to the lovely woman he'd married. But that wasn't enough to appease his bride. She'd been a dreamer, a scholar, more suited to reading books than manual labor. Even before Eve Pierce arrived on Prudence Island, his parents' marriage had been in trouble. But neither of them would admit to making a mistake. Instead, they had allowed their differences to fester between them. They had argued often, their rows becoming frequent and bitter. Both growing more and more unhappy with each passing year.

As a child, Samuel had silently watched his family deteriorate. He'd been a helpless bystander in a battle he barely understood, wondering if in some way he were to blame for their troubles. Wondering, if it hadn't been for him, would they have stayed together as long as they had? When they'd first boarded the *Marianna* that morning, he'd believed that a life with Jessie would be fated to end in the same way. That she would prove as unwilling to compromise as his mother had been.

Now he wasn't so sure.

Instead of giving up, she seemed determined to fit in. After her scare with the snakefish, she had swallowed her fear as well as her pride and had rejoined

Jacob and Billy in their chores. What she had lacked in skill, she made up with tenacity. He could find no fault with her efforts.

The thought left him oddly unsettled. It should please him that she was trying so hard. That she hadn't spurned the life he led. That she hadn't abandoned him.

But he wasn't pleased.

If anything he was more apprehensive than ever. He felt as though a weight was pressing against his chest. It would have been easier for him if Jessie had turned on her heel and run after her first taste of a shrimper's life. Easier for him to distance himself from her.

Now he was faced with the disquieting truth: if he were to push Jessie away, it wouldn't be because she wasn't willing to accept him for what he was; it would be because he wasn't ready to accept her.

Chapter 12

Gull's Cottage has been so quiet for so long, it appears abandoned. No one answered my knock. I'll just search the grounds. There's Jessie's BMW, parked in the shed near the house.

The bitch hasn't left Prudence Island after all.

Despite the clouds that played cat and mouse with the midday sun, tourists swarmed the beach like bees around a hive. With their tanned, bathing-suit-clad bodies, they spilled out in all directions, obscuring a clear view of the docks. Stepping away from the annoying crowd, no longer able to use them as a shield, the watcher moved closer to the pier, scanning its length.

One by one, the boats were returning to shore. But there was no sign of the *Marianna*. It had not yet docked. Curling fingers into fists of impatience, the figure stepped back, melding into the cover of the crowd once again.

Yesterday too many risks were taken. First, the

break-in. The timing needed to be perfect. The rage was unplanned, unfortunate. Valuable time was lost.

Heat and anger was the driving force, not caution.

But last night, the shots in the dark were the ultimate show of control. Cool, calculating control.

The warning—the last of its kind—has been given.

In the distance, the familiar blue and white colors of the *Marianna* came into view. Slowly the boat chugged into port. Samuel was at the helm in the pilothouse. Two figures moved on the deck. The first was Samuel's right-hand man, Jacob Winters. The second was young Billy Bowen, a boy still learning his trade.

No one else is aboard. The bitch may still be on the island, but she isn't with Samuel, after all.

An unexpected movement on the deck of the *Marianna* caught the watcher's eye. Someone stepped out of the hold. Someone small and slender with dark hair.

No, it can't be…dammit. Jessie is aboard, after all. Nothing has changed. My carefully placed warning has been ignored.

The two of them are still together.

The *Marianna* bumped to a stop against the dock. Jacob and Billy jumped down to secure the lines. Cutting the engine, Samuel stepped out of the pilothouse and joined the laughing group on the deck. The clouds parted, and sunshine streamed down from the heavens. Samuel's blond hair glistened like spun gold beneath its rays. His smile was slow in coming, but he joined the festivities nonetheless.

With her dark eyes glittering, looking beautiful and innocent, Jessie smiled up at him; her expression, a reflection of undeniable tenderness and care.

A silent scream of outrage bubbled up in the watcher's throat. A group of tourists approached. They stopped, pausing to cast wary glances. Swallowing hard at the vile taste of bitterness, the watcher turned away, fighting for control once again.

The warnings have not been heeded.

There is nothing more to be done.

Swiftly and surely, the ultimate punishment must be carried out. The bitch cannot be free to ruin any more lives. She must not be allowed to repeat the sins of the past.

Jessie unsuccessfully hid a yawn behind her hand.

"It's been a long day," Samuel said, startling her with his closeness. She hadn't realized he'd been watching her.

With a self-deprecating smile, she murmured, "I guess I'm not used to working this hard."

Samuel studied her, looking as though he would like to comment. Instead, he said, "I'm sure you're anxious to get back to Gull's Cottage."

Oddly enough, she wasn't anxious at all. The thought of returning to the house that had been the scene of such turmoil left her feeling apprehensive. The only thing she craved was a hot bath to wash away the pungent scent of the sea from her skin. Shrugging, she said, "Whenever you're ready."

He hesitated, glancing down at his stained work-clothes. "Would you mind if we stopped by my house first? I'd like to shower and change."

"No, I don't mind," she said, hoping she didn't sound as eager as she felt. Going to Samuel's house would serve a dual purpose. She would avoid spending time at Gull's Cottage. And, perhaps even more important, it would give her a glimpse into his private life. She'd be lying if she said she wasn't anxious to learn more about Samuel.

Samuel turned to Jacob, who was watching them from the stern of the boat. With a wave of his hand, he called out, "We're off."

"I'll see you on Monday, Samuel. Have a good weekend," the older man said, giving him a mock salute. He gave Jessie a wide grin. "Anytime you want to help out, you're welcome aboard, Miss Jessie. The *Marianna* can always use an extra hand. Especially one as pretty as you."

Blushing, she bade Jacob good-night. Then, with Samuel's help she climbed onto the dock. Used to the constant undulation of the boat beneath her feet, the motionless dock caught her off balance. Swaying, she reached out, using Samuel's solid strength to steady herself.

Gripping her arms and holding her tight, he looked down at her, his concern obvious. "Are you all right?"

It had been hours since he'd last touched her. Hours since he'd even acted as though he'd wanted her near. The unexpected contact sent a delicious shiver throughout her body.

"I will be…as soon as I get my land legs," she stammered, flustered by the sudden intimacy that held them. Sure that he could see the longing in her eyes, she reluctantly stepped out of the circle of his embrace. Taking a moment to regain her composure, she glanced up and saw Jacob disappear into the hold of the boat. "Isn't Jacob leaving for the day?"

"Jacob lives on the boat," Samuel said, still watching her.

"On the boat?" She frowned. "Doesn't he have a home?"

"The *Marianna* is his home. It has been for years."
As though sensing her surprise, he explained, "In
exchange for keeping an eye on the boat, his rent is
free. He has a place to stay, and I know the boat is
safe. It's been a good arrangement for both of us."

"But it seems so...so lonely."

"Not when your first love is the sea." He gave a
rueful smile. "Unlike the people who try to tame it,
the ocean doesn't care about your past. It doesn't care
if you've made mistakes, only how you treat it now.
The ocean can be a forgiving companion."

With that, he turned to leave. Jessie considered his
explanation as she followed him to the truck. A handful
of fishermen were still at work, storing their nets,
checking on supplies and preparing for tomorrow's day
of rest. A few called out their goodbyes as they passed.
Samuel raised a hand in response. And Jessie realized
that not all the residents of Prudence Island had
shunned him for his troubled past. There were still people in this town that accepted Samuel for who he was,
a good and honest man. She wondered if he realized
this for himself.

The parking lot was nearly empty. Samuel's truck
stood alone on the far side. Despite the clouds that
filled the sky, late-day heat radiated up from the
ground. A brisk wind blew dust across the crushed-
shell lot, chalking their clothes, making Jessie feel even
more gritty beneath a day's worth of grime.

Samuel opened the door for her, and she slid into
the front seat, conscious of his watchful gaze. Being
alone with him had the power to set her stomach fluttering with uncertainty. Despite the intimacy they'd
shared the night before, for most of the day Samuel
had purposefully distanced himself from her. Instead of

bringing them closer, becoming lovers had only complicated matters. She no longer knew what he expected from her, or how to behave around him.

The short drive to Samuel's home was made in strained silence, telling her she wasn't the only one feeling uncomfortable. As soon as she spotted the house, however, an unexpected calm settled over her.

The cedar shingles on the sides of the Cape Cod house were painted a creamy yellow. Dark green shutters flanked the windows. Brightly colored flowers spilled out from window boxes. A rustic brick walkway led to the front door, inviting a person to enter. Samuel's house held none of the darkness that surrounded Gull's Cottage. It felt cozy and warm, fitting her fantasy of the perfect family home.

Samuel pulled into the driveway and cut the engine. Without a word, or a glance her way, he popped open the door and slung himself out of the truck.

Following at a slower pace, Jessie opened her door and stepped outside to join him. The air felt fresh, scented with the saltiness of the ocean and the sweetness of tea roses and honeysuckles. In the distance, waves crashed against the beach. A cooling breeze streamed off the ocean. She breathed deeply, letting the soothing ambiance work its magic on her frazzled nerves.

"This shouldn't take long," he said, as he moved toward the house. He bypassed the front pathway, opting instead to circle around to the back, where the view of the ocean beyond the dunes was almost as breathtaking as her own at Gull's Cottage.

Her tennis shoes slipped against the sand-and-gravel path as she stopped to look around. Nestled on the undeveloped side of town, Samuel's nearest neighbor was almost a mile away. In the yard, a pair of white-washed Adirondack chairs faced the ocean. Half barrels of flowers lined both sides of the wide porch. Here, unlike her own cottage, someone had made this home a haven of peace and solitude.

The screen door at the rear of the house squeaked on its hinges as Samuel pulled it open. Unlocking a wood-framed glass door, he stepped back and waited for her to enter.

Climbing the porch, she went inside. The door opened to a small utility room, where a washer and dryer had been installed. Just beyond was a large kitchen. With the sun setting on the opposite side of the house, the rooms were dark. It took a moment for her eyes to adjust. When they did, she liked what she saw.

The walls of the kitchen were painted antique-white. Yellow gingham curtains lined the windows. Ladder-back chairs and a large pine table were centered in the middle of the room. The cabinets were dusty green. Despite the fading sunlight, the room appeared bright, cheerful.

Samuel switched on an overhead light, casting the room in a soft glow. He stepped out of his boots, leaving them outside the door. In the utility room he pulled his T-shirt over his head and tossed it into the waiting washer. Jessie swallowed hard. She had the unnerving impression that if it weren't for her presence the rest of his clothes might have found a similar fate. As it was, the sight of his bare chest sent erotic images flooding her mind. Touching him, making love to him, seemed like a lifetime ago. It took all of her willpower not to reach out and run her fingers over the rippling muscles of his chest.

"There's plenty of food in the pantry and drinks in the refrigerator," he said, bringing her thoughts crashing back to reality. He closed the distance between them, setting her body humming with awareness. "I'm sure you must be starved. Help yourself to whatever you need."

"What I need is a shower," she blurted out. Grimacing, she tugged at her sticky shirt. "I've been doused with fish water and who knows what else all day long. I must look a fright."

"You're anything but," he said, scanning her from head to toe. His silent gaze of appreciation sent slivers of desire racing through her body.

Jessie's mouth went dry. She swallowed hard, yet couldn't find the words to answer, too afraid of ruining the moment. Instead, she stared at him mutely, yearning for his touch.

As though he'd read her mind, he lifted a hand and brushed a strand of hair from her face, tucking it behind her ear. Slowly he ran his fingers over the curve of her cheekbone, resting them on the tip of her chin. Tenderly he lifted her head to look at him. As he held her gaze, she saw a battle for control brewing behind his blue eyes.

Then, to her disappointment, he drew in a quick breath and dropped his hand. "I'm sorry, Jessie. I shouldn't have—"

"No, I'm the one who should be sorry," she interrupted, not wanting to hear any more. Rejecting her was bad enough. Apologizing for his actions was more than she could bear. Her face burned with embarrassment. "Goodness knows, I've disrupted your life enough already. If it wasn't for me, you wouldn't have been dragged into this whole mess. If you hadn't felt obligated to watch over me, I wouldn't have been under your feet all day.''

"Is that what you think? That I'm here with you out of some sense of honor?'' He shook his head, giving a short, mirthless laugh. "You give me too much credit, Jessie. If I were truly an honorable man, I'd stay the hell away from you.''

His words left her reeling. She blinked in confusion. "I...I don't understand.''

"Don't you?'' He stared at her, a vein pulsing at his temple. His voice strained, he said, "You must know what you do to me, Jessie. Today, all day, you were so close...I could barely keep my hands to myself. If it weren't for Jacob and Billy, I would have made love to you right on the deck of the *Marianna*.''

"And would that have been so wrong?'' she asked, unable to keep the hurt from her tone, feeling the tears of frustration sting her eyes.

"It's wrong because there's no future for us.''

The bluntness of his words hit like a blow, stealing her breath away. "H-how can you say that?''

"I can say it, because it's true,'' he said, his tone heavy with resignation. "What happens after we solve the mystery behind your mother's death? Are you telling me that you plan to stay on Prudence Island? That you'll make Gull's Cottage your home?''

She wanted to say yes, that anything was possible. But she couldn't lie to him. Gull's Cottage stood for everything that had gone wrong in her life. She knew in her heart she couldn't live with its haunting memories indefinitely.

Her silence speaking volumes, he continued, "Prudence Island is where I live. It's where I work. I could never leave here, any more than you could stay.''

Knowing better than to argue with the truth, she quietly said, "I never asked for a commitment, Samuel."

"No, but you deserve more than just a casual affair."

Raising her chin, she met his fiery gaze with a steely defiance. "I only want what you can give me."

He shook his head, looking unconvinced.

Frustration churned inside her. Trying one last time, she said, "Don't you understand, Samuel? I'd rather have a handful of minutes with you, than a lifetime of regrets. I want to be with you now...no matter how long it might last."

Clenching his jaw, he released his breath. He looked so angry—angry with her or angry with himself, she wasn't sure which—she thought he would turn away. Instead, with a quickness that took her by surprise, he snagged a hand around her waist and pulled her roughly toward him.

Jessie gasped as he took her mouth in a kiss so explosive, so intimate, she nearly melted beneath its heat. Her hands were sandwiched between them, pressing against the warm, bare skin of his chest. She could feel each erratic beat of his heart, each ragged inhalation of his breath. He smelled of the sun and sea, of sweat and hard work. She longed to run her hands over his body, to touch him, to have her fill of him.

He shifted, giving himself room to maneuver. Slipping a hand beneath her shirt, he sought the soft warmth of her hidden flesh. In a rush of self-consciousness, she remembered the day's worth of perspiration and grime she'd accumulated.

"Samuel, no..." she murmured halfheartedly, dragging her mouth from his. Her heart pounded in her ears.

She felt breathless, as though she'd just run five miles. "I'm such a mess. I need a bath."

"A bath? Do you think that matters to me?" he asked, looking amused. "Jessie, we've both been out on the *Marianna* today. I don't expect either of us to be as fresh as a rose garden."

"It might not matter to you, but it does to me," she said, averting her gaze, feeling her face warm.

Thoughtfully, he said, "Then I guess we'd better find a way to take care of this problem...fast."

Before she could protest, he lifted her in his arms as if she was weightless and carried her through the kitchen. Kicking open the swinging door, he strode down a narrow hall. She caught brief glimpses of family pictures lining the walls. Her heart fluttering in her chest, she asked, "Samuel, where in the world—"

Her question was answered before she even finished asking. A short way down the hall, he stopped, flicking on the lights in the bathroom. The floors were white tile with black trim. An old-fashioned clawfoot tub stood to one side.

Wordlessly, Samuel lowered her feet to the floor, until she was standing unsteadily beside him. Turning on the taps, he allowed the water to flow into the tub. Then he turned to her and slowly began to undress her.

With an impatience matching her own, he slipped off her tank top and unfastened her bra, dropping them both to the floor. The air felt cool against her clammy skin. Letting his eyes, not his hands, caress her, he took off her tennis shoes, then undid the button of her cutoffs. Jessie trembled as he slid them down, past her hips and over her thighs. He steadied her as she stepped out of them. They joined the quickly growing pile of clothes. When he hooked his fingers around the band of her panties, a delicious thrill coursed through her. Slipping them off, he dropped them, too.

Steam rose from the tub, filling the room with moist clouds. When she reached for the zipper of his jeans, he brushed her hands away. Stripping out of his clothes, he tossed them aside and paused long enough to allow a moment for them to study each other.

Then, taking her hand in his, together they stepped into the tub. Slowly they lowered themselves into the soothing hot water, positioning themselves so that they faced each other. Tilting her head back, Jessie sluiced water through her hair. Samuel reached for the shampoo, pouring it into his cupped hand. Turning her around, with her back to him, he gently worked the suds into her silky strands. Jessie closed her eyes and gave in to the sensations flowing through her body, cataloging each new feeling and storing it in her mind for a later day. For if this were to be their last time together, she didn't want to forget even a moment of it.

Lowering her head, he rinsed away the shampoo under the tap. Then, he traded places with her, shampooing his own hair, letting the steamy water wash away the bubbles.

They took turns soaping each other. Their hands slippery as they glided their fingers over each other's body. Not an inch of skin went untended. Carefully they cleansed away the remnants of the day's toil, reveling in the moans of pleasure their ministrations brought. By the time they were finished, Jessie felt weak with wanting him, weak with a need only he could fulfill.

Samuel unplugged the drain and stepped out of the tub. Grabbing a towel, he hurried to wrap her in its cocoon of warmth. Impatiently he hitched another towel around his waist, then half led, half carried her out of the bathroom.

With their lips melded in a kiss, they stumbled into a bedroom that Jessie knew must be his. Tangled in each other's arms, the boxsprings sighed as they fell across the length of the brass bed.

Flicking aside his skimpy towel, Jessie indulged herself in an orgy of touching and exploring. Closing his eyes, Samuel lay back against the bedspread and gave in to her caresses. She ran her fingers through the damp hair of his chest, past the smooth flatness of his stomach, stopping only to cover him with her hand. Slowly, with a boldness she'd never felt before, she gave him pleasure.

Until he could stand no more. With a low moan, he rolled to his side and pushed her down onto the bed. His impatient touch stoked a fire in her belly, making her hot and breathless with desire.

By the time he entered her, she was warm and moist and past the point of readiness. She nearly cried out, overwhelmed by the emotions of the moment as he filled her. Did in fact, when he thrust himself even deeper.

They mated with a fierceness that startled yet thrilled her. There was an urgency that wasn't there before, an urgency that came from not knowing what tomorrow might bring. For all she knew, this very well might be their last chance to make love. Neither of them, it seemed, wanted to waste a second of their time together.

All too soon the world shattered around her. Jessie's breath quickened, catching in her throat. Her pulse throbbed in her veins. Raking her fingers down his back, heat flushed her body as she reached the shuddering point of climax. Her limbs still shaking from the impact, she wrapped herself around him and clung to him.

When it was over, they lay exhausted in each other's arms.

Jessie listened to the sound of his breath as it slowly returned to normal. She measured the beat of his heart next to hers. The damp towels were sodden beneath them. Her hair was still wet, curling about her face. Her stomach ached with hunger. But none of the discomforts mattered.

Not as long as he still held her.

She knew she would always be safe in his arms.

Chapter 13

"The key is the diary," Jessie insisted.

With the memory of making love to her still fresh in his mind, Samuel frowned, finding it hard to concentrate as she moved about his kitchen dressed in one of his T-shirts. Her own clothes were in the washer, being cleaned as they prepared omelettes for dinner. While the T-shirt skimmed the tops of her knees, it did little to hide her lush curves. But that wasn't what bothered him. What bothered him was the fact that she wore nothing underneath.

She cracked an egg into a mixing bowl, adding it to the others already waiting. Pouring in milk, she picked up a fork and whisked the mixture into a froth. "Dora said my mother had many admirers. Her killer could have been any of them. If we could only find the diary, then maybe we could identify a man who might have been harassing her...someone who didn't want to take no for an answer."

Samuel shook his head. "We're grasping at straws. We don't even know for sure that there is a diary. We only have Dora's word that it exists."

"That's why we have to look for it," she insisted.

"Jessie, even if we found the diary, who's to say there'll be proof in it that Eve was being harassed?"

"What else could it have been?" she demanded, her fork clicking rapidly against the sides of the bowl. "My mother had just moved into Gull's Cottage for the summer. She wasn't here long enough to make an enemy."

"What about a jealous wife?" he pointed out. "Dora also said that the women of the town had clamped down on their husbands' wayward activities. What if one of these husbands didn't want to comply with his wife's wishes?"

Her hand stilled. She bit her lower lip, considering the possibility. Shrugging, she said, "I suppose there's a chance...you know what they say about a woman scorned." She looked at him, her gaze anxious. "Can you remember anything anyone might have said back then? Any gossip that might have been going around town?"

"You mean, gossip other than about my own parents?" he asked, unable to keep the bitterness from his tone.

Jessie's enthusiasm faltered. A contrite expression crossed her face. "I'm sorry, Samuel."

Not as sorry as he was. No matter what they did, no matter how many different angles they looked at the situation from, it didn't change the facts. The trail to Eve Pierce's murderer always seemed to lead to his father.

Perhaps it was time to give up, Samuel told himself.

Time to end this fruitless search. Time to admit the truth—that his father had been the man who had killed Jessie's mother.

"It wasn't your father," Jessie said softly, as though she had read his mind.

He met her gaze, holding it for a long moment. "How can you be so sure? Everyone else seems to believe he was guilty."

"Not everyone…Dora doesn't believe it."

He sighed. "Dora was my father's friend. They'd known each other since they were children. She'll never think the worst of him."

"There are others, Samuel. Not everyone on this island has abandoned you and your family. Just because Sheriff Broward is so adamant—"

"Sheriff Broward?" Samuel frowned. The mention of his name struck a nerve, leaving him uneasy. There was something about the man, more than just his swaggering conceit, that bothered Samuel. The night of the shooting at Gull's Cottage, Broward had seemed defensive, angry when they'd questioned his investigation into Eve Pierce's death. It was more than just protecting his integrity. He'd acted like a man fighting his way out of a corner.

"Sheriff Broward is a pompous jerk. I don't care what he says," Jessie said, interrupting his thoughts. "Your father wasn't guilty, Samuel. Any man who could have raised a son as good and honest as you are couldn't possibly have lifted a hand to kill another person. No matter what the circumstances might have been."

He stared at her, wanting to believe it.

At his silence she continued, "What about the break-in? And the shooting? If your father was the killer, then how do you explain them? Don't you see, Samuel? Someone believes we're getting too close to the truth."

He hesitated, considering the possibility.

"Samuel, you know I'm right. If we weren't making someone nervous, then why would they go to the trouble of trying to hurt us?"

"Not hurt us, scare us," he said thoughtfully. "Whoever's behind the break-in and the shooting, they had no intention of hurting either of us. If they had, we wouldn't be standing here now. It was a warning, Jessie, nothing more."

"A warning about what?"

"About sifting through the past. Someone out there is afraid of what we might turn up."

"What we'll turn up is the truth behind my mother's murder," Jessie insisted.

"Or just a scandal that someone would rather keep buried," Samuel returned, forcing himself to be the voice of reason. "I'll agree, this person—whoever it is that's been harassing us—might be guilty. But they may not be guilty of murder."

Carefully Jessie placed the fork on the counter. She folded her hands at her waist and studied him, her expression defensive. "Why are you doing this, Samuel? Why are you trying to discourage me?"

"I'm not trying to discourage you." With a sigh Samuel rose from his seat at the table. He closed the distance between them and placed his hands on her shoulders. She held herself stiff, refusing to give in to his embrace. "Jessie, all that I'm trying to say is that I don't want either of us to build up our hopes too high. We need to be prepared for the worst. We need to keep our minds open to all possibilities, including the fact that the past cannot be changed."

"So, you're ready to believe Sheriff Broward. You want to give up on proving your father's innocence."

"No," he said, suddenly feeling very tired. "I'm telling you that I've been through this before. I've already tried to clear my father's name. I don't savor the idea of failing him again."

"You haven't failed him, Samuel," she whispered. Lifting a hand, she brushed her fingers through his hair and looked at him with a tenderness that made his heart melt. "You were a boy when he died. There was only so much you could do."

"I'm not a child anymore," he said, meeting her gaze. "And I still can't seem to do anything to help him."

"That's why we can't give up," she said, with a determination he did not share. "No matter what our search uncovers, no matter how unpleasant it might be, we still have to know the truth. We can't live like this anymore. At least, *I* can't—" Her voice broke. Clearing her throat, she said, "Samuel, I need to find out who the monster is in my dream, the one that won't let me sleep."

Quietly he said, "And what if the monster in your dream is my father?"

She swallowed hard. He saw the muscles working in her slender throat, the uncertainty shadowing her eyes. "Then that is something we will have to deal with when the time comes."

If their search uncovered the fact that his father was guilty of the crime for which he'd been convicted, what sort of future did that leave for him and Jessie? Surely not one in which they could be together. For how could they face each other without their loyalties being challenged? How could they live with a constant reminder of such a horrible event?

He'd been right all along.

No matter how much he cared for her, it was hopeless. He and Jessie had no future. They never did have.

Numbly he said, "You'll stay here tonight, where I can keep an eye on you. I'll sleep better knowing you're safe. In the morning we'll keep digging. We won't quit, no matter what we turn up."

Her brow furrowed into a cautious frown. "Are you sure this is what you want, Samuel?"

"No, I'm not sure of anything," he admitted, his voice echoing the hollowness of his heart. "But it's too late to stop now...even if we wanted to."

The next morning a long shiver racked Jessie's body as they approached Gull's Cottage. She attributed her disquiet to lack of sleep. Last night, despite the reassuring warmth of Samuel's body next to hers, she'd been unable to escape the terror of her nightmares.

The monster in her dream would not let her rest.

Instead, she'd lain awake, watching as Samuel slept. She'd counted down the minutes until dawn, listening to each soft breath he drew. Her rapt gaze had followed the rise and fall of his chest. Silently she had marveled at the strength and power of his body, wishing she had the courage to wake him.

Then, as the golden rays of dawn filtered in through the closed curtains, Samuel had finally stirred. They'd made love one last time. And, when it was over, neither of them had commented on the desperation that had fueled their passion. But she suspected they both knew its source had been fear. Fear that their time together was near an end.

Now, in his truck, with clouds crowded in the morning sky, she looked in bleary-eyed dismay at the house that was hers. Compared to Samuel's warm and cozy home, Gull's Cottage seemed so cold and uninviting. Though she would never admit it to Samuel, she dreaded the thought of going back inside.

Gravel crunched beneath the tires, as he pulled the truck into the driveway. Turning off the ignition, he sat in silence and stared at the house. Finally he glanced beside him, focusing his gaze upon her. "Ready?"

"As ready as I'll ever be," she said, striving for a light tone and failing. At Samuel's frown of concern, she forced herself to move. Pushing open the door, she stepped outside beneath the cloud-filled sky.

A rumble of thunder, warning of an approaching storm, sounded as Samuel joined her on the stone path. Together they strode to the front door, their feet scraping against the uneven walkway. The small square of plywood covering the broken window in the door brought a chilling reminder. Last night, safely ensconced in Samuel's protective arms, even though she'd had her nightmares, the break-in and the shooting had seemed ages ago. She'd almost forgotten the vulnerability, the horror she'd felt at such a violation.

Pushing the troubling thought from her mind, she unlocked the front door and swung it open. When she started to enter, Samuel placed a staying hand on her arm. Jessie looked at him questioningly.

"Let me go first," he said quietly, "just to be on the safe side."

Trying not to let her relief show, Jessie nodded, stepping back to let him pass. With Samuel in the lead, they moved into the foyer. An eerie silence welcomed them, marred only by the erratic thumping of her heart.

Because of the inclement weather, the rooms were dark, forbidding. Samuel snapped on an overhead light and stepped into the living room.

Jessie hesitated, feeling rooted to the spot in the middle of the foyer. Instead of following him, she stood frozen, listening as he moved about the house, chiding herself for letting her fears get the better of her. Whoever had broken into Gull's Cottage had done so when no one was home, she told herself. The shooting had occurred at night, under the cover of darkness. Obviously the person harassing her and Samuel didn't want to be identified. There was no need for her to worry that she would be harmed in the middle of the day.

Samuel's footsteps grew louder as he returned to the foyer. His expression grim, he said, "It's all clear."

"Good," she said with a sigh of relief.

His gaze narrowed as he searched her face. "Maybe this isn't such a good idea."

"Don't be silly, Samuel. You need to check on the boat. You said it was important, right?"

"Right," he said, averting his gaze, shifting uncomfortably from one foot to the other.

Jessie frowned. If she didn't know better, she would say Samuel wasn't being completely honest with her. But why? What possible reason would he have to lie? Brushing aside the unsettling thought, she said, "Samuel, you need to leave. And I want to start looking for the diary. Both of us can't be together in two different places at the same time."

Scowling, he glanced around the house, taking in the ruined couch and the torn pictures. "What if something happens? I won't be here to help you."

"Nothing will happen," she said with more conviction than she actually felt. While she was touched by his concern, it was time for her to learn to stand up for herself. With their future so uncertain, she couldn't become dependent upon him. ''Besides, Dora's just next door. If I need to, I can always go to her.''

Jessie's face warmed at the lie. Her neighbor was the last person she'd turn to for help. Dora might be Samuel's friend, but she had yet to feel comfortable in the other woman's presence. There'd been something distasteful about the pleasure Dora had taken in revealing to Jessie her mother's sordid reputation.

''Look, Samuel, what I'm trying to say is…we just can't be together every second of the day. Our lives can't be put on hold indefinitely.''

He sighed. ''All right, I'll go. But I shouldn't be long.''

''Take your time,'' she said, forcing a smile. ''There's no need to rush.''

His gaze lingered on her face, as though searching for the truth. Reluctantly he turned to go. Two steps away from the door, with his hand on the knob, he hesitated. Whirling to face her, he said sternly, ''Make sure you lock the door behind me.''

''Samuel, I'll be fine…. Go,'' she said, rolling her eyes at his concern.

Finally, without another word, he did as she'd asked. He stepped outside, closing the door behind him. At his departure, an emptiness as vast as the ocean outside her door enveloped her.

For the first time in days Jessie was completely alone.

Slowly she glanced around the rooms. Somehow they seemed even darker, as though the storm clouds had settled inside the house as well as outside. The silence echoed in her ears. Jessie wrapped her arms around her waist and hugged herself tight. She felt Samuel's absence like a raw aching spot in her heart.

When had it happened?

When had her feelings for him gone beyond the mutual need to find the truth behind their pasts?

When had she fallen in love with him?

Shuddering, more from trepidation over an uncertain future than from the actual chill of the rooms, Jessie hurried to the door and bolted the lock. Feeling weak and tired, she leaned her head against its solid strength.

From the beginning she'd known that her relationship with Samuel would not be an easy one. She'd tried hard not to let her heart become involved. But now it was too late.

No matter what the outcome might be, she knew she would not come out of this time with him unscathed.

Samuel's grip tightened around the steering wheel as he maneuvered the truck over the narrow, rutted lane leading away from Gull's Cottage. Leaving Jessie behind, lying to her, had been the hardest thing he'd ever had to do. Even though the lie was one of omission, meant to protect rather than to hurt.

Samuel wasn't going to the boat this morning. He had no intention of going anywhere near the docks. Instead he was headed for town and a long-overdue confrontation.

Since last night Samuel had been troubled by his conversation with Jessie. Other than leaving things unfinished between them, something else had bothered him. It had been the mention of Sheriff Broward and his reaction to their investigation into Eve's murder that had nagged at his growing suspicions.

For too many years he'd endured the sheriff's disdain, telling himself that he'd brought on the older man's censure by his youthful years of rebellion. After his parents' deaths, Samuel had wanted to lash out, to find someone to blame for what had happened to his family.

His rage had centered on Sheriff Gilbert Broward.

Who better to blame than the man responsible for bringing his father to so-called justice? If it hadn't been for Sheriff Broward and his flimsy evidence, his father would never have gone to trial. He'd never have been sentenced to a life in prison. His mother's heart wouldn't have been broken. Nor would she have died at her own hand.

If it wasn't for Sheriff Broward, Samuel's life wouldn't have been destroyed.

The truck's motor heaved in protest. The tires spun out, slipping on roadside gravel as Samuel lurched onto the blacktopped highway. Regaining control, he tromped his foot down onto the gas pedal and sped toward town.

As a teenager, he'd found a way to vent his anger through pointless destruction and by lashing out at the town's sheriff. As an adult, though Samuel had learned to control his emotions, he'd never found the strength to forgive the man he thought of as his nemesis.

The animosity between him and Sheriff Broward remained as potent today as it had twenty years earlier. If anything, it had grown even stronger. The only difference was that Samuel had learned to bite his tongue and not indulge himself in the battle of wills the sheriff seemed so bent upon engaging in.

Instead he'd taken years of verbal abuse from the mouth of a man who was supposed to be his protector.

He would take no more.

The gray brick building that housed the sheriff's department stood on the outside of town. Patrol cars and various other county vehicles clogged the small parking lot. Samuel slid into an empty space beside a black-and-white patrol car. Slamming the gear into Park, he cut the engine and scrambled out of the truck.

Lightning crackled in the sky, followed closely by the rumble of thunder. The sky's electrically charged display matched his own agitated mood, serving as a perfect foil to the storm brewing deep inside him. Thrusting open the glass door, he entered the one-story building.

A deputy, a man Samuel had gone to school with, stood at the front counter. He glanced up from a stack of papers. His gaze narrowed in recognition. "Morning, Samuel. What can I do for you, today?"

Samuel wasted no time on niceties. "Is Broward in?"

"Yeah, but—"

Not waiting for further explanation, Samuel pushed open the swinging half door that separated the lobby from the rest of the building. He strode purposefully down the center aisle of the large outer room toward the hall leading to the sheriff's back office.

"Samuel, wait," the deputy called after him. "You can't just barge in—"

"I can and I will," Samuel growled, setting his jaw in a determined line, daring the man to stop him.

At the commotion, other deputies looked up from their desks. Some rose to their feet, snapping to attention at the first sign of trouble. Others stood staring in surprise, caught off guard by the intrusion.

Samuel didn't wait for an armed escort off the premises. He continued walking, not stopping until he came to the closed door of the office marked Sheriff. Without knocking, he threw open the door and startled its lone occupant.

Sheriff Gilbert Broward was seated at his desk, talking on the phone. The conversation stopped abruptly. His expression hardened at the sight of his unannounced visitor.

"Sheriff, we need to talk," Samuel said, hearing the ominous tone of his own voice.

For just a moment Samuel thought he saw fear flicker in the other man's eyes. Recovering his aplomb, the sheriff glared at him as he spoke into the phone, "Harold, I'll have to call you back. I've got a small problem to deal with."

Footsteps sounded behind Samuel, alerting him to the approach of others. Two large deputies stepped up beside him, each grabbing him by an arm.

The deputy from the front desk scowled his impatience. With a contrite glance at his boss, he said, "Sorry, Sheriff. He got by me before I could stop him."

"That's all right, Jimmy," the sheriff said, his shrewd gaze never leaving Samuel. "I'll handle this myself. Let him go."

Reluctantly both deputies did as they were bade: they released their iron grips. Samuel resisted the urge to rub the circulation back into his arms. Stepping away from the door, but leaving it open, the men disappeared down the corridor.

"Sit down, Samuel," the sheriff barked, his face a mask of stony defiance. "Let's hear what you have to say, so you can get the hell out of my office."

Samuel almost smiled at the other man's agitation, but he thought better of it. Enough tension filled the

office. Samuel knew he was outnumbered and outgun-
ned. There was no point in forcing the sheriff into a
battle he would only lose.

Instead, he seated himself on the chair in front of
the desk. Once settled, he looked at the sheriff and said,
"I want to know what's been done regarding the break-
in and shooting at Gull's Cottage."

"Been done?" the sheriff snapped, looking appalled
by the question. "We're handling it. Just as we'd handle any other incident on the island."

"Have you found anything new? Anything at all?"
Samuel persisted.

The sheriff hesitated, uncertain whether or not to di-
vulge the information he'd obtained. Then, with a
shrug, he said, "Nothing useful. The ballistics test
came back on the bullets. A .22 gauge rifle was used
for the shooting. Which, as you know, is about as common a rifle among hunters as you'll find in these
parts."

"Convenient," Samuel mused.

The sheriff's face flushed a deeper hue. "What's this
all about?"

Ignoring the question, Samuel asked, "What else are
you doing to protect Jessie?"

"Jessie Pierce isn't my only concern on this island,"
the sheriff said, his tone defensive. "I'm responsible
for the hundreds of tourists visiting our community—"

"So, in other words, you're doing nothing."

"I'm doing everything possible," the sheriff said,
clenching his teeth. He rose to his feet and leaned forward, placing his hands on the desktop before him.
"I've beefed up patrols in the area. And my men have
been keeping a close eye on Gull's Cottage." With a
smug smile of amusement, he added, "Close enough

to know that our Ms. Pierce didn't sleep in her own bed last night.''

Samuel froze. His muscles stiffened at the innuendo. He refused to allow the sheriff to bait him into a fight, or to distract him from the purpose of his visit. Deciding that he'd wasted enough time on small talk, he came to the real point of his inquiry. ''How well did you know Eve Pierce?''

The sheriff's smile faded. Instantly wariness returned. ''What the hell is this all about?''

''It's about you and a murder investigation in which you had a conflict of interest,'' Samuel said coldly. ''You were involved with Eve Pierce before she died, weren't you?''

The sheriff's mouth snapped shut with a click. His jaw tightened in agitation. A vein pulsed angrily along the side of his thick bull neck.

Knowing he'd gone too far, but unable to stop himself, Samuel continued, ''I know that you spent a great deal of time at Gull's Cottage, checking on Eve's well-being before she died. She was a beautiful woman. She had many admirers. It wouldn't be a surprise if you were among them.''

''That's none of your damn business.''

''It is if you allowed your feelings for Eve to influence the way you handled the investigation into her death.''

The sheriff's face turned a deep crimson. ''Son, I think you'd better be careful what you're implying.''

''I'm not implying anything, Sheriff.'' Samuel leaned forward in his chair, forcing himself to remain calm in the face of the other man's growing anger. ''I'm telling you…I find it convenient that you were the first to arrive at the scene of the murder. I find it even more convenient that no one ever found key evidence, Eve's diary. There certainly would have been ample opportunity for a law official—say, someone who was afraid of what the diary might reveal—to slip it out of the house with no one being the wiser.''

"Diary? What diary?'' Broward sputtered, his brows furrowed in confusion.

"Eve's diary,'' Samuel repeated. ''I want to know what happened to it.''

"If there was a diary, this is the first I've heard of it,'' the sheriff insisted, his bewilderment too real to be feigned.

Samuel frowned, his confidence wavering. ''You're lying. I know the police searched the cottage for Eve's diary.''

"Who in the hell told you that?'' the sheriff growled. Striding to the filing cabinets flanking a wall, he pulled open one of the drawers. ''If there'd been a search for a diary, it would have been in the reports. But it isn't there, because there was no search.'' Taking a file from the drawer, he tossed it onto the desk, spreading its contents out before him. ''If you don't believe me, take a look for yourself.''

At first Samuel didn't move. His hesitant gaze traveled from the file to the sheriff's adamant expression, then back again. Slowly, he picked up the file. Unease found root inside him, growing with each passing moment as he leafed through the documents.

The course of the investigation was outlined in detailed notes. The evidence that convicted his father was set down in carefully typed print: a hat belonging to his father was found in the cottage; his father's fingerprints were in the kitchen at the scene of the crime; testimony of Eve's neighbor, Dora Hawkins, put Sam-

uel's father at Gull's Cottage on the night of the murder. Though the evidence seemed circumstantial, it had
been enough to convict him of the murder by a jury of
his peers.

But what was in the files wasn't as important as what
was missing. There was no mention of the diary. Nothing about a search for the diary, or even of its existence
in the first place.

"Samuel—" the sheriff said gruffly, startling him
out of his runaway thoughts. "If there was a diary, this
is the first I've heard of it. I don't know who's been
filling your head with these wild stories, but they're
wrong—"

Panic pressed against his chest, making it hard to
breathe. Who'd been filling his head with stories?

Someone he thought he could trust.

Someone who had no reason to lie, unless...

"No..." Samuel surged to his feet, spilling the contents of the file to floor. Ignoring the irritable response
from the sheriff, he turned on his heel and strode to
the door.

Broward caught up with him, grabbing his arm to
stop him. "Samuel, where the hell are you going
now?"

"Jessie...she's alone," Samuel ground out harshly,
knowing he wasn't making any sense. But he didn't
have the time to explain. "I left her alone with the
monster."

Shaking off the sheriff's restraining hand, he turned
and hurried from the office.

Chapter 14

Unnerved at being alone, Jessie filled the gaping silence by keeping busy. Despite the constant reminders, she refused to allow herself to dwell on the events that had happened in Gull's Cottage. Avoiding the kitchen, which seemed to be at the heart of her fears, she began a search of the house. In the bathroom, she searched the closet, restacking sheets to one side, towels to another. The shelves were bare of toiletries, except for her own. Still, she found no sign of the diary.

An inspection of the bedrooms turned up much the same. Other than a few forgotten photos, a hat, a pair of flip flops and a scarf, there was nothing else of her mother's left behind. Disappointed, Jessie drifted into the living room, wondering if she was wasting her time. She paused to frown at the bookshelves, then sighed in resignation. As she was about to begin the daunting task of taking down each book to inspect one at a time, Jessie heard a noise coming from the kitchen.

She stood still, her heart in her throat, as she listened to the sound of the back door being tried, then opened.

Heavy, rubber-soled footsteps squeaked against the tiled floor. Then the door clicked as it closed shut. And once again, stillness descended upon the house.

Jessie's heart pounded in her chest. The raspy sound of her own breath filled her ears. Shaking off her fears, she told herself she was going to look silly standing in the middle of the room with a panic-stricken look on her face when she discovered Samuel at her back door.

"Samuel?" she called out as she took a tentative step toward the kitchen.

No one answered.

"Samuel? Is that you?" she repeated, louder this time, wondering if the noise had been a product of her overactive imagination.

Then she heard it again. The squeak of shoes on the ceramic tiled floor. Someone was definitely in the house.

Jessie hesitated at the doorway of the kitchen, scanning the shadowy room, ready to turn and run if necessary. With the storm gathering outside and choking out the day's light, she almost didn't see the figure standing in the cover of darkness. Lightning flashed, illuminating the room with a blinding brightness. Snapping on the overhead lamp, she drew in a startled breath as she recognized her visitor.

"Dora?"

Dora's round glasses glinted beneath the harsh light. She blinked, her square face and round body making her look like an owl. Dressed in her usual uniform of loose-fitting khaki pants and an oversize polo shirt, she stepped forward into the halo of light. "I didn't think anyone was home. I'd have knocked, if I'd known."

Thunder rumbled, sounding closer this time. Frowning in confusion, Jessie stepped farther into the kitchen. "Dora, what are you doing here?"

"The other night I saw all the police cars. That's when I heard about the break-in and the shooting. Such terrible things," she said, tsking loudly. She tilted her head to one side, eyeing Jessie curiously. "You've been gone a long time, Jessie. I've kept an eye on the house for you. A moment ago I thought I saw a light in a back bedroom. I thought it'd be best if I checked it out."

"Of course," Jessie said, with a heartfelt sigh of relief. "I mean, that's very kind of you, Dora. But it was only me."

Dora nodded. Then, with a frown of concern, she asked, "Are you all right, dear?"

"I—I'm fine," Jessie lied, willing her pounding heart to still. "Just a little jittery, considering…"

"Yes…considering all that's happened," Dora murmured, finishing the thought, as she stepped closer. Carefully she added, "I suppose you'll be leaving soon. You won't want to stay on Prudence Island now that it's become too dangerous for you."

Jessie stared at her, mesmerized by the lilt of Dora's hypnotic voice. She felt as though she was being drawn into a spidery web of unreality. Outside, the wind howled in protest, pushing its weight against the windows of the house, startling her out of her trance. "No, I won't be leaving Prudence Island. At least, not anytime soon. Especially now…"

She stopped, her voice breaking abruptly.

"Especially now?" Dora prompted.

Jessie stared at her, startled by the urgency behind

the words. Was it her imagination, or did Dora sound scared?

Dora's eyes never left her face. ''What's happened to make you want to stay?''

Jessie hesitated, not sure how much she should reveal. Prudence Island was a small community. Word traveled fast within its borders. But this was Dora, Samuel's friend, one of the few friends who had stood by him and his family throughout the ordeal of his father's murder trial. Surely Jessie would be safe confiding in her, of all people. ''My memory...it's returning.''

''Your memory?'' The words sounded sharp, agitated. ''What do you remember?''

Jessie's stomach fluttered with unease. She shook her head, fighting the urge to run away. ''Just...just bits and pieces. Mostly of the night my mother died.''

''How much do you remember?'' Dora demanded, her frantic voice triggering an unwanted memory from the recesses of Jessie's mind.

Voices.

Loud, angry voices woke her.

Confused and uncertain, Jessie climbed from her bed. Stumbling, following the night-darkened hallway here, in Gull's Cottage, she hurried toward the sound of shouting. Her movements were clumsy. Her feet were leaden, making her feel as though she was walking in slow motion. Her heart raced, fluttering in her chest like a butterfly's wing.

The voices grew louder. Emotion distorted their timbre, making it hard for her to identify them.

She stepped into the shadowy kitchen, where she saw her mother struggling with an intruder. Frightened, she pressed her small body against the cabinets and inched her way to the pantry, where she hid.

Through a crack in the door she watched as the shadow person struck out against her mother. Her stomach clenched as she heard the sickening thud of an object striking flesh and bone. Then, her mother fell heavily to the floor.

And an unbearable silence filled the room.

A beam of light sliced through the inky night, blinding her, paralyzing her with fear....

A shape, large and frightening, coming closer, closer...

It was the intruder that approached, drawing nearer, looming in the darkness. A shaft of moonlight streamed in through the kitchen window. For just a moment the intruder stepped through the light, and a face emerged from the shadows.

The face of a monster.

Her heart leaping in her chest, young Jessie stumbled backward, closing the door of the pantry behind her. One step, two, until she couldn't go any farther. Curling herself into a tight ball of invisibility, she hid in the corner of the closet, where there was no light, only darkness. Complete and terrifying darkness...

Cowering in the dark, she waited for her mother's attacker to find her.

The monster of her dreams finally had a face. A face that left her shuddering in fear.

It was the face of Dora Hawkins.

Lightning splintered the sky outside, bringing Jessie crashing back to the present. She stared at the woman who had killed her mother and realized that Dora had guessed the truth. That her secret was no longer safe. With an ominous peal of thunder shaking the floor beneath her feet, Jessie met Dora's fierce gaze without flinching. "Why, Dora? Why did you kill my mother?"

At first Dora looked as though she might deny the accusation. Then rancor washed over her, making her plain face even more unattractive. In a voice that shook with barely controlled emotion, she said, "I had spent my entire life waiting for a man to notice me. And along comes your mother, all pretty and dainty." She spit out the words as though they'd left a bad taste in her mouth. "From the moment she arrived on this island, the men followed her around as though she were a queen bee needing to be tended."

Wind lashed against the windows. The air crackled with the approaching storm and with the force of Dora's hatred. Jessie's mouth went dry. She swallowed hard at the lump of fear in her throat. It was as if Dora had become consumed with bitterness.

Dora's hollow laugh sent a chill down Jessie's spine. The words spilled out as she continued her twisted tale. "The worst part was that your mother didn't even care about all the attention. She was still mourning the loss of her husband. She truly was a grieving widow. But when Samuel Conners came calling...I knew it was different."

Dora's voice grew quiet, taking on a soft, faraway quality. "I had always loved Samuel. I had lost him to one woman already. But everyone knew his marriage was a mistake. It was only a matter of time before he would come to his senses and see that I was the one who was meant to be with him. That is...until Eve Pierce came to town."

Dora fell silent, her eyes glazed. She looked at Jessie as though she were staring through her. Not really seeing her, but seeing a distant memory. Seizing the opportunity, Jessie backstepped, moving away from the other woman, jockeying for a better position to turn and run.

More lightning streaked the sky. Thunder boomed, shattering the silence. Dora blinked, bringing her eyes into focus. Jessie froze midstep, watching as the woman shivered as though trying to rid herself of an unpleasant memory. Then, as if nothing had happened, she continued speaking. ''Samuel was infatuated with Eve. He forgot all about me, about everything that truly mattered in his life. When he wouldn't listen to my warnings about Eve, wouldn't stay away from her, I knew my dreams of a future with him were pointless.'' Her voice trembled with anger. ''I lost Samuel forever, and all because of a tart like your mother.''

Large raindrops pelted the windows. Jessie's instincts screamed out to run now, to escape while she still had the chance. Dora seemed at the brink of losing complete control. She teetered on the verge of a blinding rage. It was only a matter of time before Dora realized how much danger she'd put herself in by finally confessing her crime. It was only a matter of time before she lashed out at the one person who could condemn her.

But Jessie couldn't bring herself to turn away. For over twenty years, she'd wondered about the cause of her nightmares. She couldn't hide now, not when she was so close to learning the truth.

''I never meant to kill her,'' Dora said, startling Jessie, bringing her reeling back to the present. ''I'd come to Gull's Cottage to warn her to stay away from Samuel, to leave Prudence Island. But she wouldn't listen. She ordered me to leave her house.'' Dora looked down at her empty hand. She clenched her fist, as though holding an unseen object. "I'd brought the flashlight to guide me on the walk over to Gull's Cottage. When I swung out, I never realized the power behind the blow…" Her gaze drifted to the floor, to the spot where Jessie's mother had died. "Not until Eve crumbled before me."

Jessie shuddered at the memory. The horror of it felt so clear, so real. As though it had just happened.

Dora lifted her gaze to Jessie. "I knew you were in the house. But I wasn't sure just how much you'd heard…or seen. I was going to look for you, but a car pulled into the driveway." She shook her head, giving a short bark of a laugh. "It was Deputy Broward, that randy old goat, taking another shot at seducing your mother. So I left. I ran out the kitchen door and never looked back…not until you returned to Prudence Island."

Jessie felt winded by the full impact of Dora's revelation. If it hadn't been for Sheriff Broward's intervention, she had no doubt that Dora would have killed her, too. Suddenly Jessie realized that the other woman's attention was no longer focused on the past, it was focused upon her.

"Imagine my surprise when you joined forces with Samuel to ferret out your mother's killer. Samuel, of all people! You wanted to turn him against me, just like your mother had turned his father against me."

Jessie flinched. The shrillness of Dora's voice grated against her overwrought nerves, putting her on an instant alert.

"I didn't know what to do," Dora said. "I couldn't hurt Samuel, but I had to stop you from snooping. Tearing up your house didn't scare you off. I thought if you knew the truth about what a slut your mother was, you'd leave the island in shame…but you stayed. And your hold on Samuel grew even stronger.''

"If you cared about Samuel, then why did you try to shoot us?" Jessie blurted out, finally finding her voice, breaking the spell of fear that had held her.

"The shooting was a warning." Dora smiled, a haunting smile of amusement. "I'd hunted with my father from the time I was a young girl. I'm an excellent shot. If I'd wanted to kill you, we wouldn't be having this conversation now."

"What about the diary?" Jessie persisted. Dora was at the breaking point. It wouldn't take much to push her over the edge. But Jessie needed to know the truth, the final piece to the puzzle. "Does my mother's diary really exist?"

"Of course not." Dora laughed again, that strange barking laugh. Rain drummed against the roof. Water trickled down the windows in narrow rivulets. "It was a decoy. I needed time to figure out what to do. I thought I'd buy myself some of that time by throwing you off the search. But you didn't take the bait like I'd hoped. You used my warnings as an excuse to get your hooks even deeper into Samuel. Did you think I wouldn't know of the nights you'd spent with him?" Her look was one of pure disgust. "You're just as much a slut as your mother."

Jessie had heard enough. It was time to go—now—before it was too late. Dora stood in the center of the kitchen, blocking her path to the back door. So Jessie whirled on her heel, heading in the opposite direction, bent on making her escape through the front of the house. Her mistake was in misjudging the older woman's nimbleness.

Quickly closing the distance between them, Dora grabbed a handful of Jessie's hair.

Jessie cried out in pain, stopping short as her head was viciously jerked back. Tears stung her eyes. She flailed her arms in vain. Twisting herself around, she tried to loosen the other woman's claw-like grip.

Dora slammed her into the kitchen cabinet, the impact loosening her hold. Pinpoints of light danced before her eyes. The room spun beneath her feet. For a moment she thought she might lose consciousness.

Gasping for air, she gathered her flagging strength. With a yell of outrage, she threw herself at Dora, refusing to cower in fear.

But Dora had size in her favor. When Jessie's shoulder connected with Dora's chest, it barely made an impact against Dora's thick muscular body. Cursing, Dora pushed her away and swatted Jessie with the back of her hand, the blow landing squarely against her jaw.

Jessie heard the crack of bone against bone. She felt the searing pain ricochet up her cheek, blinding her with its intensity. Falling backward, she retreated against another attack.

Taking the advantage, Dora shoved her hard, this time pushing her into the pantry. Before Jessie could react, Dora slammed the door shut, clicking the lock into place.

The pantry was pitch-black. The light switch was outside the closet. She was trapped in darkness. Panic filled Jessie's chest, making it hard to breathe as she realized that she was reliving the nightmare of her past.

Her lungs burned from lack of oxygen. Until that moment she hadn't realized she'd been holding her breath. Struggling against confusion, she gulped in air. Shaking off the mind-numbing fear that threatened to

engulf her, Jessie reached out blindly, feeling her way
in the darkness, searching for the handle to the door.
Grasping the knob, she jiggled it and found its lock
secure.

Unwilling to give up, she threw her shoulder against
the wooden door. Fresh pain spiraled through her body
where she'd already been bruised and battered by
Dora's blows. The door was solid, holding fast against
her attempts to escape. Thumping a hand against the
door, Jessie closed her eyes and uttered a soft moan of
despair.

Through the thick door, she heard Dora moving
about the kitchen. Pans clattered. Drawers were being
pulled open, the contents clattering as they spilled out
onto the ceramic floor. All the while, Dora kept up an
angry, hissing monologue. Jessie pressed her ear
against the door and strained to listen, but could make
no sense of the garbled words.

Suddenly a whoosh of a noise sounded on the other
side of the door. Jessie froze in terror, unable to fathom
what was happening. A crackling, like the sound of
paper being crumpled into a ball, filled the pantry.
Smoke curled under the door.

And Jessie realized that Dora had set fire to the
house.

In that moment of panic her thoughts turned to Samuel. Regret tore through her as she recalled their last
parting, how she'd left things unfinished between them.
She'd allowed her fears and her uncertainties to get in
the way of telling him how she really felt…how much
she cared for him.

"No!" Jessie shouted, shaking off the maudlin stu-
por.

Anger took the place of remorse, renewing her resolve to survive. Dora had nearly destroyed her life once before. She would not allow the woman to stand in her way of a second chance at happiness.

She would fight. She would find a way to escape this nightmare.

And when she did, she would let nothing get in the way of telling Samuel how much she loved him.

Chapter 15

Fat drops of rain splattered against the windows of the truck as Samuel sped down the highway. The windshield wipers thumped unevenly, each unsteady beat working on his already-strained nerves. Behind him a siren wailed. Red lights flashed in his rearview mirror. But he ignored Sheriff Broward's attempts to pull him aside.

He had to get to Jessie before it was too late.

Numbly he looked out at the rain-soaked highway, recalling their last conversation.

"What if something happens?" he'd asked. "I won't be here to help you."

"Nothing will happen," she'd insisted, her smile brave. But he'd seen the uncertainty in her eyes. He knew she hadn't wanted to be left behind. "Besides, Dora's just next door. If I need to, I can always go to her."

Dora was just next door.

She was Jessie's closest neighbor. Eve's closest neighbor. His father, Eve, Jessie, even himself…they had all trusted her, confided in her, turned to her for advice.

Dora had played them all for fools.

Blithely she'd given him and Jessie clues that had led them on a wild-goose chase. She'd told them of a diary that had probably never existed in the first place, letting them believe it held the secret to a killer's identity. On the day of the break-in, she'd met them while coming up the path from the beach. A path that led directly to Jessie's house. She'd been a gracious hostess, while only minutes before she'd nearly destroyed Gull's Cottage. Dora was an excellent marksman. Once he'd seen her shoot the center out of a silver dollar as it was tossed into the air. She certainly had the skill to shoot an unmoving target.

Dora had ample opportunity to destroy their lives.

If only he knew her motive.

It was his fault that Jessie was in danger. His fault that she was alone. If he hadn't been so blinded by his own needs, so determined to guard his heart against the pain of caring too much, he'd have seen the truth standing right before his eyes.

Dora Hawkins had pretended to care about him and his family. All these years, all these wasted years of living his life alone and miserable, she'd stood by and had allowed him to struggle to prove his father's innocence, knowing that one word from her and his suffering would have been over.

How could he have been so gullible?

Samuel slammed his fist against the steering wheel, welcoming the punishing pain. Lightning zigzagged through the sky, making his pulse quicken. Thunder growled, matching his fierce mood.

First his father, then his mother…and now, Jessie. Once again, he'd failed to protect someone he loved.

God help him if he was too late to save her.

The back end of his truck fishtailed as he made the turn into Jessie's driveway too quickly. Correcting himself before he spun into one of the tall oak trees lining the road, he straightened the wheel and headed in the direction of Gull's Cottage. The truck bounced over the rutted lane, its bottom scraping against the ground.

Sheriff Broward's patrol car reappeared in his mirror; his car lights bobbed up and down as he bounced over the ruts. His siren continued to wail in angry protest.

While the other man's presence meant he would have help in the face of trouble, it did little to ease Samuel's fears. Jessie had been alone in the cottage for over an hour, with Dora only a stone's throw away. It was more than enough time for a madwoman to wreak her vengeance.

No matter how quickly he and Sheriff Broward hurried, they both could be arriving too late.

His worst fears were confirmed as he drew closer to the cottage. The acrid smell of smoke clung to the air. Through the clearing in the woods, he saw a billow of black smoke curling up into the sky. He pulled the truck to a lurching stop in front of the house and saw the flames licking its roof.

For a moment, he stared, frozen in disbelief.

Jessie's house was on fire.

Slamming the truck into Park, he shouldered open the door and threw himself outside. Rain peppered his skin, dampening his clothes. But the meager drops of water did little to slow the intensity of the blaze.

Heat radiated from the wooden house like a red-hot stove. Windows popped and shattered. Shards of glass rained down upon the ground. Heedless of the danger, Samuel hurried toward the cottage, toward Jessie...

Until Dora appeared in the front doorway.

Samuel halted, too shocked to move.

Sheriff Broward's patrol car skidded to a stop. The siren squawked as it was cut short. The cherry lights throbbed like a heartbeat against the day's gloom. With an angry string of curse words, the sheriff rolled out of his car. Staring at the house, shaking his head in disbelief, he demanded, "Conners, you want to tell me what's going on here?"

Samuel didn't answer. Instead, he kept his gaze focused on the woman who stood between him and Jessie.

"You're free," Dora told him. She smiled, the look on her face tender, like that of a lover's. "You're finally free, Samuel. Eve won't be bothering us again."

"Eve?" Samuel blinked in confusion. Dora wasn't making any sense. Surely she didn't believe Jessie to be Eve?

Gravel crunched beneath his boots, as Sheriff Broward stepped up beside him. Beneath his breath, he muttered, "Is she crazy? What the hell is she talking about?"

Time was running out. Samuel ignored the man, concentrating on Dora. With an impatience fueled by the fire consuming the house, he said, "Not Eve, Dora...Jessie. What have you done to Jessie?"

Dora shrank back at the harshness of his voice. "I

did it for you, Samuel. I did everything for you. Don't you see? I love you…I've always loved you.''

Sickened by the words, Samuel realized he was wasting his time trying to make sense of Dora's rambling declaration of love. Determined, he strode to the doorway. But Dora blocked his path.

She snatched at his arm, stopping him, surprising him with the strength of her grip. Patting his face with her free hand, she murmured, "Samuel…my dear, sweet Samuel. You've been gone for so long. Stay with me…don't ever leave me again.''

Understanding struck like a blow to his gut, winding him. Dora believed him to be his father.

"My God, you are insane," Samuel said, his voice incredulous. He tried to shake her off, but she clung to him, wrapping her arms around him, holding on tight, like a tenacious strand of seaweed.

"Dora, let him go," Sheriff Broward commanded. Samuel never thought he'd be so glad to hear the sound of Sheriff Broward's voice. The other man stepped up beside them. He took Dora by the shoulders and yanked her away from Samuel.

The woman screamed in outrage, fighting the sheriff's restraining hands.

Free at last, Samuel didn't look back as he ran into the burning house.

Jessie pounded on the door, hoping against hope that someone might hear her. The wood felt hot against the palm of her hand. Smoke filled the pantry, choking her.

Coughing, she called out, "Is anyone there?"

Only the roar of the fire outside the door answered.

It was hopeless. She was trapped. There was no way anyone would find her in time.

"Oh, Samuel, Samuel...I'm so sorry," Jessie murmured, feeling light-headed from the smoke and the lack of oxygen. Pounding her fist one last time against the door, slowly she slumped to the floor.

By the time it was over and done, she told herself, there would be one more reason for Samuel to blame himself for what had happened. She didn't want to die. But even more, she didn't want Samuel to suffer.

He'd been through enough pain in his lifetime.

He didn't need to add her death to his already overburdened conscience.

The smoke grew thicker by the second. Wheezing, she struggled to find air. Too weak to fight any longer, she closed her eyes and let her head fall back. It thumped against the wooden panel of the door.

At the sound, a muffled voice called out to her, "Jessie!"

Jessie's eyes flew open. The deep voice sounded so familiar. But was it real? Or was it merely a figment of her smoke-clouded imagination?

Footsteps sounded outside the door—sharp, heavy footsteps against the tiled floor. Once again the voice called out her name, "Jessie!"

"Samuel," she said, her voice hoarse from inhaling the black smoke. Clumsily she turned, rising to her knees. She lifted her fist, striking weakly against the door. "Samuel!"

"Jessie, thank God! Everything's going to be all right now. I'm going to get you out of there," Samuel's deep voice assured her.

She wanted to believe him. More than anything else in the world, she wanted everything to be right.

The knob rattled. The lock clicked free. And finally the door swung open. Wincing from the searing rush

of heat, she blinked hard, clearing the hot smoke from
her eyes. Framed by the flames, Samuel stood in the
doorway, his arms extended, reaching for her.

Tears of relief welled up in her eyes. Nearly col-
lapsing, she fell forward, letting him take on her
weight. Half leading, half carrying her, Samuel hurried
her through the smoke-filled kitchen to the safety of
the back door.

They stepped outside. Holding on to each other,
gasping in cleansing breaths of air, they didn't stop
until they saw Dora standing on the edge of the porch.

Dora's clothes were stained with dirt and ashes. Her
glasses were gone. An angry red bruise marked her
cheek. She stared at Samuel, her eyes blinking in disbelief. "Samuel…no. How could you do this? How
could you betray me?"

"Dora, I haven't betrayed you," Samuel said, his
voice sounding tired, defeated. He frowned. "What
happened? Where's Sheriff Broward?"

Dora gave a dismissive wave of her hand. "Gone.
He thought he could stop me."

Samuel stared at her. "You aren't well. You need
help."

The older woman shook her head. "No, Samuel. I
need you."

"Dora, I'm not who you think I am." He sighed.
"I'm not my father."

"No, no, I won't listen." Dora clapped her hands
over her ears. Trembling, she screamed, "Eve must die.
It's not too late. We can still be together."

"It *is* too late," Samuel insisted, the pitch of his
voice rising. Releasing his grip around Jessie, he
pushed her behind him, making sure she was out of
harm's way. Unable to find the strength to stop him,

Jessie watched as he stepped toward the other woman, toward danger. "Dora, we can't change the past. It's time we faced the future. No matter what it might bring." He held out his hand. "Come with me, Dora. I'll make sure that you're safe."

"No...I don't believe you. You don't care about me." Dora backed away, shaking her head. Her eyes wild, she swung her gaze to Jessie. "All you care about is that...that tramp." Tears glistened in her eyes as she turned back to Samuel. "How could you have done this to me, Samuel? How?"

Before he could stop her, she whirled on her heel and ran into the flaming house.

"Dora, no..."

Samuel's stunned voice echoed in Jessie's ears. She reached out to stop him, but he moved too quickly. Jessie cried out in alarm as he ran into the house after Dora.

Chapter 16

Jessie stood by the empty patrol car, huddled in a scratchy wool blanket, shivering uncontrollably as she watched Gull's Cottage burn to the ground. She felt chilled from the inside out. The narrow lane was clogged with fire trucks, police cars and an ambulance. A crowd of people gathered, pressing against the yellow, crime-scene tape for a better view of the destruction.

A shudder of revulsion shook her body. A bitter taste filled her mouth. She felt sick to her stomach. Sick at the loss. Sick at the utter waste of human lives.

Too many people had died because of one woman's twisted fantasy.

Dora Hawkins had killed her mother. For years, she'd covered up her crime, allowing the man she'd professed to love to take the blame. In doing so, she had destroyed his life and the lives of his family.

Jessie's eyes searched the crowd. Relief poured

through her as she spotted Samuel standing by the ambulance, talking to Sheriff Broward.

His blond hair was dirty and tousled. Black grime smudged his face. His clothes were coated with a thick layer of dust and ash. He wore a bandage on his arm—the white dressing standing out against his tanned skin—where a falling timber had singed him. But other than that one small injury, he'd come out of the burning building unscathed.

A miracle had brought him back to her.

When he'd disappeared into Gull's Cottage that last time, she truly believed she'd lost him for good. Her heart nearly ripped in two at the thought of facing life without him. So devastated at the prospect, she'd almost thrown herself into the flames after him.

Sheriff Broward had stopped her. He'd held her back, telling her it was too late. The flames were too strong. No one could survive the ordeal.

But Samuel had survived. He'd walked out of the cottage empty-handed, unable to save Dora.

Guilt pricked Jessie's heart. Guilt because she could not bring herself to mourn the loss of the woman who had brought so much suffering into her life. Bitterly she acknowledged that the only emotion she could muster was pity. Pity for the pathetic lie Dora had forced them all to live.

As though sensing her troubled thoughts, Samuel glanced at Jessie, a worried frown on his brow. He turned to Sheriff Broward, speaking words she could not hear. The sheriff nodded. Then both men made their way toward her.

With his hands stuffed in his back pockets, Samuel came to an awkward halt in front of her. "Sheriff Broward says it's all right for us to leave."

Jessie nodded, feeling numb inside, confused by the distance he kept between them. Too much had happened. Too much had been risked. She longed for the reassurance of Samuel's touch.

"Samuel's truck will be blocked in for quite some time. Purty will drive you home," Sheriff Broward said, nodding at the deputy who stood waiting nearby. Hesitating, he cleared his throat and stared at the scorched remains of Gull's Cottage, unable to meet their eyes. "About this mess, I...I wanted to tell you, I'm sorry. I have no excuse for not listening to you when you tried to come to me for help. No excuse, except for being mule-headed."

"Sheriff..." Jessie began softly.

"No, let me finish," he said, brushing away her attempt to stop him. The big man shifted uncomfortably, his boots scraping against the soot-blackened gravel. "Jessie, when your mother was still alive, I was young and cocky. I thought I had the whole world by its throat. Eve was the prettiest woman I'd ever laid eyes on. I fell hard for her. So hard, I couldn't believe she wasn't interested in me. Seeing her with Samuel's daddy only made matters worse. Knowing she'd preferred him over me—"

He closed his mouth with a click, his jaw clenching and unclenching as he worked his way through an unreadable emotion. "Well, let's just say the green-eyed monster got the better of me. I let my feelings influence my judgment. So much so, I couldn't see what was really happening. Because of me, an innocent man was convicted of a crime he didn't commit." His cautious gaze shifted from her to Samuel. "Samuel, I'm not proud of the way I've treated you. I've taken a lot of my frustrations out on you all these years. And I put both of you in danger by being so pigheaded. For that I'm truly sorry.''

Jessie didn't say a word. It had taken a great deal of courage for the sheriff to admit he'd been wrong. She held her breath, waiting to see how Samuel would respond.

''The past is over,'' Samuel finally said, his voice tired. He blew out a slow, resigned breath. ''We can't change it. We can't let it weigh us down, either. All we can do is get on with our lives the best we can.''

Sheriff Broward listened thoughtfully. Then, with a curt nod of his head, he said, ''Right. Well, I'd best be letting the two of you go. We'll talk again, once things have settled down.'' Squaring his shoulders, he turned on his heel and strode away from them.

Finally alone, Jessie looked up into Samuel's eyes. There she saw myriad confusing emotions—relief, sadness, tender concern and bitter regret.

Before she could question him on the latter, he glanced away, scanning the growing crowd of onlookers. With a disgusted note to his voice, he said, ''Let's get out of here.''

Jessie didn't move, realizing for the first time that she had no place to go. Gull's Cottage was gone forever. A fact which, not surprisingly, she didn't regret. To her, Gull's Cottage had represented everything bad in her life. In her mind it would always be the house where her mother had died. Not once had she ever felt safe within its walls. Now, after all that had happened, Atlanta seemed a vague and distant memory. Returning to her former life seemed as unappealing as the loneliness it promised.

The truth was she had no place to call her own.

She had no home.

"Jessie?"

Startled, Jessie looked up to see Samuel watching her, his concern obvious. Frowning, he asked, "Is something wrong?"

She gave a stilted smile. "I was just trying to decide where I'm supposed to go."

"You can come home with me...for now."

Not quite the response she'd hoped. Wounded but not defeated she refused to look away. "And later? Where should I go then?"

For a long moment their gazes clashed in an unspoken battle of wills. The silence strained between them. His lack of response spoke volumes, answering her question more clearly than any excuse he could possibly give.

Samuel wanted her to leave Prudence Island.

"It's finished," he said finally, his flat tone shattering the silence. "Gull's Cottage is gone. Your mother's death has been solved. There's no reason for you to stay. Whenever you're ready, you'll go home to Atlanta."

"Is that what you want?" she asked, unable to keep the bitterness from her voice. She had thought he cared for her. They'd been through so much together. And now he was ready to push her out of his life—forever—without so much as a second thought. "Do you want me to leave Prudence Island?"

"No, dammit," he ground out, his jaw tightening with barely controlled emotion. Glancing at the crowd, he lowered his voice and said, "That's not what I want at all."

Her vision blurred with unwanted tears. She shook her head, feeling ridiculously close to blubbering like a baby. "First you tell me I should leave. Then you tell me you want me to stay. I don't understand, Samuel."

"Don't you?" He caught her gaze, holding it with his. "I love you, Jessie. I want you to stay here with me more than anything else in the world. But you don't belong here. Dammit, Jessie! I'm nothing but a shrimper, living a hand-to-mouth existence. What kind of life is that to offer?"

"Do you think that matters to me?" Hot tears welled up in her eyes. This time, she allowed them freedom. Teardrops streaming down her face, her voice trembling, she said, "Nothing matters but being with you." At his look of surprise, she smiled. "I do love you, Samuel. I can't think of anything I'd rather do than to make my home here with you...if you'll have me."

"If I'll have you?" He gave an incredulous laugh. "Jessie, I didn't know how I was ever going to let you go."

"Oh, Samuel...I wouldn't want you to."

Ignoring the curious crowd of onlookers, the man who'd spent his life worrying about what others thought of him pulled her into his arms and kissed her thoroughly. She melted into his embrace, savoring the feel of his powerful body close to hers. By the time the kiss ended, both of them were breathless.

Refusing to let her go, he said, "I've been alone for too long, Jessie. From the minute I saw you, I wanted you to be a part of my life. We've got more than just a past to make up for. We've got a future to live. I promise you I'll do my best to make it a happy one."

"As long as we're together it will be," she whispered.

Closing her eyes and holding him tight, she let the soft tide of contentment wash over her.

Epilogue

"Hurry or we're going to be late," Jessie gently chided the toddler, unable to keep the amusement from her voice. The little girl had dark hair like her mother's, pale blue eyes like her father's and the face of an angel.

Not to mention the curiosity of a kitten.

As Jessie hurried down the dock toward the *Marianna,* her daughter, Grace, named because her appearance in their lives had been an answer to their prayers, had other ideas. A sundial, washed onto shore, had caught her eye. Pointing a chubby finger, she cooed, "Pretty, Mommy. Pretty."

"Yes, Grace. It's very pretty." She scooped the squirming child up into her arms, breathing in the sweet scent of her tiny body. "But right now, we have to find Daddy."

"Daddy," Grace repeated, her face lighting with a cherubic smile.

Jessie gave a contented sigh. Five years had passed

since the fire at Gull's Cottage. During which time Prudence Island had become her home. She and Samuel had married, making their vow to stay together official. Samuel's shrimping business had flourished. So much so, he was considering the purchase of a second boat. Her illustrations were selling well. Last year she'd authored her first children's book as well as illustrating it. Two years ago Grace arrived, making their world complete.

Over the years there had been many changes in their lives. Now Jessie wondered how Samuel would feel about one more.

Placing a hand on her tummy, she calmed a bout of butterflies. Her tennis shoes slapped against the wooden dock as she quickened her step. Up ahead, she saw the blue and white colors of the *Marianna*.

Jacob waved from the deck of the boat. His salt-and-pepper beard contained more salt than ever before. But he was still spry on his feet, and the most knowledgeable seaman Jessie had ever met. And he loved to dote on Grace, as proud as any surrogate grandfather. "We were worried about you," he said, clucking his tongue. "Just about ready to send out the Coast Guard for a search."

"I'm sorry, Jacob," Jessie said, handing Grace up to him on the deck. Once her hands were free, she clambered onboard. "My appointment ran longer than expected."

Jacob rubbed one of Grace's plump cheeks. "This little one's gotten some sun. She's as pink as a rose petal."

"Not from the sun, I'm afraid. She had a temper tantrum on the way to the car. Seems she didn't want to pass up the swings in the park across from the doctor's building."

"Stubborn little thing." Jacob chuckled, as he passed the child back to Jessie. With a conspiratorial wink, he nodded toward the pilothouse. "Reminds ya of someone else, doesn't she?"

Jessie smiled as she glanced over to where Samuel stood watching them intently, an impatient expression on his handsome face. Her stomach lurched with awareness. Smiling, she realized that even after all these years, he still had the power to make her feel as giddy as a schoolgirl. Drawing in a steadying breath, she stepped toward her husband.

"Well?" he asked, his voice gruff, though Jessie saw the tender concern in his blue eyes. He really was just a softy at heart. "What did the doctor say?"

"Well," Jessie said slowly, prolonging his agony. "He said I was as healthy as a horse. Not a cough, not a sniffle...just perfect."

He raised a brow. "And?"

"And...I'm pregnant. Eight weeks to be exact. How does a winter baby sound to you?"

"Sounds wonderful," he said, pulling both her and Grace into a bear hug.

Grace giggled, used to being the middle of a human sandwich. She wrapped her arms around her father's neck and squeezed as tightly as she could.

Chuckling, Samuel took her from Jessie's arms. Before releasing her, he bent to help himself to a kiss from his wife, his lips lingering with the promise of more to come later. Reluctantly he stepped away. Calling out to Jacob and Billy that it was time to cast off, he carefully suited up Grace in her own tiny life vest.

Once finished, he seated himself at the wheel, placing his daughter on his lap.

Jessie watched from the doorway, marveling at the change in Samuel. Since Grace's birth, he'd become more sure of himself, more outgoing than she'd ever imagined. Given the opportunity, he made a pest of himself, showing off his daughter to fellow fishermen. Trips into town became a chance to pass around the latest baby photos. He was the most obnoxiously proud father she had ever met.

And she loved him for it.

And Grace...well Grace was truly a fisherman's daughter. She was born with sea legs, feeling more at ease on the boat than she did in her own crib at home. Even at her young age, she swam like a fish. So tempted by the lure of the water, Jessie had to keep a careful watch to make sure Grace didn't indulge herself in an unexpected dip in the ocean.

"She's going to make a good big sister," Samuel said, drawing Jessie out of her musings.

Jessie smiled. "How can you be sure?"

"Because she has her mother's nurturing nature," he said, with a grin. "And because no one should have to grow up alone."

The words ended on a bittersweet note.

"She'll never be alone, Samuel. We will always be there for her. You do know that, don't you?"

"I know," he whispered, pressing his lips to the top of his daughter's head. "It's just...sometimes it's hard for me to believe that one man can be so happy. Sometimes I feel as though I don't deserve all of this. I'm afraid something might happen. That you and Grace...it'll be taken away from me."

"Nothing will happen," Jessie said, impatient for

the first time. "You've paid your dues, Samuel. We both have. We deserve every bit of happiness we can find. And I don't ever want to hear you to say anything else."

Samuel grimaced, holding his hands up in mock surrender. "Don't worry, Jessie. I wouldn't dare cross you."

She raised her chin, tilting her head to one side. "I'll remember you said that."

Starting the engine, he slowly steered the boat from shore. Once on the open sea he gave the motor its head. The boat skimmed across the ocean. Wind and a fine spray of water buffeted their faces.

And Jessie felt a contentment that she'd never imagined possible. Gone were the dreams that had haunted her most of her adult life.

Here on Prudence Island, with Samuel, she had finally found her peace.

Loving him, she had finally found her second chance at happiness.

* * * * *

If you enjoyed what you just read,
then we've got an offer you can't resist!

Take 2 bestselling love stories FREE!

Plus get a FREE surprise gift!

Look Who's Celebrating Our 20th Anniversary:

"Working with Silhouette has always been a privilege—I've known the nicest people, and I've been delighted by the way the books have grown and changed with time. I've had the opportunity to take chances…and I'm grateful for the books I've done with the company. Bravo! And onward, Silhouette, to the new millennium."

—*New York Times* bestselling author
Heather Graham Pozzessere

"Twenty years of laughter and love... It's not hard to imagine Silhouette Books celebrating twenty years of quality publishing, but it is hard to imagine a publishing world without it. Congratulations..."

—International bestselling author
Emilie Richards

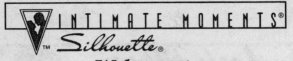

SILHOUETTE'S 20TH ANNIVERSARY CONTEST
OFFICIAL RULES
NO PURCHASE NECESSARY TO ENTER

1. To enter, follow directions published in the offer to which you are responding. Contest begins 1/1/00 and ends on 8/24/00 (the "Promotion Period"). Method of entry may vary. Mailed entries must be postmarked by 8/24/00, and received by 8/31/00.

2. During the Promotion Period, the Contest may be presented via the Internet. Entry via the Internet may be restricted to residents of certain geographic areas that are disclosed on the Web site. To enter via the Internet, if you are a resident of a geographic area in which Internet entry is permissible, follow the directions displayed on-line, including typing your essay of 100 words or fewer telling us "Where In The World Your Love Will Come Alive." On-line entries must be received by 11:59 p.m. Eastern Standard time on 8/24/00. Limit one e-mail entry per person, household and e-mail address per day, per presentation. If you are a resident of a geographic area in which entry via the Internet is permissible, you may, in lieu of submitting an entry on-line, enter by mail, by hand-printing your name, address, telephone number and contest number/name on an 8"x 11" plain piece of paper and telling us in 100 words or fewer "Where In The World Your Love Will Come Alive," and mailing via first-class mail to: Silhouette 20th Anniversary Contest, (in the U.S.) P.O. Box 9069, Buffalo, NY 14269-9069; (In Canada) P.O. Box 637, Fort Erie, Ontario, Canada L2A 5X3. Limit one 8"x 11" mailed entry per person, household and e-mail address per day. On-line and/or 8"x 11" mailed entries received from persons residing in geographic areas in which Internet entry is not permissible will be disqualified. No liability is assumed for lost, late, incomplete, inaccurate, nondelivered or misdirected mail, or misdirected e-mail, for technical, hardware or software failures of any kind, lost or unavailable network connection, or failed, incomplete, garbled or delayed computer transmission or any human error which may occur in the receipt or processing of the entries in the contest.

3. Essays will be judged by a panel of members of the Silhouette editorial and marketing staff based on the following criteria:

   > Sincerity (believability, credibility)—50%
   >
   > Originality (freshness, creativity)—30%
   >
   > Aptness (appropriateness to contest ideas)—20%

   Purchase or acceptance of a product offer does not improve your chances of winning. In the event of a tie, duplicate prizes will be awarded.

4. All entries become the property of Harlequin Enterprises Ltd., and will not be returned. Winner will be determined no later than 10/31/00 and will be notified by mail. Grand Prize winner will be required to sign and return Affidavit of Eligibility within 15 days of receipt of notification. Noncompliance within the time period may result in disqualification and an alternative winner may be selected. All municipal, provincial, federal, state and local laws and regulations apply. Contest open only to residents of the U.S. and Canada who are 18 years of age or older, and is void wherever prohibited by law. Internet entry is restricted solely to residents of those geographical areas in which Internet entry is permissible. Employees of Torstar Corp., their affiliates, agents and members of their immediate families are not eligible. Taxes on the prizes are the sole responsibility of winners. Entry and acceptance of any prize offered constitutes permission to use winner's name, photograph or other likeness for the purposes of advertising, trade and promotion on behalf of Torstar Corp. without further compensation to the winner, unless prohibited by law. Torstar Corp and D.L. Blair, Inc., their parents, affiliates and subsidiaries, are not responsible for errors in printing or electronic presentation of contest or entries. In the event of printing or other errors which may result in unintended prize values or duplication of prizes, all affected contest materials or entries shall be null and void. If for any reason the Internet portion of the contest is not capable of running as planned, including infection by computer virus, bugs, tampering, unauthorized intervention, fraud, technical failures, or any other causes beyond the control of Torstar Corp. which corrupt or affect the administration, secrecy, fairness, integrity or proper conduct of the contest, Torstar Corp. reserves the right, at its sole discretion, to disqualify any individual who tampers with the entry process and to cancel, terminate, modify or suspend the contest or the Internet portion thereof. In the event of a dispute regarding an on-line entry, the entry will be deemed submitted by the authorized holder of the e-mail account submitted at the time of entry. Authorized account holder is defined as the natural person who is assigned to an e-mail address by an Internet access provider, on-line service provider or other organization that is responsible for arranging e-mail address for the domain associated with the submitted e-mail address.

5. Prizes: Grand Prize—a $10,000 vacation to anywhere in the world. Travelers (at least one must be 18 years of age or older) and parent or guardian if one traveler is a minor, must sign and return a Release of Liability prior to departure. Travel must be completed by December 31, 2001, and is subject to space and accommodations availability. Two hundred (200) Second Prizes—a two-book limited edition autographed collector set from one of the Silhouette Anniversary authors: Nora Roberts, Diana Palmer, Linda Howard or Annette Broadrick (value $10.00 each set). All prizes are valued in U.S. dollars.

6. For a list of winners (available after 10/31/00), send a self-addressed, stamped envelope to: Harlequin Silhouette 20th Anniversary Winners, P.O. Box 4200, Blair, NE 68009-4200.

Contest sponsored by Torstar Corp., P.O. Box 9042, Buffalo, NY 14269-9042.

PS20RULES